Elaynna

A MOVING STORY OF A YOUNG GIRL AND A LOST EDUCATION

Elaynna

MUSART ELLAAHI

authorHOUSE®

AuthorHouse™ UK Ltd.
1663 Liberty Drive
Bloomington, IN 47403 USA
www.authorhouse.co.uk
Phone: 0800.197.4150

Published by AuthorHouse   05/09/2014

ISBN: 978-1-4969-8036-6 (sc)
ISBN: 978-1-4969-8035-9 (hc)
ISBN: 978-1-4969-8037-3 (e)

DEDICATED TO

MALALA YOUSAFZAI

MY LOVING PARENTS

AND

MY SUPPORTIVE HUSBAND

NASEER UDDIN

"IF A MAN GAINS KNOWLEDGE

THEN HIS KNOWLEDGE WILL REMAIN WITHIN THE

HOME,

IF A WOMAN GAINS KNOWLEDGE,

THEN HER KNOWLEDGE WILL SPREAD TO

GENERATIONS".

HAZRAT ALI RA

MAY ALLAH BE PLEASED WITH HIM

CHAPTER 1

Elaynna didn't know how to react when her brother caught her missing school. Elaynna was nine years old, the eldest with two younger brothers, only a year between each of them. Elaynna and her brother were both born in Birmingham, England. However, due to family circumstances, the family had to fly back to Pakistan beginning their early education there. Elaynna's Grandmother was diagnosed hepatitis when she was born. Their father, Abdul Aziz, being the eldest of his family, had to return to Pakistan to help finance for his mother's medical treatment.

Elaynna was a quiet child who hated the classroom. She'd look for any excuse to escape. Elaynna had made a verbal contract with her teachers that she would do their chores for them in return from being excused from her homework.

The day her brother caught her, Elaynna was washing dishes with a bucket full of soapy water under a shady tree near her school. Being the month of June, lessons started early just after sunrise and finished at noon.

Rahim was sent by his mother to investigate his sister's whereabouts. Elaynna hadn't noticed that the other girls had left already; she was so consumed in getting the burnt pots clean she had lost track of time. An obstinate burnt stain would not shift. She didn't notice her brother until he said "Baji?" Elaynna froze and slowly looked up. She silently gazed at her brother and looked around at the school court yard amazed to find it empty. All the class room doors were shut, the school gate too. She stared at the school gate in amazement. How had she lost track of time? The word came again "Baji". She looked at Rahim nervously. "Oh . . . Rahim, I didn't notice you there, Mm-miss Shazia, jujus-just asked the the class who who would he-help her with her dishes, she was jujus-just here a minute ago . . . . umm and I offered to to help her . . . . that's all . . ." Rahim gave her a funny look as if to say do you think I'm stupid "Baji, did I ask you anything? It has been nearly two hours that you haven't come home, Ammi sent me to find you. Everyone has been so worried about you and you're sitting here washing dishes?!" Rahim kicked the bucket full of water and began pulling Elaynna by the arm all the way home. Elaynna's mind was fixated on the last dirty pot worrying about the burnt stain that she couldn't get clean. Miss Shazia won't be pleased she thought.

When they reached home Rahim took Elaynna straight through the courtyard to the open kitchen where her mum was lighting the tan door. Elaynna's mother Yasmin got up slowly holding her back, a 7 months pregnant belly hanging forward. Yasmin was 26. Yasmin was quite fair with full lips, big eyes with broad cheek bones. "What took you two so long?" she asked firmly. Before Elaynna even opened her mouth Rahim started talking. "I found Elaynna outside the school washing Miss Shazias dishes. I don't think she attended class there were so many pots and plates. She didn't even have her school bag."

"I think I know where that is." answered Yasmin crossly. Elaynna stood there silently looking down. Too scared to say anything, being caught out. A sudden strong palm hit her across the face. "I have been doing everything to keep this house in order, when you know that I am expecting, rather than coming home to help your own mother you are washing dishes for your teachers! You disgusting little bitch!" Elaynna stood there listening to the abuse, tears rolling down her oval shaped face. Her cheek felt sore, itching to feel it she dared not to touch it.

Elaynna was a beautiful girl, she had high cheek bones with oval shaped hazel eyes and long curly eyelashes. Her chestnut hair, the envy of the village, went down to her elbows. Without realizing it, Yasmin dragged Elaynna to the wheat room where the whole wheat was stored for the chapatti flour. Yasmin shoved Elaynna locking her in. Elaynna woke to reality when her mother closed the doors leaving her in the dark, "Please Ammi! Please Ammi open the door! Its scary in here! I promise I will do as you say!" She pleaded.

Upon hearing no response she walked back until her back hit the wall, scraping the wall she sat down on the floor curling up her knees towards her chest, she cried silently in the dark. All she could see was the streak of light that came through the crack in the double doors. Her mother had never taken such a drastic decision like this before. She would get the odd slap or the ear twisting here and there but never this. Realising she had made a terrible mistake to be given such a firm punishment.

Yasmin warned everyone about letting Elaynna out without her permission if they did they would be served the same punishment. Rahim dusted his hands cunningly giving an unnoticeable smirk, then went to join his cousins who invited him to a game of cricket.

Her brother Kareem, watching his sister's punishment felt sorry for her. Kareem was 7 yrs old, he wasn't as good looking as his older brother or sister but he was the wisest of the three. He had a close bond with Elaynna, the only one who understood her. Kareem fearful of his fathers temper, ran to tell his Grandmother. Jannat was her name. Jannat adored and you could even say favoured Elaynna. Kareem was out of breath by the time he reached his Grandmother. "Dadi! Dadi!" he panted. Jannat's face fell pale of worry. "What's the matter my love? Is everything ok?"

"Dadi . . ." Kareem finally caught his breath. "Dadi, Ammi has locked Elaynna in the wheat room because she was caught washing dishes outside her school by Rahim, she didn't even let Elaynna speak or explain herself. She's been in there a while now I am worried she might be unconscious there is no window in there! Ammi also warned us that if any of was to help her we will be in big trouble too, I didn't interfere and just came looking for you, Ammi only listens to you."

Without a moments hesitation Jannat held Kareems hand heading home. She stormed into the court yard rushing to the wheat room releasing the lock, she pushed the doors open. Elaynna lay unconscious on the floor, her body dripping with sweat. Jannat shouted at Kareem to bring some water gently taking Elaynna onto her lap. Yasmin lay having her afternoon nap under the empress tree in the courtyard.

Awoken by all the commotion, Yasmin rubbed her eyes looking across the courtyard only to find the wheat room doors open, squinting she saw her mother in law trying to bring Elaynna to consciousness.

"Elaynna, beta get up, get up! It's your Dadi come on Beta you can do it." Yasmin quickly got up to run across to help, tripping over the basket that was covering the newly hatched chicks, she fell on her tummy on the hard concrete ground. Kareem handed his grandmother a clay cup of water. Jannat splashed the contents onto Elaynna's face. Finally Elaynna awoke. "Dadi . . ." she gasped in a daze. Slowly sitting up she saw her mother lying on the ground clutching her tummy. "AMMI!" she screamed, quickly getting up running towards her. Jannat and Kareem rushed after. Jannat noticed blood zigzagging on the floor following the lines of the brick laded ground.

With Elaynna's help Jannat quickly picked up Yasmin and took her into the house. She ordered Elaynna to call her sister and Kareem to get the midwife.

Elaynna ran out to call her Grand aunt Imtiaz. Fortunately the midwife and Imtiaz lived only five minutes away. "Dadi Imtiaz! Dadi Imtiaz!" Elaynna panted. Imtiaz was busy making rotis in the tan door with her daughter in law Sakeena. Imtiaz rose from her seat and stared at Elaynna. "What's wrong my dear why do you look so worried?"

"Ammi fell over in the court yard and there was blood everywhere I helped Dadi take her in the house Dadi asked me to call you at once!" Imtiaz was well experienced in delivering babies, an expert on how to deal with miscarriages. Imtiaz left the last two rotis to burn in the tan door and quickly ran into the house. She brought out a special dried flower which she had brought back from Hajj. She carefully placed the flower in the jug, pouring water over it. This special flower was believed to help women in labour. If it bloomed in the water the birth would not be difficult for the mother also the child would be saved. If it didn't then the opposite would happen. Imtiaz had kept this flower for many years so far it had always bloomed, when taken out and left to dry it turned back into its original curled position. She left the jug on the outside kitchen wall and told Sakeena to keep an eye on it and to also pray.

Imtiaz followed Elaynna home. Yasmin clutching Jannats hand, Amina the midwife had examined her already.

"Where have you been Imtiaz? What took you so long?!" asked Jannat crossly. "I'm sorry" replied Imtiaz. Imtiaz went to Yasmin, held her other hand and stroked her hair. "Is everything ok?" she inquired the midwife. "In shaa Allah everything will be ok" replied Amina. "I think Yasmin has got the dates wrong I feel this baby isn't early at all, I think she is exactly 9 months. Yasmin is just smaller than before which is why I have been misguided by her measurements. Also her waters have broken which came along with the bleeding". Amina had studied midwifery in London and Pakistan. She knew what she was talking about. Midwives didn't usually measure with a tape measure in Pakistan nor did they scan they just felt the mothers tummy making rough guesses. Jannat and Imtiaz let out a grateful sigh at the same time, they trusted Amina, she had a good reputation in the town, although this was the first time she was delivering a baby in their family. Elaynna walked in with her hot ruffled face. She was so worried about her mother, feeling all of this was her fault. She walked to her mother and started crying. "I'm so sorry Ammi, it's all my fault." she sobbed. Yasmin was panting in pain, she asked Elaynna to leave. Jannat took Elaynna by the hand and led her outside. She also asked her to fetch some hot water and told her everything would be alright.

Back at Imtiaz's house the tan door was catching fire. Sakeena panicked, without thinking she threw the jug of water onto it. Sakeena finally calmed down as the fire died out. Suddenly realising what she had done she panicked again. Luckily the flower had bloomed fully. It was stuck in the jug like a small wooden ship in a glass bottle. Sakeena raised the jug above her head and looked at it in amazement.

Elayna was crouching on her feet with her arms crossed over her knees watching the pot of water on the stove. Suddenly Imtiaz ran out shouting. "Allah O Akbar! The baby is born! It's a boy!" Elaynna ran out of the kitchen straight into the store room. Yasmin was smiling and Jannat was holding the baby wrapped up in a white towel. The baby was very healthy and fair skinned. He looked a lot like Elaynna. Elaynna looked at the baby and couldn't help smiling. She was so happy that tears began rolling down her cheeks. If such a dear fragile being had been lost. She would have been to blame. If only she had attended school, if only she hadn't been washing dishes, if only . . .

Elaynna fell in a trance, suddenly Jannat gave her a nudge to hold her baby brother. Quickly wiping her tears she gave her mother a smile. Yasmin smiled back. Elaynna sat down on the bed beside her mother. Yasmin stroked Elaynna's hair lovingly. Elaynna's worries disappeared at the feel of her mother caressing her hair, feeling she had been forgiven. Jannat placed the baby in Elaynna's arms. Elaynna, looked into his big blue eyes. He was wide awake looking straight at her. "This is your baji Elaynna" said Yasmin. "She has been working very hard to save you today, you must thank her one day." Elaynna's eyes beamed with happiness upon hearing a compliment from her mother's lips for the first time. "Yes I agree" replied Imtiaz. "She came quickly to me waiting for me to leave with her."

"If it had been anyone else they would have given the message and ran away" added Jannat. Elaynna's eyes blurred with tears. No one had ever given her a compliment no matter how hard she worked, apart from Kareem. A tear dropped on the baby's forehead. "Beta don't cry it's all ok now." comforted Yasmin, the daughter she had locked in the wheat room. She could have gained one child and lost her only daughter all in one day. She was grateful no tragedy occured.

"I will go and get the hot water. We can bathe the baby and clean up Yasmin before Bhai Abdul gets home" interrupted Amina. "The azaan is yet to be done in the baby's ears." Everyone helped Amina bathe the baby, so Yasmin could get some rest. Elaynna and her brothers also took a bath, it was a very hot day.

It was nearly 7pm when Abdul arrived on his motor bike. He worked as a Police officer in Rawalpindi. It was an hour's journey for him every day. Upon hearing their father's motorbike enter the court yard the children ran towards him. They all shouted excitedly "Abu! Abu! Abu!!" Jannat unable to contain herself, joined her grandchildren from the kitchen, holding a wooden spoon, she had been cooking for the family as well as making a non spicy dish for Yasmin. Imtiaz came out of the store room holding the baby in her arms. Abdul parked his motorbike quickly pacing towards his aunt. He gave the box of barfis and gulab jamun which he had brought coincidently, to Elaynna. "Mashallah!" he exclaimed stroking the baby's cheek. "It's a boy!" Squeeled Imtiaz.

"Mubarak my dear." She then passed the baby gently into his arms so he could say the Azaan. Abdul said the azaan in both of his son's ears.

Jannat hugged her son and kissed him on his forehead. "Mubarak beta." she said taking the sweets from Elaynna. Abdul then went into the house to see his wife. Jannat divided the sweets into small bags to hand out around the village. As was the custom in Pakistan if there was any kind of big news sweets were handed to the nearby neighbours and relatives. Jannat left some sweets for the whole family to eat after dinner. As there weren't many left she cut them up in small pieces; she didn't want to disappoint the children. Jannat then called Rahim, Kareem and Elaynna handing them a couple of bags each. "Elayna you hand these bags out at the top of the village, Rahim you give these ones to Amina and your uncle's house. Kareem you go and give these to Dadi Imtiaz's family and your aunts."

They set out like three musketeers on a mission. They were so happy feeling responsible for being given such an important task. Half of the village of Chaman Pur already knew that a son was born in the Aziz household. Amina had passed on the good news on her way home.

The sun was setting in the sky as the children returned from their sweet delivery. It was dinner time. Elaynna laid out the dinner mat on the floor outside the kitchen and Abdul lit the lanterns around the house. Abdul had paid for electricity for his brother's and sister's household, but not his own. This upset Yasmin however she never said anything. Abdul's family all had fans for their homes as well as other little luxuries, but Yasmin never complained. She made do with the shady tree in the day time and everyone slept outside in the evening to get a cool night's sleep. In Pakistan, when a mother gave birth, she's not allowed to leave the house or her bedroom unless absolutely necessary for forty days. Yasmin was worried what she would do this time, her other children were born in winter. Elaynna and Rahim were born in England. It was much easier there. Amina had advised that a cool temperature was necessary for such a small baby otherwise the baby could suffocate. This gave Yasmin the courage to speak to Abdul. Afterall she had a very good excuse. Also she knew that Jannat would stick by her.

Elaynna began to lay out the plates while her brothers and father went to wash their hands. Jannat went inside to Yasmin's room to give her milk mixed with turmeric powder and a bowl of butter and flour halwa. These were nutritious foods to help Yasmin heal from labour and to help her produce more milk. Elaynna then poured the chicken curry in a pot. Being it a day of joy Jannat had slaughtered one of their chickens. They all sat down together apart from Yasmin, Abdul made a special dua thanking Allah for a healthy son and the food waiting out in front of them.

When they finally began eating Jannat asked the family for names for the new baby. "How about Aziz?" asked Rahim. "No, we can't have Aziz" replied Abdul "Aziz is our surname we can't have Aziz Aziz." Everyone laughed except Elaynna who just smiled coyly. "How about Shazia?" Rahim asked cheekily looking at Elaynna in a teasing way. Elaynna felt her cheeks burn with embarrassment. Jannat darted Rahim a sharp disappointing look. "Rahim, Shazia is a girl's name we have a brother not a sister." replied Kareem sternly. "Yes Rahim now stop being silly and eat your food".

Abdul had the final word, Rahim knew he had to shut up. The muezzin called the Isha azaan, the evening prayer.

Elaynna cleared up the plates and went to wash up in the courtyard. Filling one bucket full of soapy water and another full of plain. Kareem kindly followed with a lantern to help her see in the dark. As Elaynna laid out the dishes on the muddy floor squatting on her feet. Kareem also sat beside her with the lantern in his hand until she had finished. Kareem knew she had had a rough day and thought this would be a good time to talk to her. "Thank you Kareem." Elaynna said. "Baji can I ask you something?" he gently said to Elaynna understanding his sisters reserve. "Yes" replied Elaynna looking away. "Why did you wash Miss Shazia's dishes today? How long have the teachers been bullying you?"

"It's not their fault Kareem, it's me. I hated getting hit so I offered to do things for them." Kareem knew his sister would never find fault in anyone. She didn't realise that the teachers were jealous of her beauty and her English nationality.

They would make up that she had always got her answers wrong when she hadn't. They would blackmail her to do their household chores or else they would tell her father. Elaynna, innocent as she was, would accept this abuse every day. "But why did they hit you so much that you offered to do their chores?"

Elaynna's eyes filled up with tears and her lips began to tremble. Kareem lifted the lantern up to Elaynna's face, her wet face glistened in the light. "Hey baji, I'm so sorry, did I upset you? Please don't cry I can't take it when you're upset." Kareem took out his handkerchief and wiped Elaynna's cheeks. Elaynna took the handkerchief and blew her nose. "Thank you Kareem, it's not you. I just feel that I am so stupid, nobody likes me, I don't have many friends. Ammi is always shouting at me. I feel nobody loves me apart from you Kareem."

"Don't be silly you're not stupid, I am not the only one who loves you Ammi loves you, see how proud she was of you today. She shouts at me and Rahim too. Dadi loves you more than anyone. You know when Ammi locked you in the wheat room Dadi was so cross she came running." Elaynna stayed quiet and smiled a little. "Look Baji what ever happens I will always be there for you . . ."

"Kareem! Elaynna! Rahim! Come here quickly we have chosen a name for your little brother!" Abdul called out. At that point Abdul's and Yasmin's extended family walked in through the gates cheering. "MUBARAK! MUBARAK!" Abdul's brothers Yaqoob and Yasin patted their older brother on the back and exchanged embraces. Their wives Shenaz and Asiya followed Jannat to Yasmin's room. Slowly the courtyard began to fill up with the villagers and their children. There were lanterns glowing everywhere. It looked like New Years in China, without the dragons of course.

The villagers kept coming in and congratulating Abdul and his family. It is a custom in Pakistani culture for neighbors and families to come in and share their family or neighbors happiness or sadness by visiting them in their homes unexpected. If there was a member or a neighbor that didn't turn up it would be seen as disrespect. Chatter and laughter echoed all around the court yard.

Yasmin was tired of smiling and repeating her birth story again and again. Abdul's announcement of his son's name was frequently delayed. Kareem and Rahim were busy passing around the sweets their guests had brought and Elaynna ran around serving tea.

Finally when everyone had arrived and were served Abdul finally announced his son's name. "Listen everyone, thank you so much for coming tonight and lighting up my home with your presence, it truly feels special to be home today to be blessed with a beautiful son, Alhamdulillah! I would like to announce my son's name." Everyone quietened telling their children to sit quietly. Yasmin opened her window wider to hear what her husband had decided. "I have decided to name him Qasim Aziz!" Everyone cheered, the men opened fires with their magazines. Abdul hated guns even though he was in the police force. He hated violence altogether. Abdul asked the men to stop opening fires and to kindly put their guns away. He didn't want to scare the children. The men quickly did as they were told, they highly respected Abdul. Abdul was the most respected man in the family as well as his town because he had made many generous sacrifices for his peers.

The men apologized and congratulated Abdul once more.

They all thought that it was a beautiful name. Everyone left one by one and said their goodbyes as Elaynna and Jannat laid out their beds in the courtyard, it was too hot to sleep inside. Jannat laid out Yasmins bed in the veranda, she knew it would be too hot for her grandson, remembering Amina's advice. Yasmin gave Jannat a wishful look of a fan. Jannat understood her daughter in law instantly while she prepared her bed covers on the roped wooden bed. Jannat lay out thick quilts under the sheets to soften it. Jannat held Yasmins face and softly said "Sab theek ho jaye ga" meaning everything will be alright. Yasmin brought out Qasim and sat on her bed. The wind blew softly across their faces, Yasmin leaned on the wall behind her and held Qasim to her chest. He was fast asleep. Yasmin stole the opportunity to properly look at her son, she didn't have a peaceful moment alone with him the whole day.

Yasmin analysed his features in the dim light trying to recognise who he resembled the most. This was their first mother and son moment. Yasmin realised he didn't resemble anyone. He was rather fair like his father but with bigger blue eyes and pouted lips. He would have easily passed as a girl. Yasmin smiled to herself at the thought of this. Pleased to know that he would grow up to be a handsome man like his father. Yasmin looked across the courtyard at the five beds laid out in a row.

Her children were fast asleep. Jannat was sitting up in her bed holding a tasbih, praying silently to herself. Yasmin's gaze fell back to Elaynna. Looking at her made her stomach churn with guilt and despair. How she nearly killed her own daughter! Allah would have never forgave her, maybe that's why she fell over and had such a risky delivery, maybe it was Allah's way of punishing her. She didn't understand why she was so hard on her and expecting so much of her when she was always trying her best to impress her.

Yasmins mind traced back to Elaynna's birth. It had been winter, 9th of November 1967 Birmingham, England. Elaynna had a premature birth, being small in height and low in weight, only three pounds in weight and thirty centimetres in height. She was so weak and fragile that she had to be kept in the hospital for three months to reach a stable weight. Having to have a oxygen mask to help her breathe. She was fed on formula milk being too weak to suck on her mother's breast. Yasmin remembered how hard it was to look at her and wonder if she would survive. Abdul had reassured her that Allah was watching over her and she will pull through. She remembered crying and praying every night that the doctors would discharge Elaynna and let her be with her at home like any other child, but most of all to be like a normal baby of her age. Yasmin remembered making promises to Allah that she would look after her daughter and always keep her happy. Which she did until they returned to Pakistan, why did the move make her change drastically? Yasmin tried to place what went wrong. She realised how much she appreciated her more then, than she did now. An unexpected tear trickled down her face until she was suddenly shaken by Abdul. "Yasmin? Are you ok? You seem rather distant."

"I'm fine Abdul ji. Just a couple of old memories came to haunt me."

"Anything you would like to talk about?" inquired Abdul, wondering if he had done anything wrong. Yasmin shook her head and told him to rest. Abdul kissed Yasmin and Qasim on the cheek good night.

CHAPTER 2

The cockerel woke the village at dawn. The sun was still hiding, the fajr adhan followed after the sound of the cockerel. Jannat was the first to wake up to perform morning prayers, the shortest prayers of the day. Abdul awoke soon after to wash heading towards the masjid. Jannat awoke the children lovingly; Elaynna first, her duty to take over her mother's side of chores. Elaynna put the tea on and made buttered chapattis. It was Thursday, another school day. Elaynna's hands trembled with fear while she served breakfast, she was dreading to go to school. She knew that Miss Shazia will give her a bollocking, for leaving the dishes incomplete.

Elaynna couldn't help worrying; to deter her mind she slowly continued to complete the chores pretending she had forgotten it was a school day. Kareem knew what his sister was up to, he began to observe her closely when he sat to eat his breakfast. Rahim sat next to Kareem and whispered. "Look at Elaynna, bet she wont go to school today." he giggled to himself. Kareem gave his brother an annoyed look, "Shut up and eat your breakfast." Rahim ignored his brother's outburst, he cheekily smiled picking his cup of tea.

Jannat saw Elaynna sweeping the courtyard and looked around for her son, he hadn't returned from the masjid yet. Where could he be? she pondered, he will be late for work. She didn't near enough think about Elaynna not being ready for school yet, being grateful for the help.

Rahim and Kareem left for school with their backpacks. Elaynna watched them leave with excitement. I might just get away with not going to school today she said to herself. Elaynna started folding the bed covers and clearing away the dishes. Jannat sat on Yasmin's bed and woke her up gently for her breakfast holding her milk with turmeric powder, and a bowl of wheat flour pudding to help heal her wounds. Jannat held Qasim while Yasmin ate. Both still unaware whether Elaynna went to school, the first lesson would have already begun.

Jannat asked Yasmin if she knew where Abdul was. Yasmin responded that she saw him leave in the morning as soon as the muezzin called for prayer. He didn't tell her anything. Now both of them began worrying. It was almost 7am now, still no sign of Abdul. Yasmin lost her appetite for a bit, until she saw Elaynna washing the dishes in the hot sun. Yasmin looked at Jannat. "Aj Elayna school nahi gahi?" as in didn't Elaynna go to school today? Jannat squirmed at this, and admitted she had forgotten to send Elaynna to school. "I'm sorry Yasmin, I was too consumed in my own thoughts that I forgot about Elaynna. Do you want me to take her now? Shes late already, and bless her shes done everything this morning. Bechari works so hard . . . You are too hard on her sometimes. Especially what happened yesterday, that was so unnecessary. You almost killed her, she could have died of suffocation."

Yasmin instantly felt nauseous. "I know I'm sorry. I don't know what got into me." She muttered. Biting her bottom lip Yasmin made a suggestion.

"Ammi I feel that Elaynna should be home schooled, I will teach her to sew and to read the Quran. I am worried that the outside world would take advantage of her. Shes so vulnerable and I am worried she will end up like Jawaids daughter. You know the one who ran away from home? What do you think? She doesn't like her teachers or school, shes always looking for ways to avoid her books. I don't understand why? She would even go so far in to washing dishes for them. That's what made me so furious yesterday." Jannat gave a long sigh of agreement, looking down at Qasims face.

"Yes I do agree, shes nearly ten now and it will give her time to learn to cook properly. Being the eldest it will help her to learn to be more responsible."

"Do you think Abdul would mind?" Yasmin asked nervously.

"I will take care of that, don't you worry." Suddenly Abdul appeared through the courtyard entrance. Both looked at each other with relieved smile. Abdul looked really hot and bothered. Elaynna saw her father and worried she might be caught out. Quickly pouring him a glass of water from the water cooler she handed it over to him as he sat down. Picking up the hand held netted fan she fanned him until he was no longer hot. Abdul drank his water in three big gulps. He cupped a handful of water with which he poured into his right palm wiping his face cool. He smiled at Elaynna patting her head. "You're a good daughter, meri jaan". Elaynna smiled back. Jannat interrupted asking where he had been. "I had some important business to take care of."

"Haye Allah! Is everything ok?" panicked Jannat. "No, no nothing is wrong, Ammi ji, I was helping a couple of electricians." He answered casually while he loosend a buckle of his sandals.

"Electricians?" asked Jannat out of confusion. Abdul smiled to himself and winked at his daughter. Elaynna took the glass from her father's hand and went to warm him some breakfast. Abdul leaned back on his chair stretching his arms above his head. "Aren't you going to work today?"

"No Ammi ji, I called the inspector in charge and informed him of Qasim's birth. He has given me permission to take a few days off till Monday. They would cope he confirmed, it wasn't so busy. Inspector Hameed is so nice alhamdullilah. It's all Allah's mercy."

Jannat was delighted to hear this. Especially Yasmin, who was listening from her bed, she counted the days on her fingers till Monday. She would have four whole days with her husband! Yasmin couldn't stop smiling to herself, she rarely got quality time to spend with him due to his work. Yasmin cherished every moment with him. Although he was thirteen years her senior, this did not bother Yasmin, because of the way he respected and adored her. This stopped Yasmin to be a nagging wife, it made her feel guilty to ask him of anything. Her husband adored her that was enough.

Abdul ate his breakfast while Elaynna stood next to him. "Why aren't you at school today?" he looked at her curiously. Still unaware of the incident that took place the day before, nobody had dared to tell him. Elaynna looked down at her feet not knowing what to say. Jannat quickly answered before Abdul could inquire further.

"She wanted to stay and help out because of Yasmin." Jannat began to conceal her own mistake. Elaynna snuck away while her grandmother and father continued talking. She decided to go and ask if her mother needed anything. Really she wanted to hold Qasim and smell his baby smell. Yasmin was just changing Qasim's washable nappy, wrapping an rectangular muslin around his bottom and pinned it in place with a safety pin. Elaynna observed her mother's actions, patiently waiting for her to finish. "Ammi ji can I hold him?"

"Of course, here take him." Yasmin gently handed him to Elaynna. Elaynna took him carefully, holding him close to her chest she sat down next to her mother.

"So how come you are not at school today madam?" asked Yasmin. "I-I-I-. . ." stuttered Elaynna.

"Don't be nervous, I am not having a go at you."

"Your Dadi and I have decided that its best you stay at home, what do you think?" Elaynna unexpected to hear this didn't know how to express her joy.

"What about Abu, what would he say?" Elaynna exclaimed. "Your Dadi will talk to your father, she will take care of it. That doesn't mean you won't study at all, ok? I will teach you the Quran and how to cook properly and how to sew. You better pay attention. I know how your concentration span is like a goldfish."

"Don't worry Ammi I won't let you down. I don't mind staying at home. At least I will get to spend more time with Qasim and you will

20

get all the rest you need." Yasmin smiled at her daughter's innocence. Jannat walked in interrupting with a grin on her face. "You won't believe it Yasmin, Allah has answered your prayers!"

"Why? What do you mean?"

"Abdul has just gone out with two men. They are installing electricity in our village! It will take all week to go around each house to install a meter and electricity wires, what not. Ours will have electricity tonight!" Yasmin leaped up from her seat and let out a squeal like a school girl. Jannat told her to behave appropriately; it wasn't good for her to jump up and down she just had a baby. The women embraced each other and Yasmin's eyes filled with tears of joy. She had the urge to embrace her husband too but she knew she couldn't as it was frowned upon for a man and wife to show their affection openly.

Elaynna hearing the commotion she couldn't help being excited. "That means we can have fans through the day and night now and not have to light up the lanterns anymore in the house?!" asked Elaynna innocently.

"Yes, yes there are so many possibilities now my dear!" Jannat answered with excitement in her voice. Elaynna quickly passed Qasim back to her mother and ran out to hug her father to thank him. He was busy with the electricians, answering their questions and passing the tools. Yasmin couldn't help wishing she could do the same while she saw Elaynna embrace her father.

Abdul hugged Elaynna back; he felt Yasmin was watching, trying to meet his gaze. He gave her a assuring smile. "Go and play now I'm busy sweetheart." Yasmin shyly smiled back and returned inside to tend to Qasim.

Jannat began preparing lunch. She made a potatoe curry with peas. Elaynna went out to play with the other village girls. Jannat called out to Elaynna to be back by lunch time. "No Dadi Ji I am not so hungry! I am sure Nurjahan would have brought me something she always does!" Jannat waved back her approval, she couldn't wait to see her friends.

A group of girls were playing with their cloth homemade dolls under a shaded tree. The three girls were Elaynna's best friends; Nurjahan, Shaista and Tasleem. Nurjahan was chubby and round. She had a round face with small eyes and a short bob of hair. Her mother tried to be modern, because Nurjahan's father had his own business in Islamabad, he very rarely visited, he only sent money for their well being, there was a rumor he had settled with a rich woman in the city. However Nurjahan had the sweetest smile with dimples that enhanced her features. Shaista and Tasleem always teased her. Nurjahan didn't care much; when the teasing did upset her Elaynna knew how to cheer her up. Shaista was the youngest in her family. Shaista was the cheeky one of the three who always got the others in trouble. Shaista had a china doll like face, with sharp features and shiny skin with a fringe.

Tasleem was petite she was short for her age and of very small build too. She always wore her hair in pig tails and had a button like nose. Her mother always scolded her to eat more so she could fill out and grow tall. However much she ate she hardly put much weight on or grew any taller. The three girls were very excited to see Elaynna.

They missed her at school today. They did everything together. Elaynna even copied their homework sometimes when they weren't looking. "ELAYNNA!" they screamed when they saw Elaynna skipping towards them. They all stood up and began jumping up and down. As soon as Elaynna reached them they had a group hug and jumped up and down dancing in a circle.

"Where were you today?" asked Nurjahan. "Bet she got caught doing the dishes for Miss Shazia." Shaista and Tasleem giggled teasingly. "Shut up!" snapped Nurjahan. "Let her speak, you two don't know when to stop being annoying do you?" Shaista and Tasleem hid behind their scarves and stood quietly, the first time Nurjahan stood up to them. "Well where were you? These two have been on my case all day, Miss Shazia was asking for you too."

"Well . . . Shaista and Tasleem are right. I was caught washing the dishes. Ammi was really angry and locked me in the wheat room. Then Qasim was born."

"We know about your baby brother, Elaynna, our mothers told us, but why didn't you come into school today?" Elaynna looked up smiling. "Ammi said I don't have to go to school anymore, she will teach me at home. And now that Qasim is born Ammi needs even more help now." Tasleem and Shaista couldn't help feeling a bit jealous. "Wow! Lucky you no more homework or going to school in this heat!" Tasleem gasped. "How is that lucky? We won't be able to see Elaynna much like we used to and she won't learn anything." Nurjahan interrupted the excitement trying to put a plug to let the others know how bad it actually was. Elaynna made a funny face behind Nurjahan imitating her actions.

"Ammi said she will teach me at home, so I won't miss anything."

"Come on let's play!" Cut in Shaista as she could see the tension growing on Nurjahan's face. Nurjahan was small but very intelligent. She cared more about Elaynna than the other girls. The girls played lots of games together all day, sharing the snacks that Nurjahan bought.

Jannat watched them from the terrace, after hearing the sound of their innocent giggles. Jannat stopped separating the spices for a few minutes, she couldnt help worrying about her granddaughter's future. Elaynna clearly couldn't fend for herself or had learnt to read or write other than her name yet. All she could do was recognize the letters. The other girls were able to do their homework without any difficulty. These thoughts made Jannat overwhelm with helplessness, as a grandmother she couldn't help her granddaughter in any way, having been illiterate herself.

Abdul saw his mother in lost thoughts and placed a hand on her shoulder. "What's wrong Ammi?" "Kuchwini (nothing)" replied Jannat wiping the nearly fallen tears. "Aren't you happy about the electricity?" Jannats face lightened up. "Is it ready?!"

"Yes Ammi it is!" Abdul shouted from the roof tops to call Elaynna home. "Elaynna!! The sun is going down come home now!" Elaynna dropped what she was doing waving goodbye to her friends she ran home. The other girls waved back walking home together. "So what do you think will come of Elaynna?" asked Shaista playfully. Tasleem looked down at her doll "My mother told me if you don't study no one will want to marry you." Nurjahan looked at Tasleem with an agitated look. "Sorry to say but your mum dropped out of school when she was younger than your age!" Tasleem was offended but realized she shouldn't bother arguing, Nurjahan was Elaynna's best friend, she wasn't going to take nonsense from anyone today. "I didn't mean that Nuri, I'm just saying what my mum said." Shaista cut in. "Look we are worried about Elaynna as much as you and we will miss her too at school, what Tasleem is saying could be true, I'm sure she means nice boys wouldn't come for our hands in marriage if we are not educated." Nurjahan's face softened a little but stress still showed on her forehead. Deep down she knew her friends were right. Nurjahan shrugged and walked off home in the near darkness without saying goodbye.

CHAPTER 3

Elaynna ran into her courtyard, quickly splashing water on her face. It was almost dark. Elaynna remembered it was time to light the lanterns, or they would not be able to see anything. Upon reaching the kitchen, all of a sudden there was light everywhere. Her family exclaimed "BIJLI!" (Electricity). Elaynna couldn't believe her eyes! There was electricity in their house! Elaynna's mouth dropped in amazement. This was what electricity looked like? It seemed like another world. Elaynna's imagination began to wonder, she imagined herself as a princess and Miss Shazia as her servant. Elaynna dreamed of giving Miss Shazia orders, "Wash my brother's nappy and make sure you do it properly!" She imagined Miss Shazia trembling and running to do the chore. Then she would make her do another upon another. "Where are you lost?" Rahim asked as he shook her "You look so goofy!" he cackled in her face. Elaynna blushed with embarrassment and walked to her grandmother, father and mother who were standing outside in the courtyard admiring the beauty of the lights. Jannat held her palms out in the air gesturing to thank Allah that tears wouldn't resist her eyes.

Abdul and Yasmin couldn't help crying tears of joy themselves. Rahim's heart melted looking at his mother's face. He went up to Yasmin quietly slipping his hand in hers squeezing it tight. He knew this was her ultimate wish that Allah had mercifully granted. To cut the emotion Rahim all of a sudden blurted "I'm hungry, are tears on the menu tonight?" Everyone burst out laughing. Jannat wiped her tears whilst laughing and called Rahim a "gaddah" (a donkey). Jannat and Elaynna quickly lay out the floor mat to serve dinner. Lamb pilaf and raita was on the menu tonight. It was quite rare when the Aziz household would have meat for dinner. Abdul had bought the meat especially to celebrate Qasim's birth. Pilaf was the family's favorite. Elaynna handed everyone a plate and sat in her usual seat. Jannat brought out the dinner. Rahim was enchanted by the smell of the pilaf, he sniffed in the smell and closed his eyes like he was floating. When Jannat put the rice down bending down on her knees, the three of them gasped in excitement as the rice glistened under the bright light bulb. Rahim ran up to Jannat giving her a hug in excitement. Kareem coughed "kiss arse" under his breath. "Bet he's hugging Dadi so he gets it first" Thought Kareem. "Did you say something?" snapped Rahim. "No, no nothing I just coughed" Kareem answered back with a sarcastic smile. Rahim knew what he said and Kareem's smirk confirmed his suspicion.

"It's ok sit down now Rahim, I know it's your favorite you can have it first". Knew it! What an ass! Kareem thought. Rahim gave Kareem an innocent smile with a raised eyebrow. "Thank you Dadi jaan." Rahim added while tucking into his plate.

Yasmin came out holding Qasim, she couldn't resist the lovely aroma of the pilaf. "Ammi jee, please can I have some? I can't remember when I last had Pilaf!"

"NO!" Jannat snapped at once. "You will give Qasim a stomach ache, rice causes bloatedness and Qasim is only two days old, his stomach

27

won't digest it. I have made wheat halwa that is perfect for both of you. Qasim was born yesterday! You must be careful what you eat!" Yasmin got annoyed at this and tried again "Ammi, how about I eat a little bit and I can have ajwain kawa straight after that should be ok wouldn't it? I have been eating halwa since yesterday and mild stuff before his birth . . . . Please please Ammi can I have some?" Jannat raised her eyebrows, as in go and fight your case somewhere else, I am not letting you have any. Yasmin recognized the look and didn't ask again. Jannat brought out the halwa in a plate and escorted Yasmin back to her room. Meanwhile Elaynna served the rest of the family, serving herself last.

"Abu thank you for the lights. Our house feels like a palace." Elaynna told her father as she took in a morsel.

Abdul smiled at her in a loving way "Thank Allah beta, it's all his doing." Jannat joined the rest of the family. "Ammi the food is really tasty, after a long time we are having pilaf, eating pilaf in the new given light feels like a real blessing."

"I agree, Mashallah." nodded Jannat talking with her mouth almost full. Without another word everyone tucked into their meal, eating in silence helping themselves to second portions. Every mouthful tasted different, fresh and new.

Kareem helped to clear the dishes away. Elaynna and Rahim laid out the beds. Elaynna put a blanket on each bed. "Elaynna put your mum's bed further out on the veranda. It's too hot tonight." Abdul called out. "Jee Abu Jee" replied Elaynna. Abdul wanted some time alone with his wife. He hadn't spoken to her properly for two days or got the chance to hold her. He was pining for her company.

Jannat lovingly locked her eyes at Qasim in her arms when she carried him out. He was fast asleep. Yasmin settled herself outside while Kareem helped Elaynna push their brother's crib out.

Yasmin yawned and stretched her arms out ready to sleep. She noticed Abdul stealing glances at her, locking her eyes on him she smiled coyly. Their loving glances were being noticed by Jannat, everything was on full show with the bright light!

Jannat turned her back towards the veranda to give them privacy. Abdul took the chance to go to Yasmin, not realizing Jannat did this on purpose! Abdul turned the veranda light off and put the courtyard light on, so the shadows of the outside light shimmered in the veranda and they could no longer be seen. Abdul placed one hand beneath Yasmins and closed it over with his other hand, enclosing her hand tightly. Finally asking how she was feeling. Yasmin blushed at the gesture, playfully replied "Even better now that you are here". The pair continued whispering sweet nothings whilst Jannat kept the children entertained. The children fought over who could hold their little brother. "My turn to hold him now!" Rahim would try to snatch him from Kareem. Worried for her grandson Jannat decided to intervene "Stop it, hes not a doll!" Jannat scolded.

Taking Qasim gently, she laid him down on the bed. "He's only little, give him a year he will be wrestling himself with you!" Jannat couldn't help laughing at her own joke.

"I am going to lay him here so you all can have a look at him." They all sat around the bed looking at him adoringly. "Dadi, did I look like that when I was little?" asked Rahim. "Yes the three of you looked the same when you were born, hes a bit fairer than you and has a sharper nose I think, but babies change all the time when they grow up." Jannat continued to remind them of their early years.

"The three of you were really different when you were little. Rahim you were round and chubby the more you grew, Kareem you kept changing like the wind!" they all laughed at their Grandmother's jokes. "Elaynna you were the size of your mother's palm when you were born, you had to stay in a box for three months because you were in a rush to come to this world! You were born two months early. And now mashallah you're a beautiful girl." Elaynna shied away under her dubatta at her Grandmother's compliment. Her brothers nodded their heads in approval.

"Beautiful but would let anyone walk all over her." Rahim answered back not being able to stay quiet.

"Chup kar!" (shut up)

"She doesn't let anyone walk all over her she's just a helpful person." Kareem snapped at Rahim, standing up for his sister. Jannat nodded her head in agreement. Out of annoyance, Rahim went to his bed to lie down and put one arm under his head. "Look I know I sound harsh, its because I care for her. I am just worried about her that's all. If you saw how she was being used by her teachers, the way she was sweating in the heat washing their dishes? It angered me so much that I didn't know sooner! I would have sorted the teachers out! How dare they make my sister work like a donkey!" Kareem was surprised to see his brother's rage, showing a tender and a warm side that he never ever expressed. Even Jannat was taken aback. Elaynna was touched by her brother's rage, maybe he wasn't as bad as she thought he was. After all he was her brother too, for once she felt fortunate to have a brother who looked out for her.

Rahim hardly ever showed he cared, Elaynna wanted to cherish this moment as long as she could, hoping he would say more but he didn't.

As Jannat lay down on her bed, Yasmin came to take Qasim back to his crib. Elaynna's bed was between Jannat and her brothers. Elaynna liked having her bed between everyone, this made her feel secure. She was terrified of the dark, this all stemmed from her terrible encounter with the jinns.

Elaynna woke up one night screaming uncontrollably and hurting herself. Abdul held her until she calmed down whilst reciting quotations from the Quran to control the evil spirit. Elaynna all of a sudden stopped falling unconscious.

The following day Jannat and Abdul took Elaynna to see a Holy saint who gave her a blessed pendant, he strictly instructed for her to wear at all times. He advised Abdul to keep a close eye on her she had been casted an evil eye by an evil spirit. The Saint advised Abdul and Jannat to not to allow young unmarried girls to bathe at the local lake which was where evil spirits resided and would be able to take over their innocence. Also adding that they should advise the rest of the family and friends the same, due to illiteracy and ignorance people made these silly mistakes. Abdul thanked the Saint and promised to warn everyone he knew.

From that night on Elaynna was too afraid to be alone in the dark.

Elaynna retired to her bed that night, she gazed at the clear sky admiring its beauty. Every star looked like it had a story to tell. She noticed one star the biggest of them all. It seemed like it was getting bigger and bigger as she looked at it. Wanting to show the others, she looked to her left and right everyone had fallen asleep. However her father's bed was still empty. Elaynna sat up in her bed wondering his whereabouts, finally seeing her father perform the Isha prayer in the veranda, she watched him for a few minutes with admiration. She observed him opening the holy Quran quietly reading in a tone not higher than a whisper, reading these scripts made Abdul feel content and close to his Lord.

Elaynna wished she could read the holy Quran as smoothly as her father or even as well as her brothers. Being the eldest she could just about read it, this made her feel ashamed of herself. She knew she could only master this technique if she practiced but somehow something always got in the way. She then put her head down on her pillow diverting her attention to the stars that soothed her to sleep.

CHAPTER 4

Elaynna's awoke from her slumber to the sound of mysterious giggling. Quickly looking around the darkness she saw a glimpse of a candle light in the kitchen. The shadows frightened Elaynna, instantly covering her head with her blanket in a panic. Elaynna started to quiver and shake with beads of sweat rolling down her forehead, her hands started to feel clammy. She was almost certain it was a Jinn trying to call her. She cupped her ears and started reciting all that she knew from the Quran to protect her.

To Elaynna's surprise she was awoken by the sound of the cockerel. Obviously she had fallen asleep after all that commotion. It surprised her that no one else woke up with her in the middle of the night.

She looked around confused rubbing her eyes, hurrying herself to the bathroom. Maybe it was just a dream, she thought to herself as she looked at herself in the mirror. Replaying the incident in her mind made her heart race like she had run a hundred meters, she could see the reflection of the previous night's incident in the mirror. She imagined the giggling could have been a witch that came into their kitchen last night or worse a Jinn.

Elaynna recollected her thoughts when her father called her to hurry up he was getting late. Elaynna quickly washed up and then slowly walked into the kitchen trembling with fear, worried the Jinn would still be there.

Jannat had already started making breakfast. This made her feel at ease. She wanted Kareem to wake u so she could tell him what had happened. She was too scared to tell Abdul or Jannat. Jannat looked at Elaynna curiously when she just sat there quietly. She usually would feed the animals upon waking up, but she looked lost.

"Whats wrong beta?" Jannat asked softly whilst stirring the pot of tea. "Nothing . . . Dadi" mumbled Elaynna back. Remembering her chores she got up to take care of them. She finally sat down for breakfast, she still had loads to do. After attending to the animals Kareem and Rahim joined for breakfast.

The three of them sat squatted on the floor. Jannat gave them each a cup of tea and a buttered chapati. Before Elaynna was about to put a morsel in her mouth, Jannat prompted her to give breakfast to her parents. Elaynna nodded obediently taking the breakfast carefully, she put her fathers breakfast on his bed next to him as he sat there reciting the Quran. He smiled at her and put his hand on her head out of appreciation. For a moment Elaynna felt she could tell her father about the incident she witnessed. "Abu . . . last night I saw shadows in the kitchen. It sounded like a woman's laughter." She blurted out whilst looking down, still being frightened of repeating the incident out loud. She looked up waiting for a reaction. Looking up she saw her father was no longer there. Worried maybe she shouldn't have said anything. She looked around her father had gone inside to put the Holy Quran away.

"Elaynna! Stop daydreaming!" shouted Jannat. "Come and give your mother her breakfast!" Elaynna ran to the kitchen to handle the next task, Jannat especially made an ajwain buttered chappati for her mother. Ajwain seeds are used to cure stomach pains and to avoid stomach cramps or colic in babies. When newly mothers used ajwain seeds in their diet this helped their breast milk to be more tender on their babies stomachs. Women in Pakistan take great care of their diet when they give birth as these old remedies help them to be strong again and helped avoid colic, wind etc in babies.

Yasmin instructed Elaynna to watch her brother while she went to wash up. Elaynna willingly sat next to her brother and saw that he was wide awake looking at the ceiling.

Elaynna started to kiss him, to her horror he started to wail in a high pitched voice. This made Elaynna jump with fear. Her parents rushed in looking worried. "What happened?" asked Abdul. "He's probably just hungry." assured Yasmin picking him up to calm him down. Elaynna began to have disturbing thoughts, she thought the evil spirit had probably taken over her spirit the night before when she saw the light. She shouldn't have said anything, her brother could sense the evil spirit on her. Babies and animals had a sixth sense to detect such things, her grandmother once told her.

Elaynna slouched down on the floor and began to weep silent tears. Abdul surprised at his daughter's actions, pulled her up by the arms asking what was wrong. "Im cursed! Qasim doesn't like me!" Abdul shocked upon hearing the words that came out of his daughter's mouth. "Why do you say such a thing? You are not cursed, has anyone said anything to you, was it Rahim?" Abdul asked with a tone of anger in his voice. "No Abu it's not Rahim, last night I saw something that I shouldn't have seen." Abduls face dropped. Qasim was still screaming in a high pitch voice. Jannat came rushing to his aid. Jannat picked him up and checked his stomach. His stomach felt hard as a rock, he was awfully bloated. Jannat started rubbing it in a clockwise motion, he stopped crying and released some wind. Jannat began to wonder why the poor boy had so much wind.

Jannat then noticed Elaynna in tears after she had calmed Qasim down, questioned Abdul what was going on. Abdul filled his mother in. She also mentioned to Abdul that she thought Elaynna wasn't her usual self that morning. Turning to her granddaughter she sat her down and inquired what she saw. "I saw a small light in the kitchen last night and heard some giggling. It sounded like a woman." Abdul burst out laughing. Yasmin's face turned red with embarrassment. Jannat and Elaynna exchanged confused expressions. "Pagal! That was your Ammi in the kitchen last night!" Abdul gasped through all the laughter.

Jannat understood immedietly why Qasim had a bad stomach ache. She glared at Yasmin angrily. Yasmin couldn't meet her gaze knowing she had been caught out. Elaynna was relieved being assured it wasn't an evil spirit after all. Jannat ushered Elaynna to eat her breakfast.

Jannat raised her hand to slap Yasmin but Abdul took hold of it in time, asking why was she getting so worked up over a little thing?

"Your laadli wife *had* to have rice last night, that's why Qasim was screaming, he was suffering in so much pain. His stomach was as hard as a stone!" Abdul looked at Yasmin, he couldn't help laughing again. He couldn't believe Yasmin had been so immature that she sneaked in to eat the rice in the middle of the night. "And poor Elaynna thought she saw a ghost!" Jannat exclaimed.

After listening to herself, Jannat also couldn't help laughing. Yasmin started to join in the giggling. Jannat told her to shut up and to eat the ajwain chappati. Yasmin stopped laughing instantly and quickly began to eat. Jannat scolded her for eating quickly and told her to eat slowly and chew every morsel as much as she could.

Jannat came back to the kitchen to join her grandchildren. Rahim asked Elaynna why did she look like she had been crying. Jannat informed them of the incident of the previous night and Qasim's stomach ache. Rahim and Kareem exchanged glances and burst out laughing. Elaynna couldn't help laughing at her silliness.

The two brothers rushed out to play cricket after finishing their breakfast. It was Friday, no school today. Elaynna and Jannat continued drinking their cold tea. Jannat looked into the cooking pot where the rice had been, it was empty! Jannat's temper rose again. No wonder Qasim was screaming so badly. My poor grandson, she thought. She cursed Yasmin under her breath. "What a witch of a mother! Allah keep my grandson well."

"Did you say something, Dadi?" Jannat shook her head and gesturing to tidy up. Abdul handed his cup and chakor to Elaynna as she was heading out the kitchen.

Abdul remembered that it was Friday and asked if his Jummah prayer clothes were ready. Fridays were a day of blessing, so it was important to dress well. Abdul never failed to meet the requirement. He had a special outfit set aside for these prayers. He only wore this outfit on Fridays and made a scene if it wasn't ready or ironed properly.

Jannat went inside to check on Qasim. Yasmin had finished eating, she was trying to calm Qasim, he was crying in a high pitch voice again. "You greedy woman! You ate all of the rice that was in the pot! Do you want more?!" she took Qasim and whacked Yasmin hard on the head. Yasmin did not react other than a remorseful look to her son. She knew Jannat was only concerned, she wished she had not caved in to her temptation. Now her beautiful son was suffering as a result of it.

"Go and give Abdul his clothes!" Yasmin jumped up following orders. "And take the bartan (dishes) with you! You expect your dad to come and pick these up!" Yasmin scooped the dishes quickly, accidently putting her slippers on the wrong foot whilst rushing out. "Bismillah, bismillah . . ." cooed Jannat to her Grandson. She rocked him in her arms gently and then lay him down on the bed. She picked up the sesame oil bottle from the shelf and put a little in her left palm. With the other hand she undid his safety pin and lifted his vest. She gently massaged around his belly button with the oil, the belly button was still sore where the ambilicol cord was tied tight, two inches away from the stomach.

This area would be avoided completely of water and cared for with extra care. She did well in avoiding the sensitive area. As she massaged his stomach she kept saying "Aaoozoo-Billahe-Minashaitan-Niraajeem-Bismillahir-Rahman ir-Rahim". (I seek refuge in Allah from the Satan-In the name of God, most Gracious, most Compassionate).

Qasim calmed down falling quiet. He looked at Jannat, the wind that released from his bottom made him smile. Jannat smiled back at him and started cooing while she continued massaging around his stomach and pressed gently onto his pelvis. His stomach was completely soft now. Jannat sighed, feeling proud of her maternity skills. Singing him a lullaby, he fell asleep.

Yasmin had tears in her eyes when she went to give Abdul his clothes. "Here are your jummah clothes, jee." walking into his room. He was getting ready to show the electricians the next house for electricity line up. Abdul noticed Yasmin looking upset. He rolled up his sleeves observing her lovingly. Yasmin wasn't paying any attention to him. She stood frozen in her steps feeling anxious about Qasim, and Elaynna's incident haunted her once more. A tear dropped from her eyes, Abdul caught it in his palm in time and wiped it over his locks.

"Why is my Jaan losing my special pearls that I have tried to keep safe? I know you have been missing me is that it?" He teased her. Yasmin put her hands on her face and started sobbing uncontrollably. Abdul put his arm around Yasmin, leaning her head on his shoulder he stroked her hair. "Whats wrong janeman?" he whispered gently. "Im such a bad mother!" she sobbed. Abdul smiled thinking she was suffering from post natal depression. He learned how to handle this form of depression in England when Elaynna was born. He squeezed her tighter this time. "Is it because of the pilaf?" Yasmin released herself gently, wiping her tears letting out a little giggle. "Yes . . ." she replied with tears still rolling down her broad cheeks.

Abdul just assured her it was normal. He reminded her of the time of Rahim's birth, how nobody was there to teach her what to eat and how she ate everything the doctors prescribed, nothing had happened to him. Then he reminded her of when Kareem was born and no matter how careful she was with her diet, Kareem still suffered bad colic. He assured her this was the way of life and what small babies go through. However his mother was never wrong, she had five children herself and how she should trust her judgment and not get disheartened if she is cross with her.

"Ammi has your best interests at heart. You know you are her favourite, because you always respect her and take her advice. She respects you for that."

Yasmins face softened a little when she heard this. Abdul took out his handkerchief and dried her cheeks. Yasmin asked to take the handkerchief to wash. Abdul shook his head and folded his handkerchief neatly placing it in his right chest pocket. "Im taking these pearls with me, they are too precious to wash." He kissed her forehead setting off to leave, looking back before leaving the room.

Yasmin began to cry tears of joy, she couldn't believe her fortune she had been blessed with such a loving husband. Husbands were not as affectionate after they had children. However Abdul's love seemed to grow more and more.

Yasmin watched her husband through the window as he walked across the court yard, leaving the gates. Their house was inherited to Abdul from his father. It had five rooms with a veranda that was a step above the ground. The bathroom was across near the animal barns. The kitchen was at the far end of the house. The kitchen had two parts, one indoor room where all the food was kept on shelves and a cooking stove. There was an outer short wall where the tandoor was dug up and another stove to use for cooking in the summer. Abdul had started decorating his home while he was in England. Abdul wanted to complete the look with tiles and paint but he no longer had enough funds because they had to rush back to Pakistan. The court yard was very wide and the shape of a rectangle, it was big enough to hold a banquet. There were several trees planted, one lemon tree, a red bud and empress tree. There was a barn like room on the side of the house for the animals. A tall bricked wall surrounded the house and the court yard, which had broken glass along the walls to keep intruders at bay.

It was still early and the weather was cool and misty. Yasmin stood at the doorway of Abdul's room and watched her daughter bring in water from the well. Elaynna was balancing one clay pot on her head and the other on her hip. She carefully placed the clay pots in their designated place, outside the kitchen in the shade. Elaynna was tired from all the work in the morning. She poured some water in her palm and enjoyed the cold water against her lips. She then lay down on the netted bed under the Empress tree in the middle of the court yard and enjoyed the cool misty morning. Smiling to herself looking up to the sky, feeling free of all worry. No school, no Miss Shazia . . . . just me and . . . she thought . . . drifting to a deep sleep.

Jannat had fallen asleep next to Qasim. Yasmin smiled looking at the both of them, on the same bed next to the other. Qasim looked content, Jannat was snoring rhythmatically. Yasmin took the opportunity to bathe, it was Jummah Abdul would be in his best clothes, she desired to smell nice and to dress up for him. Yasmin went into the kitchen and lighted the stove to boil some water. She then took the hot water bucket to the bathroom, grabbing a cotton outfit and a towel; she picked out one of Abdul's chosen favorite outfit. Yasmin felt like a new woman after she scrubbed down every inch of her body. After getting rid of the nasty bloody smell she felt like herself again.

As she poured each tumbler of water over her forehead she felt rejuvenated, trying to wash away the negative thoughts that were troubling her.

Drying herself she got dressed in a sky blue salwar kameez. Feeling so much better she was ready to face the world. She tied up her hair in a towel and went back to her room. She noticed Jannat had left, Qasim's remained fast asleep. She bent down and kissed him gently on his delicate cheek. He reminded her of Abdul, the thought of Abdul made her kiss him again. Feeling bashful at her actions, she realized when Abdul was around she never had the courage to kiss him first.

She then applied some perfumed musk to her wrists and kohl to her eyes. Her skin was shimmering again as she applied some jasmine oil to her cheeks. She looked beautiful. Giving birth to four children hadn't aged her one bit, the men of the village envied Abdul for having such a young and a beautiful wife. On the other hand the women of the village envied Yasmin for having such a caring and a loving husband, who was not only very attractive but a learned practicing Muslim.

The women in Birmingham drooled over Abdul. They called him the George Clooney from Pakistan where he had worked in the dry cleaners factory. His features consisted of grey eyes with stark black thick eyelashes that made him look like he was wearing kohl in his eyes. His skin was fair with a hint of a golden tan. He had medium grey black hair with a grey black stubble. His body was broad with a wide chest with muscular arms, a height just an inch short from six feet tall. There were slight dimples on his cheeks when he smiled.

Yasmin's nerves began to race with guilt. If Abdul ever found out what she did the other day to Elaynna she knew he would never forgive her, she felt she was betraying him, by keeping the incident all to her self, they had no secrets between them. She was so confused in what to do. Maybe if she repented, this secret would never reach Abdul and her love would remain intact. She was worried about losing the devoted love of her husband. Maybe someone had cast an evil eye on them, the love that everyone envied.

Her thoughts were disturbed when she heard Qasim wake up for his feed. Abdul had returned from his prayers. Jannat was chopping onions for lunch and Elaynna was still fast asleep. It was nearly nine o'clock. Elaynna was still asleep for more than two hours. Kareem and Rahim returned from their games the sun was out, the temperature was increasing. Jannat took out a netted bed from inside and put it under the tree where Elaynna was sleeping so the boys and Abdul could sit. Kareem gave everyone a drink. The three of them started chatting and teasing each other. The boys were happy to be spending time with their father after a very long time. This was the first they could remember their father being at home with them for a few days. Abdul was also enjoying the quality time with his children, he asked about their school and what they had been up to.

Jannat had almost finished cooking lunch. No body had noticed Elaynna's unconsciousness. It wasn't even midday yet, everyone usually napped after lunch not before. Jannat remembered Elaynna when it came to knead the dough. She looked outside and asked the boys to wake her up to help her. Kareem went up to her and nudged her. Elaynna didn't respond. "Dadi shes not waking up!" Kareem shouted across.

"Ok leave her!" Jannat shouted back. Jannat busied herself with the rest of the cooking. It was nearly 11,oclock. Yasmin walked out of her room, holding Qasim, she sat in the veranda. Abdul watched her walk gracefully, waiting to meet her gaze. Yasmin had her hair out, letting it dry naturally. Yasmin looked up where she heard the boys laughing. Noticing that Abdul was looking at her.

Abdul turned away suddenly in a teasing way. Yasmin shook her head smiling to herself. Abdul then looked again, she was no longer there. Yasmin had joined Jannat in the kitchen. She saw Jannat had done everything alone. Yasmin grew a little annoyed when she saw that Elaynna was still asleep. Yasmin started complaining to Jannat. "It's all your love and spoiling that is making Elaynna lazy." she whined.

"What will she do when she is married? Sleep all day?!" Abdul heard the commotion and joined them.

"Whats the problem, Ammi jee?" Jannat told him that Yasmin was getting annoyed because she let her granddaughter sleep for so long. Abdul tried to soften the tension by sticking up for his daughter.

"Leave the poor thing, shes tired." he said casually. "Its your fault she hasn't slept." he teased. "She didn't sleep last night because she was so scared, you know she scares easily." Yasmin blushed with embarrassment.

"I don't care I am waking her up, she needs to get up now, or how will she sleep in the evening." Abdul watched her leave the kitchen in a huff. "You have spoilt *her*." Sighed Jannat to Abdul, taking in a deep breath.

Abdul ignored his mother, these silly actions were the reasons that made him love his wife. Abdul leaned on the door folding his arms across his chest, amusingly watching her next move. Yasmin briskly walked across the courtyard yelling, "Elaynna! Utho! Elaynna utho! . . ."

"ELAYNNA!!" when she reached her bedside shouting over her head. Elaynna didn't respond. She lay in the same position from when she had fallen asleep. Yasmin nudged her harder, "Elaynna, get up now!" Elaynna still didn't respond. Yasmin looked at Abdul worryingly, Abdul's smile faded. Elaynna usually woke up straight away, usually after the first attempt. Abdul walked briskly rushing to her side. He slapped her cheeks and checked her pulse. "Oh she has a pulse, thank Allah." he thought to himself. He tried slapping her cheeks gently at first, then harder. Still, no response. Abdul's heart started to pound with fear.

"Whats wrong?!" wailed Yasmin. "Im not sure . . ." Abdul answered breathlessly. Jannat intentively watching everything, noticing everything had gone so quiet, went to investigate what was going on.

45

She had just finished cooking the lentils. Walking out briskly she saw everyone leaning over Elaynna's bed. Jannat began to quicken her steps towards Elaynna. Fearing the worst, when saw Yasmin sobbing uncontrollably. Jannat noticed Abdul's eyes were also red with fear.

"Whats the matter?" Jannat croaked, her voice finally managing to escape her mouth. "Elaynna's not opening her eyes Ammi . . . but she has a pulse." Abdul answered finally. Rahim and Kareem helplessly watched their sister's bed in despair. She looked completely lifeless. Kareem began to cry not sure what was going on, thinking she had left them permanently. Jannat ran to the water cooler to fetch some water. She came back quickly and splashed a handful on Elaynna's face, without realizing she had thrown half of the water onto Abdul too. Elaynna moved her head to the other side. Abdul's nerves calmed down a bit. He picked her up, gently placing her head in his lap. There was no sign of her waking up. He tried slapping her again No further reaction.

He felt her forehead. It was steaming hot. As he held her, her body was becoming increasingly hot. "Why is her temperature increasing?" he asked trying to stable his trembling voice. His mother was always right. That's what he had told Yasmin today, she knew what to do.

Jannat assured him everything will be alright. She instructed him to call the doctor at once. Abdul put Elaynna down gently back to her position. He grabbed his keys from his bedroom which were in one of the displayed tea cups. He frantically ran to his motorcycle. Yasmin stayed paused in her position, she didn't move an inch, continuously crying silent tears.

Jannat sat down at Elaynna's side and held her hand. Abdul had diagnosed correctly, she was burning hot. Jannat ordered Rahim and Kareem to fetch fresh water from the well, it was where nature had water at its coldest.

Rahim and Kareem set off in a flash. They threw the bucket in the deep dark well and began pulling. Rahim realized they didn't bring anything to put the contents in. He told Kareem to hold the bucket on the reel. He ran to get an empty container.

Meanwhile Jannat darted Yasmin with venomous glares, telling her to wipe her crocodile tears. "This is all your fault! My poor Elaynna is lying here like this. What kind of mother are you? Bechari does exactly as you say and you punish her before she even has the chance to speak. Just because your mother was hard on you doesn't mean you have the right to do that to my granddaughter!" She exclaimed through her tears. Jannat saw Rahim run in empty handed. "Wheres the water?!" she shouted crossly. Rahim shaken with fear grabbed a metal pot from the kitchen, without answering he ran back outside, he didn't even dare look for a bucket, he knew the tension was building up inside.

Yasmin knew her mother in law was speaking the truth. She realized she pushed it too far this time. Her worst fear was coming true. Jannat's temper was fuming and very hurt. Jannat loved Elaynna more than her own mother ever did. Jannat's temper got worse each minute. "Your mother treated you and your sisters like soldiers, she didn't even know the meaning of the word mother, and now you are doing the same to your own daughter? People usually treat their own children with the love that they never got themselves. But you!

What the hell are you? You are a curse to be a woman? It's beyond me how my son could love such a wicked woman!" Yasmin could no longer take the insults. She ran inside crying uncontrollably. She was beginning to hate herself, Jannat was right she thought to herself, *I am turning into my mother.*

Jannat felt guilty for a second about her spoken words, but quickly changed her mind being reminded of the state she had found her granddaughter a few days ago, locked up in the dark left to die. The boys arrived back with the cold water. Jannat held the edge of her dupatta and dipped it into the utensil. She squeezed the water out of the dripping scarf and placed it over Elaynnas face. Elaynna moaned at the coolness of the water muttering "Pani . . . Pani . . ." with closed eyes. She was asking for water. Kareem got the drinking pitcher dipping it into the freezing cold water he handed it to his grandmother who then held the pitcher to Elaynna's lips and helped her drink. Elaynna drank the water half heartedly, her head felt like a burden. Elaynna then dropped back to unconsciousness.

CHAPTER 5

Yasmin's Story

Yasmin drifted back to her childhood where her mother had been so strict with her and her sisters. Yasmin was the eldest of three sisters with two older brothers. Yasmin was the daughter of Yunus Hussain. Her father was a well known man who worked very hard for his family holding a great status. He owned a carpentry shop of his own. Whenever he walked past, people would say salam to him out of respect. He held a very strict household. No matter how strict he was or the status he held outside his home, he was nothing in front of his wife, she was in charge of all of the affairs.

Yasmin's mother treated everyone like they were beneath the earth. It was very hard to impress her or to keep her satisfied. No matter how much one did for her, you wouldn't know when she would turn around and insult you. Her name was Safia Bi. A woman so sure of her self and harsh in character you wouldn't dare question her, even if you were in the right. She spoilt her sons rotten but was very hard on her daughters.

Javed, the first born son. He always took his mothers side when she had something to say. The three sisters were afraid of their brothers as much as they were of their parents. Safia educated her sons but not her daughters.

Yasmin and her sisters learnt how to read the holy Quran from their neighbor Usmaan Ali, a retired army soldier.

Yasmin remembered that her childhood consisted of work, work and more work. They would wake up at crack of dawn to fetch fresh water from the wells for their father and brothers to bathe in. Make breakfast and then go to feed the animals even before they ate themselves. Safia would just stand around with a fan in her hand and observe each chore like a colonel. If one of them fell asleep whilst doing their chores Safia would swat them with the fan like mosquitoes. If they cried out in pain Safia would punish them further. "Why does someone have to remind you to do things all the time! All you want to do is eat and sleep! When I was a little girl I had to do everything all on my own! You lazy cows!" Safia would scream with spit splurting out on their faces, her scream was so loud that even the neighbors would hear and tut their tongues. Yasmin hardly ever got screamed at, she was very quick and subtle in her work. Eager to learn and not to make mistakes. She was mindful that if she didn't do the house work properly her mother wouldn't let her go to her kind neighbor Fatima who taught her how to sew in the evenings. Yasmin was taught the holy Quran from her neighbor Usmaan Ali who had studied the holy Quran in depth and knew word for word by heart. He was a kind hearted soul and a generous man. His wife Fatima an angel in disguise, she was a tailor by trade, sewing clothes for a living for the local families. Her husband made a living teaching the Quran to the local children. The couple themselves didn't have any children so teaching young children was a delight for them.

Fatima would often tell her husband that if they didn't have the children coming in and out every day their life would be meaningless.

Even if Allah hadn't granted them with their own children they had the love and respect of all the children in the village. Every child they taught grew up to have up most respect for them that whenever anyone got married or left the village to study, upon returning they would come for a visit, they would come and visit Fatima and Usmaan first before even going to see their biological parents.

Fatima and Usmaan were so generous they often refused to take money from certain poor families in the village. They had such a long credit list of payment they never ever asked the families to pay up. Despite their generosity they were never ever short of money, they always had more than they needed. Usmaan and Fatima were devout Muslims and followed the example of the Prophet PBUH wholeheartedly. In doing so they lead peaceful lives as well as being financially stable.

All of the women in the village admired Fatima's knowledge of Islam, as well as her beauty and etiquette, even Safia thought highly of her and respected her. All of the men also admired Usmaan, who in his youth served his country and now was serving the people of the village and their children. Whenever anybody was sick or ill, the couple were the first to be there for that individual and even helped to pay for their medical costs.

Yasmin was twelve when she had completed learning to read the Holy Quran, she would have finished it earlier like the other children at nine, but due to the housework pressure it had been difficult for her to learn it on time. Fatima knew that Yasmin was very hard working and was having a rough time with her mother. So Fatima offered to teach Yasmin to sew for free in the evenings. Believing it to help her to be distracted of her mother's pressure and have something to look forward to. Safia agreed quickly, she was getting a good deal, not just saving teaching money also she thought that if Yasmin would know how to sew she would no longer have to pay a tailor.

Yasmin delighted at the prospect looked forward to her lessons every day. As the two grew close, Yasmin would pour her heart out to Fatima in the evenings. Fatima would listen contently and stroke her hair. Fatima would assure her that she was a good daughter and if she stayed patient Allah would highly reward her. "Heaven lies beneath a mothers feet, no matter how hard the mother be."

Fatima would assure her that her patience would be rewarded; Allah will reward her with a loving and a caring mother in law in return. Not that her mother didn't love her, that was just the way she was and she would have to respect her and continue being the good daughter she already was. Yasmin would force a smile wiping her tears and feel a lot better after hearing such soothing words.

Within six months Yasmin had learnt how to cut fabric elegantly and how to stitch properly. Even though she had learnt the ins and outs of sewing, Yasmin would still go to Fatima's house every evening to learn more. This time not just about sewing, sewing was an excuse, meeting Fatima had become a necessity.

Yasmin had begun to look up to Fatima as an idol. Fatima became very fond of Yasmin, she taught her about Islam and taught her something new everyday, the knowledge that Yasmin craved. Yasmin also helped Fatima with her sewing, enabling her to learn something new and explore her own creativity. Safia didn't mind because Yasmin always did her bit of chores so swiftly.

However Yasmin's younger sisters envied Yasmin's small window of independence. They still respected her like their own mother. She would sew them new outfits developing her own designs using them as templates to practice on. Which was much to their delight at their elder sister's new learnt skill.

Upon turning fifteen her parents began getting proposals from far and near. Her younger sisters Asma and Bushra would tease her that she would marry an old man because she had become so wise. Yasmin would disagree with them, saying she didn't want to get married; she inspired to study and follow Fatima's footsteps.

One evening while the girls were getting the beds ready, they overheard Safia, Yunus and Javed discussing Yasmin's marriage. The three girls leaned in to the window trying to listen in to their closed discussion. There was a candle light on the table and all they could see were the shadowed features of their parents and their older brother Javed. Safia as usual with a fan in her hand. The hand which held the fan was leaning on her bony knee which was bent against her chest. Her other leg hanging over the bed she was sitting on and her white cotton shawl draped over her shoulders and head.

Their father sat in a crossed legged position with his turban on one leg; he held the hookah in his right hand and sucking in its contents ever so tenderly, in such a way that it was priceless and would break any minute if he was not so careful. He blew into the hookah like an elegant instrument. You could hear the rumbling of the water as he sucked out the tobacco.

Yasmin, Asma and Bushra grew up with this familiar sound. They had become accustomed to the sound of it, it had become a soothing sound to them, like a lullaby to their ears. Their father would sit under the stars smoking this instrument as they lay in their beds to sleep. The sound of the water beating was the only sound in the air while everyone tossed and turned to get comfortable in their beds. The sound would drift in their eardrums like a mother humming a drowsy song helping them to fall into a deep sleep.

At times he told them stories of his youth, proudly saying how brave he had been, he had killed so many snakes without fear, how he would pick them up and tie them in a knot.

Tonight their father was inside discussing his eldest daughter's marriage and smoking the hookah without them. Javed sat facing his mother while his father sat cross legged on the chair between them. He played with the candle light on the table as he spoke to his mother. "Yasmin has now come of age to get married." Safia spoke softly for once; she didn't want anyone to hear her voice. Yunus half smiled upon hearing Safia's voice, he hadn't heard her speak softly or quietly since they were newly married.

Yasmin felt nervous butterflies in the pit of her stomach while she was eavesdropping. Asma covered her mouth in shock and Bushra held onto her eldest sister's arm and squeezed it tightly. Yasmin looked down at her and Bushra gazed up into her sister's eyes trying to give her a reassuring smile. Yasmin placed her hand on her sister's hand while they continued to listen to the conversation. "There are already lots of proposals coming for Yasmin." Javed started, trying to get a conclusion of the discussion.

"Nobody has come yet." Safia answered looking puzzled. "I mean there are people asking if she is available or if she is engaged, I have just answered that we aren't looking just as yet. That's why I thought I should come to ask you first."

Yunus nodded his head and tried to hide his wet eyes. The mere thought of giving his daughters away made him well up. He loved his daughters dearly and sneakily fulfilled their wishes without their mother's knowledge. If she ever knew that he was buying them regular gifts of jewelry or make up she would have taken them away or they would be disposed. Fortunately the girls were very good at disclosing their things. Whenever their mother wasn't home they would put make up on and imitate the women of the village.

"I want my daughter to marry a man of importance." Yunus said firmly. "He has to have a good job and be a practicing Muslim." Safia nodded in agreement. "Do you know anyone Javed?" She asked inquisitively.

"What's the rush?" Yunus asked crossly. Safia gave him an annoyed look. "Allah will send the right suitor, I am not prepared to let her go in the wrong hands, even if shes sitting here untill shes twenty!" Safia gasped beginning to fan her face even faster. "I was thirteen when I got married, my parents made the right decision." She answered back.

"My point exactly, you haven't matured." Yunus chuckled half coughing with the tobacco stuck in his throat. The girls couldn't help giggling at this. They giggled under their breath so they wouldn't be heard; the last thing they wanted was to get into trouble. They were surprised at their father's courage. Safia turned a blind eye at his comment. Javed held his laughter in by gritting his teeth and pretending to cough. Yasmin felt a lot better that their father was on their side and wanted the best for her. Maybe Fatima Aunty was right she thought.

Hearing the final thoughts of the discussion, Javed asked something all of a sudden. "Can I get married?" he asked quickly. Yunus and Safia were stunned. She stopped fanning herself and shouted "YOU WHAT?!" in shock. Yunus came to his sons defence as Safia was about to smack her son with the hand held fan. The girls trembled with fear quickly sneaking back into their beds. They knew their mother's temper all too well. However this seemed like the first time that their mother was showing any anger to her sons. They were a little taken aback at their brother's request.

Yunus took his son out of the room and led him to the other room. Safia just sat there cursing him, finally coming out taking herself to her bed that was prepared for her by the girls.

Yunus closed the door behind him. Lighting the candle on the table he opened the window for the evening breeze to blow in. Yunus firmly looked into his sons eyes and asked for an explanation. Yunus knew Javed wouldn't ever say such a thing to his mother like that. No matter how close he was to her. Yunus knew how to connect with his children. He was determined to be a good father using the knowledge he had of Islam. He knew Javed was asking for his right. Actually he was rather proud at his son's dialogue; he understood well that marriage was completing half of your religion.

He knew Javed wouldn't come out of the blue with such a request, something was up or he wanted to avoid adultery. As father and son sat in the dim light, Javed twiddled his thumbs he couldn't look back at his father. Javed respected his father greatly, a bit more than his mother.

A look of contempt from Yunus would send quivers down their spine.

Yunus tried to observe his son's face. Javed could feel his father's cold stares. He asked to be excused. "I will decide when you can leave Javed." Javed started to shiver feeling cold all of a sudden. Yunus could feel his fear growing. Yunus's face softened further as he looked deeply at his eighteen year old son. He is a grown man he thought to himself. Every man has physical needs. Yunus knew that Safia had high hopes for the boys she wanted them to study to their full potential, she wasn't against marriage, she just wasn't keen on sharing her son with another woman. Yunus was a hundred percent sure of that. Her reaction had proved it.

"Right!" Yunus finally spoke breaking the ice of silence as he placed a hand on his son's knee. "What has brought this all on?" Javed couldn't think of anything to say, this was their first father and son meeting. He pretended to not to hear, and played with his sky blue cotton kameez. "If you don't explain Javed, how do you expect me to help you?" Javeds heart started to race, feeling frightened of the outcome, but his mind confirmed that this was his only chance to tell his father. What's the worst that could happen thought Javed. His father would probably slap him, but he would bear it for the sake of his love.

"Theres this girl that I like." he said quickly and crossed his arms over his face as a shield squeezing his eyes shut. Yunus looked at him pityingly. "Who is she?" interrogated Yunus. Praying internally that his son hadn't done anything stupid, if he did he would throttle him. "Shes from our village . . . ." muttered Javed. Seeing the rage building up in his fathers eyes "Oh no no Baba jani I havent even spoken to her. I would never disgrace you." Javed quickly answered upon reading his fathers questionable eyes. Yunus thanked God under his breath. Yunus then investigated further, hoping he had gathered most of the situation already.

"So basically you like her and you want to marry her, am I right?" Javed nodded his head in agreement. "Whose daughter is she?"

"She's your friend Sheraz's daughter, shes nearly sixteen, her name is Mehnaaz."

"Oh so you have gathered all the information then?" Yunus teased. He was actually happy that his son wanted to marry some one they already knew very well, now no family background research was necessary. Javed blushed feeling embarrassed and looked down. "So do you think you are man enough to take the responsibilty of a wife? You will have to start to work and make your own money like a responsible man; it will be difficult for you to study. And if you want to marry, which I am not against you have to take full responsibilty of this family· like I have been." Javed nodded in agreement. "And remember women are either like scissors or a needle. They either cut your family or keep it together by binding it like a needle, sewing it together. It will be your responsibility to keep her intentions clean and to teach her to look after this family like her own." Javed thought for a second, pausing to nod this time.

"What about Ammi?" he asked. "Don't worry about that I will take care of her. It's about time I put her in her place. I also want you to know my son that I am extremely proud of you to have the courage to speak up, getting married is half of your deen our mazhab. Islam teaches us that marriage stops a man to look elsewhere to satisfy his needs."

After saying this Yunus got up from his chair, straightened his white kurta and walked out of the room into the moon lit darkness. He looked around the yard, everyone was fast asleep, tucked up tight under their netted blankets. Yunus stumbled on to his bed which lay on the far end with Safia on the other end. He tried to make out her expression as she snored in her sleep. She must be exhausted ordering everyone around he laughed to himself. Lying on his right side with his right hand under his ear he tucked himself in, wishing good luck to himself for the comming morning.

Javed stayed sitting there thinking about the first man to man conversation with his father. He was trembling with shock and excitement. His smile flickered in the candle light. The candle light outlined his broad face. He held his stubbled chin in his hands and then coyly ran his fingers through his hair as he imagined his wedding. Lying on the bed by the window with his hands behind his head he let the breeze caress his face whilst looking into the dark valley of the village.

The morning cockerel awoke the girls. Yunus was just returning from the masjid. The girls were doing their usual chores.

Safia was brewing tea for Yunus; he liked his tea before anything else when he returned. It was usually Yasmin's duty to do this every morning. Safia dismissed her from the kitchen and told her to help her sisters to feed the chickens and milk the goats. Yasmin was surprised at her mother's disposition when she insisted to let her do it.

Yasmin followed her mother's orders and didn't dare question her mother's unusual behaviour. Safia brought out his tea as he sat down with his hookah on his bed. She placed his tea on the small table gently that Yasmin had always put next to her father's bed every morning. Safia knew a conversation took place between father and son the previous night; she was desperate to know the details and couldn't help being jealous at their private conversation. She was regretting the way she had reacted and thought if she had been able to have kept her temper under control then she wouldn't have missed out on her son's secret.

"So what cooked between you and our beloved son last night?" she finally asked as Yunus settled himself and sipped his tea. "Beloved?" questioned Yunus trying to make her feel guilty. He took another noisy slurp on purpose.

"If he was your beloved you wouldn't have reacted the way you did when our son asked us of his personal need." Safia looked down at the floor feeling ashamed. For once she didn't speak over her husband. "He was trying to do the right thing, and us as parents have to give him his Islamic right to marriage." Yunus took another sip from his tea and stole a glance at Safia's face that had changing expressions. "So what does he want? He's only eighteen. What about his education?" Safia blurted. "Well I have told him the consequences, if this is what he wants then he has to take full responsibility. He needs to get a job. I am not letting him marry and not pull his weight around; even if Allah has blessed us with more than enough." Safia knew that arguing to let him marry and study wouldn't convince Yunus. He was a self made man who worked very hard and didn't take a penny from his own father. This independence helped them to be in a good financial position before his older siblings. Yunus himself had married when he was eighteen, he didnt let his marriage become a burden on anyone. Even when they only had one meal a day he didn't let Safia's parents or his own parents intervene.

"So who does he want to marry?" Safia further inquired after a few minutes of pause. Yunus took a deep breath and told her. He spoke softly but firmly. He told her everything.

The fathers name. The mothers name. Finally, the daughter's name. Safia's expressions changed like a chameleon. Each expression changed after each word left Yunus's mouth. To amuse himself, Yunus imagined her changing in seven different colours; Orange, yellow, blue, green, indigo, violet and finally red, the colour of rage. "You expect your petty little friend's daughter Mehnaz to be Safia Bi's daughter in law!!" she got up shouting. A drop of spit landed in his eye. Without moving his body, Yunus took out his handkerchief and wiped his face, his gaze closing onto Safia's angered face.

Surprisingly Yunus kept his cool. He didn't want to argue. "I don't want to argue Safia and I don't want to make a scene. Lower your tone of voice this instant." He said calmly through gritted teeth, laying a hard glare on her face. Safia backed down instantly, she could feel the coldness in his glare. A chill went down her spine.

Wasim was still in his bed covers almost at the opposite end. He could hear every word of the conversation and pretended to stay asleep. The morning sun was still rising: The sky was orange waiting on the horizon; the sun had not yet fully beamed through the sky.

Wasim could hear the conversation clearly, feeling impressed at his brother's request. Wasim used to tease him that no matter what he did their parents would never agree. He saw his mother calm down and sit across his father looking down like a child who was told off for being naughty. "I don't understand why I married such a jahil." Safia sat quietly for once. She knew what jahil meant and she knew that when Yunus was angered, then something must have really pushed him. The word jahil sounded like a curse. Safia wasn't educated either; she could barely read the Quran and some bits of Urdu due to the matching letters of Arabic. Yunus had tried to teach her; but he gave up because of her lack of interest. Jahil meant ignorant. When someone called you a jahil it meant you knew everything apart from common sense. An ignorant could never judge what was right or wrong. Safia instantly fell quiet upon hearing the word. She thought highly of herself, the word alone felt like a swearword to her ears. Yunus took the last sip from his tea and leaned back on the pillow behind him returning to smoke his Hookah. He noticed the tobacco was nearly finished, he took out a small pouch from his pocket, releasing the elastic band and sprinkling the contents in the small black hole at the front that was shaped like a smoking pipe, the way a chef sprinkles spices on a completed dish.

Taking out the matches from his other pocket he lit the tobacco taking in short bursts of puff. Once he was comfortable again, noticing his long pause on his wife's face he broke the silence. "Didn't you listen to a word that I said?"

"I have told Javed that if he wants to marry he has to find a job first. If his marriage is destined then he shall find a job and then we shall get him married. I don't understand why you are getting so stressed? I know he is your son. However he is a man after all. Every man has his needs." Safia didnt say a word. She just hoped that her son would change his mind. "What about his education?" she croaked her main concern.

"Well, he has to study until he finds a job."

Safia sat thinking quietly until her three daughters came in through the back door giggling. Safia came out of her silent trance when she heard them. She hadn't noticed that Yunus had left and gone inside to get ready for work. She diverted her attention at the girls, releasing her temper on them. "Who is going to tidy these beds away, they have been sitting here since dawn!" her roar shook the girls. They quickly busied themselves making breakfast and cleaning the house.

Wasim instantly got up worried it will be his turn next to get into trouble. He rubbed his eyes pretending that he just woke up. He scratched his hair and stretched his arms in the air. He grabbed his kurta from the peg and threw it over his shoulder. His father whacked the newspaper on his head from behind. "Have some shame you walk around in your vest shamelessly, you live in a house with three sisters."

"Abu jee . . . . I just woke up." Wasim replied scratching his hair and yawning. Wasim had a mind of his own. He did what he felt like and didn't care what others thought of him. Growing up as a teenager he was becoming increasingly vain.

When his father walked off in the court yard to join Safia once again with his newspaper; Wasim sneaked inside the house to look for Javed.

Their house was a five bedroom bungalow, with two bathrooms and a small kitchen. The veranda was white with a terrace all around it. The court yard was large enough to fit ten beds. Their house was rectangular in the shape of an 'L'. The terrace wall was painted white with a net in the shape of hexagon made of bricks.

Wasim finally found Javed in the last room. Javed was still asleep with his face in the same position from the night before. Wasim quietly sat next to Javed and looked at his brother's face. The morning sunlight beamed through the window. This was the coolest room in the house. It had the best view and the breeze that came through the windows. Wasim looked out the netted window and instantly shook his brother to wake up. "Javed! Its Mehnaz look!" Javed woke up suddenly.

"Where?!" Wasim stood up clapping his hands and starting to laughing hysterically. His kurta fell to the floor because he was laughing so hard. "You arse!" Javed shrieked. "I wish I didn't tell you anything." Wasim still couldn't stop laughing; he had to hold on to his stomach because it was starting to hurt.

Javed sat up and couldn't help smiling at his brother's silly joke. He loved his brother's sense of humor, which is what made them close. Javed had a serious nature, he had planned his future in detal, he knew what he wanted from life. Wasim enjoyed his carefree nature; he loved living in the present. The future didn't worry him at all. He believed in living like a free bird. And he certainly didn't believe in love.

"Javed, I can't believe you told Abu jee!" he exclaimed after calming down from all of the laughter. Javed sat with his knees closing tight towards his chest with his arms hugging his knees, he hid his face in his knees for a second. He smiled shyly at his brother brushing his shins with excitement.

"Oye hoye, all shy and why? Being shy should be Mehnaz's role not yours." He teased nudging his brother. "I heard Abu talking to Ammi this morning. Hes told her everything!" Javed sat up loosening his arms for a second.

"Brother no point getting so excited yet. Abu said you need to find a job first then you will get married." Javed smiled cheekily to himself, he already had a job in place. All he had to do was say to yes to the job proposal. He had applied in a clothes shop to be a part time assistant and to look after the accounts of the shop. He had impressed the owner with his maths skills. He even had the salary set in place. It was paying pretty well for an amateur. What he wasn't aware of was that the owner was only paying him a decent wage due to his father's reputation.

The deal was only one sided yet. Javed wanted to get his father's permission first. The owner was highly impressed by this but he was still confused as to why such a high class business man's son wanted a job. Javed already knew that his father would put that condition across if he told him of his wish to marry.

"Don't worry about that Wasim, I have that sorted already."

Wasim smiled at him and slapping his cheeks together, "Ok great! I'm happy for you." He then grabbed a towel and went into the bathroom. Javed finally got up from his bed stretching looking out of the window at the same time, hoping to see Mehnaz, but to his dismay he didn't. Safia walked in to call him for his breakfast. He quickly hugged her from behind as she was leaving. He hugged her so tight that she told him he was shameless. The hug softened her heart a little. She held his face and told him that she hoped he would do what was best for him.

Javed held her shoulders telling her not to worry. He freshend up and joined the others for breakfast. It was ghee parathas for breakfast and fresh yoghurt that Yasmin churned that morning. Safia sat down and watched her give everyone their breakfast. Safia prayed that Mehnaz be as good at housework as her daughters were, with similar intact training. Yunus left for work and .stoked his daughter's heads in a loving way. They all turned and smiled at him saying Allah Hafiz.

Wasim was the last one to eat his breakfast like always. He had finally had his morning bath and combed his hair. Setting each hair in its perfect place, making sure he used the right amount of oil. He hated the traditional wet look. He liked his hair to look fresh not greasy. Safia remained sitting until he was done eating, even if everyone else had finished their meal.

Javed rushed to his feet after he saw his father about to leave for work on his motor bike. "Abu ji, about what you said last night . . . ." Yunus nodded once, in a way to encourage him to carry on speaking. "Well I am happy to get married and I have been offered a job in town. I told the owner Omar that I would need your permission before I accept his proposal. So er . . . can I go to him today and say yes? After college, of course?" Yunus rather stunned at his son's responsible nature, "Of course you can." he then took off on his motorbike. Javed watched his father leave, feeling content at his father's reply.

Javed called for Wasim to hurry up or they will miss the morning rickshaw. "Coming Javed!" Wasim shouted back taking a last big mouthful of his paratha and getting to his feet. "Stop rushing or you will choke!" shouted his mother. The boys got ready in their white shirts and grey trousers and blue blazers. The brothers went to the private college in the town of Chakwaal; one of the highly recommended colleges in town. Safia wanted them to have a private education. So Yunus found them a good rating college. The boys waited for their morning rickshaw to pass by. Javed told Wasim his plan. Wasim patted his brother on the back for support, enjoying the content look on his brother's face.

Sitting in the rickshaw, Javed took out his maths book to check his homework. Wasim watched his brother shaking his head in disapproval. He opened his rucksack and took out his walk man and head phones and started playing his favorite singers latest album. He loved Nusrat Fateh Ali Khan. He enjoyed all of his qawalis and songs. He hid his walk man from his father. His mother had given him the money to buy it after much persistance. Whenever a new cassette came out he would sneakily run to his mother to ask for money. She hardly ever refused him, but told him off for wasting the money. He would then hide his collection of cassettes in his and Javed's wardrobe. He hid them right at the back behind his clothes in a neat row. Only he knew where he had kept them. He sat back in his seat, listening intently to each word, holding his navy Reebok rucksack to his chest. He watched nature unfold leaning back into his seat. He enjoyed watching the trees, hills going by, while the rickshaw drove on the smooth wide road. It was the only vehicle travelling at that time of the morning along their village's road.

The warm sun spreading its rays all over nature, the rickshaw reached to the end of the village road and drove on to the main road of the busy town.

Wasim watched the town go by in its hustle and bustle. He put the volume up on his walk man so that was all he could hear was the beautiful words of the song, the market stall holders noise was blocking the sound on his walk man shouting at the top of their voices to call customers to their stalls.

Javed looked up occasionally and then back to his math book again. The rickshaw stopped outside their College gates. By that time

Wasim had closed his eyes and was almost asleep with the softness of his favourite singer's voice in his ears. Javed gave the rickshaw driver his fee and shook Wasim awake. Wasim stretched his arms and yawned as he got out. He checked his hair in the rear view mirror of the rickshaw. Patting his head softly from the back making sure his hair wasn't ruined. The driver saw Wasim do this every morning and teased him everyday. "Your hair is in its place your highness, I drove very carefully to not to ruin it." before zooming off.

Wasim would shake his head laughing, both brothers then parting their ways at the entrance. Javed to the right and Wasim to the left, both would join their own group of friends. Usually disappearing and won't see each other until the end of the day.

The girls sat at home, quietly discussing what had happened the night before. They knew something was up. They whispered to each other in one of the rooms after lunch. They figured out already that Javed was eager to get married, marvelling at his outburst. Feeling excited for their brother, they agreed it would be nice having a new sister in the family.

CHAPTER 6

After college Wasim waited for his brother Javed outside the Main School gates. He leaned against the wall listening to his walkman. Above the gates hung a semi circle sign of the college's name; Javed finally came rushing to his brother's side. "What took you so long?" asked Wasim. "I was getting the exam dates from my tutor."

"Hmmm . . ." mumbled Wasim shaking his head.

"Can we go now?" Javed nodded putting his papers in his back pack. Both walked to the road waiting for their rikshaw lift. Arriving at his usual time; speeding them through the town. Javed asked him to quickly stop at the Malik Fabric shop on the way, he needed to speak to the owner. Wasim shrugged and sat back in the rikshaw while his brother hopped out to go to the shop. The rikshaw stopped in between the busy markets. Market stall holders were still shouting at the top of their throats to sell their products. Wasim enjoyed the hustle and bustle admiring the beautiful colours of the market. The town was busy as usual. The rikshaw driver got out and lit a cigarette observing the people go by.

Wasim sat back listening to his music. Javed finally came back with a big smile on his face. The rikshaw driver took a last puff of his cigarette grinding it into the ground, driving them home. Walking through their valley on their way home they saw Mehnaz walk by holding a pot of rotis, on her hip. Daring not to look up she was accustomed to keeping her gaze down. Javed watched her every move like a love sick puppy, Wasim couldn't help laughing at Javed's mouth wide open, body facing forward and his head looking back. He almost bumped into their wall. "She's gone brother! We are home now!" Wasim pushed him up the steps.

When they got home they greeted their parents. It was late afternoon. Safia as usual was fanning her face. Yunus was reading the paper and having his tea. Javed went and told his father about the job and his exam dates. He said he wanted to finish his college year before getting married. Yunus nodded in agreement, admiring his sons responsible nature. Safia huffed in dismay upon hearing this.

They both went in to change out of their uniform. Wasim had already changed and got his cricket gear out. "What about your homework!" shouted Safia. "I will be back by dinner!" Wasim shouted back running out of the door before she could make him stay. Javed couldn't help laughing when he walked out rolling up the sleeves of his kurta. He came out with his books and homework taking them to the terrace. His favorite place where he could shut himself away from the world, it was the perfect spot to watch Mehnaz. Now he was even able to recognize her footsteps. Whenever he heard her foot steps he would instantly get up and lean over the terrace wall gazing lovingly. When she would disappear he would return to his books finding it hard to concentrate and start to daydream.

"Why can't Wasim be more like Javed, hes always playing and wasting his free time; I don't understand how he manages to pass.

Javed mashallah always comes first in all of his subjects. He works so hard and is capable of going far and now he wants to mess it up by marrying that despicable Mehnaz." Safia grumbled to Yunus.

Yunus ignored her. The three sisters were in the kitchen preparing dinner they paused when they heard their mother mention Mehnaz. They knew Mehnaz. Yasmin stopped stirring the curry that she was making, Asma stopped kneading the dough and Bushra covered her mouth in astonishment. Mehnaz was really pretty and the same age as Yasmin. They didn't know her personally but she seemed very nice. They only knew her from going to each others houses once in a while or seeing her by the local well every morning. However they did seem to enjoy each others company when they were together.

That evening Yasmin as usual went to Fatima's after dinner. She hopped all the way to their house. This was her downtime. Fatima welcomed her with a hug and they both sat down to work. Fatima asked her how she was and how was her day. Yasmin told her about her mother wanting to get her married and how she heard her father sticking up for her. Fatima smiled hearing this. She also told her about her brother wanting to get married. Fatima told her to stop. She explained how it was wrong to talk about her family like that and how it was wrong to eavesdrop and ordered her to never do it again. Yasmin explained she knew backbiting was wrong but she wasn't backbiting she was only saying that her brother could be getting married soon. Fatima smiled but didn't inquire who the bride was. She hated gossiping. It was against her faith. She tried her best to avoid it. She closed the topic telling Yasmin she was happy for her happiness. Fatima could see the joy on her face when she mentioned her brother's marriage. She knew she was only expressing her good news. Fatima wanted to teach her good manners, feeling it was a duty to remind her of what was right and wrong.

The following morning Yunus took Safia to Mehnaz's house to ask for her hand in marriage.

The five siblings sat together in the courtyard. It was Friday there was no school. The sisters teased their older brother but were careful in what to say, they weren't sure how their older brother would react. This was the first time they were actually joking around with him. Usually they were too afraid to talk to him freely worried he will go back to tell their mother. But they had misjudged him. Their mother had strictly instructed them to respect their brothers and not to disturb them.

They realized that their brothers weren't as bad as they appeared to be. Javed softened to his sisters teasing, feeling happy that his dream was coming true. He was blushing with amusement. Wasim joked that he won't be their brother anymore after he got married. Javed shook his head in disapproval assuring them that he wouldn't change. In the two hours that their parents had gone, the five of them grew a close bond.

Mehnaz stood inside her bedroom looking through the barred window. Watching her parents sit with Safia and Yunus. She realized that they had come to ask for her hand in marriage. Blushing while she eavesdropped in the darkened room. Her parents looked extremely happy with the proposal. She could hear the excitement in their voices. She overheard her mother Kausar, saying they would not be able to say yes until they spoke to their daughter and seeked her permission. Yunus agreed understanding the situation; he had three daughters of his own. Safia pretended to be happy clearly forcing a smile, inwardly hoping that Mehnaz would refuse the proposal somehow. Sheraz and Kausar served them tea and rusk cakes. It was nearly midday. After their long talk, Yunus gestured Safia to get up to leave.

They got up appreciating the hospitality. Kausar offered them to stay for lunch but they refused assuring that they will come again in a few weeks for their final decision.

Mehnaz was the only sister, youngest of two brothers. Her brothers were both in college. Mehnaz's father was a builder. They weren't as well off as Yunus's family. Sheraz's sons went to the government college. Kausar and Sheraz felt that their worries were all over with their daughter getting a proposal from a well off family. An added bonus that their daughter would be in the same village, their daughter will always be nearby if they ever wanted to go to see her. When they left, Kausar went into Mehnaz's room to talk to her. Mehnaz suddenly got up and pretended to tidy up. "Sit down my love." Her mother gestured, Mehnaz without looking up sat down on a chair.

Her mother sat next to her. "Our local neighbors Yunus and Safia came today asking for your hand in marriage." Mehnaz twiddled with her dress still looking down. Her mother cupped her face in her hands and raised it towards her. She held her face close herself trying to make eye contact. Mehnaz's eyes froze looking down, she couldn't bare to look at her mother. Kausar couldn't help but to feel proud at her daughter's shy nature.

"I have told them that we have to ask your permission first before we take things further. So shall I say yes? They want the wedding to take place when their son completes this year's college; he has found a job to help out with the household expenses. He seems like a really responsible boy. I will get more information from your brothers. But what do you say my love?" Mehnaz just nodded in agreement still looking down. Kausar smiled kissing her forehead, reminding her daughter to get the lunch ready. Kausar walked briskly to her husband who was sitting under a tree smoking a cigarette whispering in his ear excitedly that their daughter had agreed to the proposal.

Sheraz smiled from ear to ear. "Let them come back and ask again. I don't want them to think we are desperate." Kausar nodded in approval and joined her daughter.

CHAPTER 7

Upon Safia and Yunus returning home, lunch was already laid on the mat outside the kitchen. They always had lunch outside, it was too hot in the kitchen, apart from in the winter. The siblings were all sitting in their seats waiting for their parents; they stopped talking instantly when they saw them walk through the gates. Yasmin had made gobi alu, potatoe with cauliflower curry. Javed eagerly looked at his fathers face hoping to hear something.

Yunus smiled at Javed in a teasing way. "They will let us know in a few weeks after they have seeked Mehnaz's permission." Javed blushed and looked down. Yunus took a bite of his dipped morsel continuing. "Don't worry son your marriage will take place. Her parents seemed happy enough, they don't have any obligation but as parents they obviously want their daughter's approval. We have to respect that." Safia ignored Yunus, she didn't wish to add anything. They all ate in silence. When they had finished eating, Yunus then told his sons to get ready for the Friday prayer. Instantly obeying and wearing their best clothes.

The girls took away the dishes and started to get ready for their Friday prayers too. The girls prayed at home while the men attended the masjid sermon. Safia joined in with the prayers. It began to get cloudy and started to rain. It was the first monsoon rain. The rain came in speeding motion. The rain hitting the ground created an aromatic muddy smell. The rain brought cold air to the three sister's cheeks as they stood in the veranda watching in awe. The three of them spread their hands out to the rain, feeling the coolness in their palms. Yasmin put both of her palms out to catch the water. She then smothered the cold water onto her face. A tingling sensation occured inside through her body, Safia came out, admiring the rain. For once smiling to herself, maybe her son getting married was a blessing after all. Safia's mood changed drastically, a hopeful feeling blooming in the pit of her stomach. Bushra daringly asked if she could play in the rain. Safia first frowned, looking at her up and down, then nodded. Yasmin and Asma tried their luck too.

Yasmin assured her mother that they will change before their brothers and father came home. Safia nodded in approval. Surprised at their mothers permission the girls charged at the rain throwing puddles and handful of rain to each other. They felt like dancing but didn't dare push it too far. Safia sat herself down on the bed under the veranda leaning against the pillow watching her three daughters giggle with each other while they played.

She watched them run back and forth drenched in the rain chasing each other. She couldn't help to laugh herself. The girls were astonished to see their mother laughing for the first time, especially so much and so loudly. They did worry for a moment or two if she had gone mad. Fatima came in, knocking at first to warn of her entrance. She sat next to Safia, shaking her umbrella, placing it onto the ground. Watching the girls play in the rain. Fatima was amused at the girl's cheerfulness. She had come to give kheer, rice pudding. Fatima always made something sweet on a Friday.

Then she would distribute a little to each household in the village. Fatima observed Safias changing expressions whilst watching her girls. Fatima couldn't help feeling disheartened for not having children of her own. Tears overwhelmed her eyes, a tear fell from her face without realizing it. She wiped it away quickly when she felt Safia turning to look at her.

"It's enough now girls go and change!" Safia ordered, the girls quickly ran inside and dried themselves. Safia took the opportunity to fill Fatima in about Javed's proposal. Fatima listened earnestly and congratulated Safia. Fatima confirmed she knew the family well also mentioning that they had a good reputation. Fatima tried to give Safia some words of wisdom. About treating her daughter in law like her own etc, Safia just nodded and changed the subject. Fatima sensed she obviously wasn't too happy about the whole arrangement. When the rain took a stop, Fatima took her leave. By that time Yunus got home it was almost 2pm. The girls remained indoors going down for an afternoon nap. Javed and Wasim trotted after their father. Safia fell asleep in the veranda on her side with her elbow under her head, with her mouth wide open. Upon enteringYunus closed it for her, and shook his head.

CHAPTER 8

The following morning the three sisters set out to go to the local well to collect the water and to tie the cow in the meadow. They usually met the girls from the village there too. Mehnaz was there too. The three sisters giggled when they saw their would be sister in law. Mehnaz couldn't help shying away in her veil. The village girls around exchanged confused looks. "Why are you getting all shy at looking at Uncle Yunus's daughters? You see them everyday you don't usually react like that?" Shenaaz teased. Mehnaz hid her face further, until Bushra innocently came over to pull it off.

All the girls began to laugh at Bushra's gesture. Mehnaz quickly covered her face with her hands turning her back to the others. Yasmin handed her clay pot to Asma and walked over to Mehnaz placing a hand on her shoulder. "Shall I take your shyness as a yes?" the rest of the clan began putting their hands on their hips and some with their hands on their chins. Mehnaz just nodded in her hands, still hiding her face. Yasmin slowly removed Mehnaz's hands from her face. Mehnaz's face had turned bright red in the morning mist.

Yasmin turned around with her arm on Mehnaz's shoulder and announced to the rest that Mehnaz was going to be their sister in law. The other girls gasped and began giggling. They all went up to Mehnaz and started teasing her even more. Yasmin told them to quieten down as the excitement grew. "Nobody knows yet so please don't say anything to anyone. Mehnaz's parents haven't confirmed it yet." She made the girls promise to not to say anything. Mehnaz nodded too. Quickly picking up her clay pot full of water; coyly leaving the others without saying a word.

The others giggled at her behavior. Bushra suddenly realised they were taking too long for their chores and worried that their mother will be in a rage. Reminding Yasmin to hurry up; Yasmin quickly filled the clay pots. Asma put one on her head. Yasmin balanced two clay pots on her head and Bushra held the smallest pot on her hip. Hurrying home like never before. Safia was already in a rage before they even stepped into the house. "Where the hell have you three been this morning? Just because I cut you some slack yesterday you think you can do what you like now eh?! Now hurry up and finish the work! Stop staring at me! Who do you thinks going to do the work, your Dad?!" the three hurried in their ways nearly dropping the clay pots out of fright, scurrying in different directions.

Safia continued her cursing while they scampered around trying to impress her. Yunus found her behavior amusing at first then eventually put cotton wool in his ears to read his paper.

Shenaaz's mother Irshad came knocking later that morning. A big smile across her round face, no secrets could be kept from Irshad. The main gossiper of the village; she had to know everything, but couldn't keep anything in her stomach. Safia had just finished combing her hair doing it in a tight plait. Taking a final glance in her hand held mirror; she heard Irshad's heavy foot steps and saw her reflection in her mirror. "Haye Allah!" she embraced Safia excitedly. "I can't believe you are getting Javed married! Many many congratulations!" Safia pretending to look amused; then began wondering how the news had gone viral in one day. At first she thought it must have been Mehnaz's parents. Until Irshad blurted that she heard it from her daughter, where Yasmin had announced it by the well. Safia's nerves began racing with anger. Somehow she managed to keep it well hidden. Not wanting to lash out at her daughters in public, she tried to conceal the news. "Well, yes we are." finally replying clearing her throat, really trying hard not to get angry. "Bhai jaan many congratulations to you too" she called to Yunus who was just leaving the house placing his topi on his head.

Yunus looked a little baffled at first, but then realized what she was on about. "Congrats will be in order when all is confirmed. We have only asked for Mehnaz's hand. I must get going, Allah hafiz." Yunus rode off on his motorbike leaving for work. Irshad started asking all sorts of questions from Safia, until Safia told her to calm down and to stop making such a commotion. "All will be settled in a few days and then we will announce it properly. I didn't want to tell anyone but obviously the news has leaked somehow." Irshad realising that Safia wasn't in a mood to talk she left her to it and took her leave.

Yasmin and her sisters started trembling while they ate their breakfast. They had heard the whole conversation between Safia and Irshad. "Yasmin why did you have to open your mouth." whispered Asma. "I was so happy I don't know what came over me. I thought I could trust Shenaz. She knows what her mother is like. I have kept all of her secrets. I hope Ammi isn't too angry." she whispered back. Her hands trembling as she sipped her tea.

Safia walked into the kitchen with rage written all over her face. "Yasmin get here now this instant!" Yasmin without looking up put her cup down, scraping her feet slowly walking outside. Safia pulled her plait and began smacking her wildly. "WHO DO YOU THINK YOU ARE EH?" she screamed spitting on her face. Yasmin covered her face to protect it. "So this is what you girls get up to early in the morning! I didn't bring you up to tell others our family matters!" Yasmin was getting hit constantly she could barely feel the pain. Safia took off her sandal and started hitting her on her sides, continuously cursing her. Bushra and Asma watched helplessly through the kitchen window, distraught at their sister's abuse.

All of a sudden Javed stepped in trying to stop his mother; shocked to see his mother in such a violent state. He grabbed Yasmin and protected her behind him. Safia tried to pull him away. Her dupatta fell off and she still wouldn't stop trying to get at Yasmin. Javed then held his mother's hands firmly and told her to calm down in the name of Allah. Safia finally calmed down and picked up her dupatta. She straightened herself up and looked into her mirror to check her hair. Javed got her some water and ushered Yasmin inside. "Why on earth all this commotion Ammi? What has got into you? What did poor Yasmin do that you were beating her to death?" Safia accepted the glass of water and drank it in one gulp. Trembling with anger, she then wiped the sweat from her forehead with her dupatta and told Javed what had happened.

Javed was appalled at his mother's behavior. "Over such a little thing you were beating your daughter to death? I know ammi it's not my place to say but one day you will regret this." Safia just shrugged.

Feeling better after taking out her rage on Yasmin, believing she deserved it.

Javed took another glass of water into the bedroom where Yasmin sat in tears. Her body stung of pain. She had never been beaten so brutally before. She put her arms on her knees with her face hiding in her arms sobbing in pain. It couldn't be felt when her mother was hitting her but now every inch of her body stung. Javed gave her the glass, she drank it slowly letting him to wipe her tears. He asked her side of the story. Yasmin admitted she was wrong between trembling tears but she couldn't help expressing her happiness to her friends when she saw Mehnaz that morning.

Javed stroked her head gently hearing her side of the story. This was the first time he shared such a moment with his sister. Rather touched at his sister's disposition. Offering her his handkerchief to blow her nose "Shhhh . . . ." he soothed. "Its ok, I appreciate your lovely gesture. Actually I am quite happy about it." Yasmin stopped crying and wiped her tears with the back of her hands.

Javed smiled gazing at her. She smiled back taking a deep breath, her body still trembling.

"Thanks to you, maybe Mehnaz has started to have feelings for me too. Now tell me what was her reaction when she saw you, what happened? What did you say? What did she say?" Yasmin looked at her brother in amazement. He was talking like a love sick puppy. My brother is in love, she thought. Not believing he was opening up to her. All these years of growing up Safia smothered her sons so much that she didn't give them any time to spend with their own sisters.

Keeping them to herself. Today finally her brother was talking about his feelings. Yasmin stopped feeling sorry for herself, then beagn telling Javed the whole story not missing out a single detail.

He sat next to her with his knees against his chest hanging on to her every word. Safia intruded into the room all of a sudden. Yasmin quickly got up straightening herself, waiting for the next punishment. "Go and take your disgusting face somewhere else! Today you are to scrub all of the floors of the house with the hand held brush. This will teach you to never to speak about our family matters to anyone ever again!" Yasmin nodded obediently putting on her scarf, briskly leaving the room without looking back at her mothers glaring eyes. She didn't want to make matters worse by not acting quickly. Javed still sat back where Yasmin had left him, leaning onto the wall whilst sitting on the floor with his knees against his chest.

"You two were looking cosy." Sneered his mother. "I tell her off and you turn it around that she wasn't in the wrong? You think I didn't hear your conversation? Stupid gadda!" now she was shouting at Javed. Getting up slowly, trying not to smile. He stood up and folded his arms across his chest trying to figure out his mother. "Look Ammi . . ." he tried cutting in. "Shut up! I don't want to hear a thing!" Safia finally broke down in tears. Safia sobbed for the first time in front of her son. He knew why she was reacting the way she was. She is jealous. He thought. She must be incredibly jealous. I am her first born.

Observing his mother sulking standing in the same position; not ready to comfort her as yet. He gazed at her lovingly he finally placed his hands on her shoulders and made her sit down. "Ammi no matter what happens I will always love you. You are my mother, you gave birth to me, you brought me into this world. You mean everything to me. And no other woman can EVER take your place." Emphasizing on the word ever quite sternly making sure she understood him well. "But Ammi you shouldn't take your anger out on Yasmin. She is your daughter. YOUR daughter. One day she will be married and you will never get the chance to be close to her again. Do you want her to have a hard life? Ammi you're a woman yourself if you can't symphasise with another woman then who are you?"

Javed had never ever spoken to his mother in this manner. But getting married had made him feel more responsible than ever. He had to learn to stand up to his mother. Even though his father never attempted to, because his father loved his mother dearly, he wouldn't dare say a thing to upset her or against her. Safia looked at her son in disgust. She couldn't believe that what he was saying was absolutely right. Feeling guilty all of a sudden, she didn't let Javed see her guilt.

Stroking his hair she held his face in one hand "When did you grow up so quickly my darling?" Javed smiled back leaving for college. Safia sat in the same position he had left her and tried to think what had made her become so heartless. Why was she continuously terrorizing her own daughters? For once she asked for repentance in her heart in the hope that Allah would forgive her.

Later that afternoon when everyone was asleep Yasmin whispered to Asma how she felt a bond between Javed that day. Asma rubbed powder on her arms for comfort when Yasmin showed her her bruises, and how much they were paining her from all the floor scrubbing. Bushra was fast asleep like a baby. They giggled when Yasmin told her about Javed's sweet gesture that morning. Usually Javed never ever got involved when their mother would hit them. This was his first time. They felt their brother was changing for the better in case their mother hit his wife. They were in a fit of laughter after that. They laughed with their palms covering their mouths as quietly as they could just in case their mother would walk in on them.

CHAPTER 9

Over the next two weeks. Yunus and Safia went again to Mehnaz's home to ask for their reply. Kausar and Sheraz welcomed them when they walked in with baskets of fruit and sweets. Greeting each other with distant hugs; Kausar pointed to their seats, gesturing for them to sit down. Kausar went in quickly to get tea and sweet treats. Sheraz and Yunus first spoke about the weather and work etc. When Kausar finally came back with the tea and treats, their conversation got down to business.

"Let's not beat around the bush, and talk about why we are actually here." Yunus finally starting the discussion; Kausar felt a little excited in the pit of her stomach and a mixture of sadness. Kausar and Sheraz exchanged looks at each other with content, looking back at Yunus they smiled and nodded in agreement. "I am hoping that you are going to say yes. Also we don't want Mehnaz to be forced into anything. You have spoken to her haven't you?" Sheraz sat upright in his chair, nodding again. He finally spoke and said "We are happy to accept your proposal. Our daughter won't get a better proposal than of your family. Yunus, my brother we have grown up together in life and you have succeeded more than me. You are a very respectable man and have never degraded anyone. I have more respect in my heart now for you as you have come to ask for my daughters hand in marriage." Sheraz finished his sentence wiping a tear from his eye. Yunus got up from his chair and couldn't help embracing him.

As a father of three daughters, he could feel the emotions that Sheraz was going through. He patted his back in a supportive way. "Right! Now where is my daughter in law!" amused at his comment Kausar went in to bring Mehnaz to meet them.

Mehnaz walked shyly with her mother; looking to the ground continuously. Mehnaz was wearing a green and pink salwar kameez. Kausar held onto Mehnaz's shoulders while they walked together, leading her like she was unable to walk. Safia smiled half heartedly, wondering what her son had seen in her, she wasn't near enough good looking as her son, she thought to herself. Yunus got up placing both of his hands gently on the top of her head like it was melon, testing its ripeness. Safia followed expressing her affection with a hug and a forced kiss. Purposefully making her sit between her and Yunus.

Keeping one arm over her shoulder and the other on the top of her hand, showing affection was not Safia's usual thing but she managed to act it out well in front of Mehnaz's parents.

Kausar returned to her seat trying to observe Safia's affection, trying really hard to work her out. Safia noticing Kausar's observance increased her affection furthermore. Yunus recognized her fake attitude, hoping internally that his wife wouldn't make a scene. "Mehnaz you are like my own daughter. I hope you will keep our family happy. We will try our best to make you feel at home." Mehnaz's mother felt satisfied, feeling that her daughter would be well looked after.

"So when can we take our daughter home?" Yunus turned to Sheraz. "Shes yours now you tell us when you are ready to take her its all down to you." Yunus was starting to enjoy the respect he was receiving. Thinking for a few minutes he tried suggesting a date. "Hmm, how about July the 3rd? That would be when Javed finishes his exams and his college year. He has a job in place as an accountant, he wont start the job officially until after a few weeks of marriage."

"But that's only a few months away?" Kausar answered with hesitation in her voice. Before she could say anything further Sheraz agreed with Yunus. He couldn't let such a good proposal slip through their hands.

"Why is there any problem? If there is we can rearrange it?" Yunus assured her. "No brother there isn't any problem it's just that you know there are so many arrangements etc, however if that is your wish, then we must contribute to it." Yunus clapped his hands in excitement. "Great! See you soon. We will be in touch!" Safia didn't say a word apart from exchanging goodbyes.

When Yunus and Safia stepped into their home, Javed had been biting his nails anxiously waiting, listening out for their footsteps. Javed quickly closed his book, quickening his steps down the terrace stairs. He tried to act as casual as possible, so he didn't look desperate.

"Asalam aleikum ammi, Asalam Aleikum abu."

"Walikam salam." They replied at once. Yasmin quickly brought them a cold drink. Handing them a glass of water first, and then brought them some tea. Javed pretended to do some chores around the house; hoping that his father would tell him if the proposal was accepted or not without him having to ask, if he asked his mother she would scold him. Trying to be more in their way so they would notice him he hung up some clothes on the peg, then shook his uniform. He pretended to read, he moved the water pots. Yunus knew what he was up to burst out laughing. "Whats wrong with you? Why you being so helpful all of a sudden? You ok?"

Javed blushed with embarrassment about to step onto the stairs to return to the terrace, Yunus called him over. "Yasmin! Asma! Busra! All come here please!" Wasim walked in from playing cricket that moment. Safia stormed inside she didn't want to listen to her misfortune again. They all sat around their father, leaning in to hear his announcement. "Well I have some news." He began.

Just then the azaan for the afternoon prayer began its calling from the masjid. Yunus sat back in his chair letting the azaan complete its call; they all sat in silence waiting impatiently. Javed hung on to each word of the azaan. His heart beating to each attribute. When it ended, his nerves were racing so fast that he could hear the sound of his heart beat in his ears.

Yunus looked at him and then turned to his other children. "As I was saying." he began again. "As you all know where we went this morning. Mehnaz's parents have said yes to our proposal, not only that but I have also set the wedding date. Javed your wedding will take place from the third of July. A few weeks after your exams, so you have time to help out with the arrangements of the wedding rituals. Are you happy now?" Javed counted the months in his head, "Yes abu ji, what ever suits you."

Wasim cheered and the girls said their congrats. Javed nodded and then briskly walked back up the stairs of the terrace. Finally alone in his private space he expressed his feelings. He started jumping up and down with joy. Whispering yes! Yes! He didn't want anyone to hear him so he tried to keep his excitement as quiet as possible. His smile wouldn't leave his face.

Remembering to be grateful he looked up to the sky and thanked God for answering his prayers. All of a sudden he heard foot steps coming up the stairs. Instantly changing his position he hid behind his book, pretending to be engrossed in his revision. Fortunately it was Wasim. "Why were you jumping?" Wasim teased. "Are you ill? Shall I call the doctor that you have a jumping illness?"

"Ha Ha very funny . . ." Javed teased back smacking the book on Wasim's head. Wasim rubbed his head laughing. "Ouch! Hold on! We will see whose head hurts more in a minute!" then chased him to get him back. They ran around in circles laughing. Javed teased him that he couldn't get him. Wasim caught up with him suddenly grabbing him from behind holding his arm against his back. "Ok . . . ok . . . your stronger my little brother." Javed gasped out of breath trying to hold his laughter. Wasim set him free and then embraced him.

Wasim couldn't help welling up, he was overjoyed to see his brother happy. He quickly dried his eyes when Javed set him free. Wasim placed a hand on his shoulder squeezing it hard. "How does it feel to have your dream come true?"

"The feeling . . . . ah . . . I can't explain it. I am so happy." Exchanging looks they burst out in fits of laughter.

Safia sat in her room until dark. Yunus eventually went to her, no body knew what he said but he managed to bring her out to eat. Every body could sense their mother's unhappiness. Yunus didn't say anything in front of the children but tried to keep things cheerful. "Tomorrow, Wasim I want you to get the sweets from the Mithai shop and we will distribute it to the whole village. What do you think Safia ji?" Safia just mumbled. Yunus gave her a look of contempt.

"Yes, yes that would be the best thing to do." Uttering her first words that day; eating her dinner in silence. That day Yunus had especially ordered lamb to be cooked to celebrate the proposal acceptance. As impatient as he was getting at Safia's behavior he didn't want push her too in case she was to make a scene at the wedding. Eventually she will accept the wedding and soften her heart he hoped.

The main thing was that she didn't create any scenes at the wedding; if she misbehaved when Mehnaz came home then he will deal with it accordingly were his ongoing thoughts.

The following morning Wasim woke up early for the first time taking out his father's orders. He came back with many assorted sweets in large boxes. He handed them to Asma who sorted them with Bushra preparing them in little bags. His father was proud at his responsible behavior and organizational skills. Both father and son distributed the sweets to the whole village. They spent all morning going to each and every house in the village. Every single house that they distributed sweets to they were offered tea and snacks as a way of congrats, ending up having many breakfasts in one day. If they refused the snacks they were blackmailed into staying for Javeds joyful news. Refusal was out of the question. By the time they got home they were completely exhausted. Wasim scraped his feet through the gates holding onto his tummy.

Beads of sweat ran down Yunus's face. They both threw themselves on the netted beds at the same time. "Abu ji, this whole marriage is not as easy as it looks." Wasim gasped managing to force words out of his mouth. His father started to laugh whilst holding his stomach that was full to the brim. Wasim joined him, laughing at his innocent joke. "It even hurts to laugh!" he said pressing down his stomach.

Yasmin came from the kitchen offering them water. The both refused waving their hands like she was bringing them poison. Yasmin couldn't help but to giggle. Yunus asked Yasmin to prepare some kawa. Yasmin understood that they had obviously eaten too much; turning towards the kitchen to follow her father's commands. Safia walked in with Asma and Bushra. The three of them had gone to see Kausar to talk about the colour scheme for the wedding to discuss what arrangements they had in mind.

Safia walked slowly fanning herself. Noticing father and son exhausted. She sat next to Wasim asking what was wrong. "Oh Ammi don't ask!" he protested. Yunus told Safia how they were force fed on every delivery. Safia tutted her tongue adding how greedy they were; they could have easily said no and had not been so greedy.

Yunus shook his head in disapproval "Its not called being greedy it's called celebrating my son's marriage! At least some of us are happy." he mumbled under his breath. "Excuse me?" Safia exclaimed. Yunus ignored her accepting Yasmin's herbal tea. She had purposefully added cardaman and fennel with the mint to reduce the bloat. Wasim

93

got up at once, he couldn't wait for it to cool, and he drank it all in three sips. Letting out a big burp. Everyone laughed apart from Safia. "Oh you shameless donkey!" shouted out his mother. "Call me what you want Ammi, I feel better now that's all that matters, I don't care if I'm shameless or shamefull!" he blurted out laughing, a few more burps following.

Safia smacked him with her fan. Yunus complimented his daughter for the lovely mixture. "It's a miracle the pain has gone. Wheres Javed?" asked Yunus all of a sudden, he hadn't seen him all day.

"I think he's studying on the roof, working hard that the exams are near." answered Yasmin taking the cups away before Safia told her to. "Mashallah, Im really proud of him, hes still working hard for his exams when his wedding is near. We are blessed with such good offspring, Alhamdulilah, if it were any other boy they would have stopped looking at their books thinking that now the wedding is sorted whats the need to study." Yunus looked up to the sky in a way like he was gesturing to God. Safia mumbled in agreement. All of a sudden smacking Wasim on the thigh and told him to follow his brother's example.

Wasim rolled over on his side trying to ignore her falling into a deep sleep, his eyelids closing in on him. "Leave him be, Safia the poor boy has been running around with me all day and hes got a stomach ache." Safia stamped her foot to the ground in anger "You're the one who is always spoiling everyone! If he doesn't pass it will be your fault. Wasim go to the terrace like your brother is studying, NOW!" she screamed in his ear.

Wasim got up angrily, forcing his feet in his shoes. "It's his wedding and I am running around like a donkey, and your complimenting him when his been on his bum all day!" he said angrily rushing up to the terrace. Javed seeing his annoyed little brother tried to make him feel better.

"What's wrong boss? Why are you so annoyed?"

"Ammi is whats wrong! I have been running around all day inviting everyone to your wedding, I got a stomach ache from the hospitality at every ones house. I was starting to feel better, Ammi starts lecturing me when Im trying to take a short nap!" he huffed lying down on one of the beds. Javed couldn't help laughing. "Is that it? Ok get some sleep, I wont tell Ammi you had a nap, I will tell her you came up and did some revising."

"Thank you." Wasim turned over to sleep. Within five minutes he was snoring like a baby. Javed got up and kissed him on his forehead. Javed continued revising until nearly sunset. Wasim awoke two hours later. He scratched his head and stretched his arms out above his head. Javed was sitting where he had left him. Wasim looked at his watch yawning again telling his brother it was time to take a break.

Javed agreed and told him he was nearly done. He had an algebra exam the following morning. He wanted to revise the formulas enough to get top marks; this was his last chance to prove to his father how serious and responsible he was. "When are your exams starting?" he asked without turning away from his exercise book.

"My exams don't start officially for another two weeks. This moment I am running around like a monkey for your wedding arrangements! Thanks for letting me sleep by the way. I feel energized! Lets go play cricket." Javed scribbled his last answer and snapped his books shut, joining his brother.

CHAPTER 10

The boys of Chakwaal Private Institute rushed out of college pulling their ties off jumping up and down. It was the end of the year, the last term. They couldn't wait to start their summer holidays. Three long months of no books or teachers, just relaxation and games awaited them.

Wasim loosend his tie placing an arm over his brother's shoulder. He turned to hug him and picked him up out of joy, his brother was getting married within a week. While the other boys were celebrating the joy of the end of the year; Javed was celebrating the beginning of his new life. Getting married to the woman he loved. He couldn't believe how quickly time flew, Mehnaz would finally be his wife.

The journey home was the norm for Wasim with his headphones in his ears gazing out of the window. This was the first journey Javed was not holding any books. The first journey home; where he looked out envisioning his future with Mehnaz. Being able to relax and stop racing through the subjects that took over his mind, letting his mind think about him for once.

A sense of ease spread over his body. He leaned back in his seat letting his eyelids close until they reached home. He invited the rickshaw driver to come to his wedding before he stopped the vehicle.

Upon entering home Javed was welcomed home like a king. The house was filled with the village women discussing his wedding. Shying at their comments when he walked past; clutching tightly onto his rucksack. They all cheered him and patted his back like he had just won a cricket match.

By the time he reached his room his nerves were racing with embarrassment, he couldn't believe how much he was blushing and this was only the beginning. Wasim teased him.

The next day was the date setting ritual. All of the men and women would go to Mehnaaz's house and set the date for the wedding. Hence why all the women were at the groom's house discussing the arrangements the night before. They laughed and joked all night. Javed hid in his room; only coming out for necessities. His brother teased him that if he was so shy now what will come of him after he was married. Javed ignored him throwing a pillow at him gesturing him to shut up.

The following morning all of the women set out to the bride's house donning white cotton clothes; taking sweets and nuts in baskets as an offering. Javed had to stay at home. He obviously wasn't allowed to go and see the bride at all untill the day of his wedding. Being grounded till his wedding day, this meant that his face will glow on his wedding day so no evil eye could touch him.

The women were welcomed in Mehnaz's house wholeheartedly. The men were escorted to sit down on the other side of the court yard while the women on the other. Between them was a big colourful sheet on a wire separating the sections for the men and women. The sheet had the colours for yellow, red and green in a symmetrical pattern.

Kausar led Safia and her family in the best seat, with cushions on a day bed and a quilt to soften the netted mattress. The bed was placed in the shade so the cool air reached it splendidly. Safia enjoyed the royal treatment. Constantly fussed over with snacks and drinks; the men began a prayer for the bride and grooms future. The women chatted away while holding their hands up in prayer.

The date was fixed for the 11th, a week away. The ceremony for the colours began. Mehnaz's female family and friends came to throw the yellow liquid colour on the groom's side of the family and friends who had to come wearing white colours especially so they could be recognized in their uniform. Safia gave a look of discontent; she didn't want to ruin her new lovely white cotton dress which she had got sewn especially from Yasmin.

Mehnaaz's aunts began throwing the yellow dye at the three sisters first who desired to be coloured fully. Safia gave the impression of only having a small corner of her scarf dipped into the colour. Mehnaaz's mother nodded in agreement, however one of Mehnaaz's aunts missed the silent conversation between Kausar and Safia.

Things got exciting and out of hand, one of the aunts threw a whole jug all over Safias top. Safia's face went from fair to hot red. Not being happy as it was with the whole wedding, this really aggravated her mood.

"I thought I made it clear that I didn't want to get covered in the yellow dye?!" she screamed. All of the women fell silent as she expressed her disapproval. "You messed up my whole suit, you stupid woman!" she spat at Mehnaz's aunt. "Im so so sorry, I promise the colour will come out, I, I will wash it for you . . ." she stammered. "There goes Safia and her anger, good luck to Kausar . . ." began whispering the women to each other. "It's her sons wedding, why is she making a scene over such a small thing." whispered another.

Kausar added an apology on her behalf, insisting to buy her a new suit to replace it. "It's not about the suit, it's about respecting your elders, I thought I made it crystal clear that I didn't want any colour apart from one corner of my scarf, doesn't mean you go around throwing colour like a lunatic!"

"Yes, Baji, I agree . . . please please come and have your lunch." Kausar ushered Safia back to her seat and handed her a cloth. She then went over to her sister and slapped her across her face in front of everyone and told her to get some food for the groom's mother. Her sister took the orders without looking up. The other women gasped and were also ushered back to their seats. Kausar didn't want to make another scene and tried to cover up the situation as much as she could, she didn't want the marriage to be ruined.

Safia appreciated Kausar's outburst, and when Kausar came to her with a glass of pink lemonade, apologizing again. Safia trying to make her self look bigger; told Kausar there was no need to slap her sister, it was probably an accident. Safia was internally pleased that she didn't have to slap her herself, Yunus would have been very cross.

Kausar's sister came with a steel tray with four plates of food, one for Safia and the rest for Yasmim, Bushra and Asma. They had beef curry with thin chapattis, sweet halwa for desert. Kausar and her sisters had cooked the meal themselves; they couldn't afford to get caterers for the day. Not having too many guests it made sense to cook it themselves. The henna night they would cook themselves again but the wedding day was organized by caterers, they wouldn't be able to cook for five hundred people.

The girls licked every inch of their plate; complimenting it was the best they had had after a long time at a wedding. Usually at weddings there was either too much oil or less meat. This time it was just right you could taste the home touch in each mouthful.

Safia nodded in agreement and hoped that Mehnaz could cook as well as her mother. The outburst was long forgotten when everyone had their appetites tended to, they couldn't get enough!

All of the women began asking Kausar tips and gave her compliments for cooking it herself. They all told her that as though it was simple they couldn't stop licking their fingers not aware of her culinary skills.

Kausar blushed at their compliements, implying further that Mehnaz could cook better than her own mother. She said this intentionally, she could feel Safia watching and eavesdropping. When she went to collect the dishes from Safia, Safia probably for the first time in her life expressed a compliment. Trying to make a come back for her behavior earlier, feeling she didn't come off too well.

Kausar accepted the compliment and asked if she wanted to go inside to see Mehnaz. "Of course, please show me where my new daughter is!" Safia and her daughters followed obediently. They were led into one of the rooms. Mehnaz sat with her scarf draped over her face; she was wearing a pale yellow outfit that expressed her innocence, sitting with her friends huddled in one corner of the room.

As soon as she saw Safia entering the room, she instantly got up to greet her. "Be happy, God bless you." Safia said kissing her forehead. Untying one corner of her scarf; she took out some money and forced it in her palm.

Yasmin went in for a hug, and the other sisters followed suit. Their mother left the room and went back to her seat with Kausar walking behind like an assistant. Yasmin and her sisters sat down with Mehnaz having a little giggle with her friends, taking part in the teasing.

Gradually everyone started to take their leave. A little boy came to Safia to give her Yunus's message to take leave. One of Mehnaz's aunts came to inform the three sisters that their mother was calling them to go home. Safia hugged Kausar, departing on good terms.

Kausar sighed with relief when she saw them stepping out of the gate. The first day of difficulty had surpassed. She thanked Allah that the day went smoothly even after the incident.

Kausar went to her sister Sameena, she hugged her and apologized for the slap. Her sister Sameena said she was willing to accept anything so long as Mehnaaz's wedding took place smoothly. The other sisters welled up at her lovely commnet. All warning each other to be careful of Safia. They didn't know what she was like yet, maybe she was older than them, that's why she behaved the way she had.

Kausar protested to her sisters to keep quiet about the scene that took place, she didn't want the men to hear of the incident, worried that if Sheraz or any of the men had found out then things could get out of hand. They promised to keep their tongues tied.

The Yunus household arrived home tired but content. There wasn't any cooking to do; Sheraz had kindly wrapped food for their family to take home in a serving dish. He handed it to Wasim on their way out, Yunus appreciated the gesture.

The girls were given orders from their mother to start preparing the *Barri* in other words the gifts that they were going to give Mehnaz and her family. They would have to press all of Mehnaz's clothes presenting them in a pretty order. The girls got to work hand sewing on the matching scarves onto the dresses in a way that the dresses and the design could be seen properly.

They laid out the clothes in order, with a gift to each of the members of the family. Safia had bought an outfit for each member of the family, including the grandparents. Mehnaz had five new outfits including the wedding dress. Yasmin had sewn all of the outfits. Not having the chance to sit down ever since her brothers wedding preparations had begun. She was expected to sew Mehnaz's clothes and all of her own family's clothes.

Working so hard she had forgotten to eat. In all of the excitement of her brothers wedding she had lost her appetite. The date ceremony was the first time she managed to actually sit down and eat properly. Yunus would scold her when he realized she was missing her meals, telling her she would not be standing on the wedding day if she carried on the way she had been. Her weight was decreasing gradually. Yasmin appreciating her father's consideration promising to eat later, but she actually forgot to eat collapsing on her bed each evening. Safia was impressed at Yasmin's hard work, didn't mind handling the kitchen for her.

It was Asma and Bushra's duty to tend to the guests as well as helping their sister with the arrangements. Yasmin was now extremely busy preparing Mehnaz's wedding dress. She had taken close measurements and was designing it herself. She used a tinsel border for the bridal scarf on the edges of the scarf, adding small details in the middle of the scarf to match the dress.

The wedding dress was blood red with antique gold detail. Yasmin then used the gold thread to make special floral designs on the necking of the dress to match the scarf.

Yasmin wanted to make the best wedding dress that was ever seen. She carefully added gold beads on the edges of the sleeves and on the scarf. The usual wedding scarves were light in weight, Yasmin wanted to make it unique to fill it up with a heavy feel. Now all she needed to do was to sew the dress to match Mehnaz's measurements, and work on the bridal scarf until the wedding day.

Asma and Bushra couldn't close their jaws in amazement every time they came in to check on their elder sister. Yasmin would tell them to stop gaping it was not yet finished. Eager to surprise her mother of her new found skill, especially her brother when he would see Mehnaz for the first time. Yasmin worked day and night until the wedding day, her eyes had sunk into their sockets at the rate she worked.

The local male tailor had come to take Javed's measurements for his outfit, a fabric merchant accompanied him bringing a selection of fabrics and buttons to choose from. Yunus picked out the fabric, choosing a thick cotton material of the colour of shiny beige. He also picked out a golden fabric asking the tailor to make a matching waist coat. He then picked out a red cotton long fabric to make his turban. He also gave orders to the tailor to bring the *sehra* which would go across Javed's turban. So no other woman would be able to look at him before Mehnaz. The tailor also took Yunus's and Wasim's measurements for their outfits. The following day was the ritual of the henna night for Javed.

Guests started to arrive at 4pm the following day. Dinner tables were arranged on the field. There was a buffet for the food. One main and one desert. Lamb curry with chapattis and sweet coloured rice being on the menu. Yunus had arranged caterers to come early they had started preparing from 9am for 400 guests. The seats were for 200 people. Everyone would have to eat in turns, the men first and the women would be served on the second serving of food.

The day consisted of welcoming the guests; the best man ceremony was to take place before the early dinner. A prayer was said on the mat with close family members and friends standing around with their hands held up joining in the prayer. Javed's best friend bought him a bracelet with dangling tinsel and ball balls. It was tied tight around his wrist by his best friend Faizan.

Javed hadn't been allowed to shave or bathe till his wedding day since the wedding date ritual. His friends would make fun of him that he was starting to reek; he shrugged their comments, believing he was prepared to sacrifice anything for his future wife.

However he would use a wet handkerchief to wipe under his armpits every morning and evening. This helped him to keep his body odour at bay; fortunately he was allowed to change out of his clothes.

The ceremony for the henna began late in the evening. Yasmin and the other women had gone to the well to fetch water in a hand decorated water pot before dinner. They then all sang songs whilst swapping to carry the water pot on their heads walking back to the groom's house. Singing wedding songs about the groom and the family, the others watched on while the rest sang and clapped their hands. They would save that water pot till the wedding day and pour it over the groom in front of everyone before he bathed to get ready in his groom outfit.

On the henna night Yunus had called *dhol* and *pipe* players, their music brought the whole village to life. "Now it feels like a wedding!" exclaimed the guests cheering. The men started to dance around Javed. Javed was seated in the middle with his best man on his side; presented with a flower garland around his neck, so you could differentiate between the groom and the best man. Almost suffocating in the smell of the sweaty men dancing around him, internally hoping it will be over soon, or at least wishing he could be on the side watching from a distance.

The women watched the fun seated from the veranda. Only the men were allowed to dance. The women were not allowed to mingle with the men, it was not allowed at all. The sound of the drumbeat excited the women, wishing they could join in the fun. They expressed their amusement by watching their husbands do silly moves.

When the men stopped dancing, Yunus began the henna ceremony. Each member of the family came to put a small amount of henna onto his palm donating a little money to the poor man who was holding the tray with the henna in a bowl and a bowl of oil.

Each guest would apply a little oil to his hair and then put a little henna on his palm. The women followed the ritual when the men had done their part. His aunts would kiss his forehead before applying any ingredients.

Faizan held a box of *meethai* to those who wished to eat it or wished to feed it to Javed. Javed beginning to get a little fed up and tired. He couldn't wait for the ceremony to end. After the ceremony the women sat on the terrace and sang songs all night while playing on an empty clay pot as an instrument. This made a lovely sound. Asma sang all night with her beautiful voice while the other women joined in. They sang; *Oh henna, oh henna, how bright are you . . . . your colours bring out joy and happiness. You will unite the bride and groom as one, and what a handsome couple they will become . . . .*

They sang wedding songs all night. Safia and the other women had sneaked Yunus's hookah, puffing smoke from it all night. Knowing that Yunus would be too busy dancing to care for it; smoking the tobacco seemed to put Safia into a good mood all evening. It helped her to drown her sorrow of her son going to show his love and care for another woman.

The night was lit up with glass lanterns along the walls. The men danced to the sound of the drum all night while the women made their melody on the terrace. Poor Yasmin was making sure there was a bed for all of the guests. She went around giving everyone blankets and pillows. She had sewn new ones especially for the guests that would be staying the few nights before the wedding, coming from miles away.

The guests were maternal and paternal aunts and uncles, their children and their children's children. There were eleven families staying with them. The work wasn't much of a burden thanks to her cousins helping her to handle the work. Yasmin thought it would be a good idea to let the women to sleep on the terrace, so she made it really comfortable using lots of pillows and quilts on the floor so there was enough room for everyone.

The women could fall asleep as soon as they finished their party. She made use of all the beds laying them out on the veranda and the courtyard for the men, hardly any space for anyone to squeeze through. The men had already begun retiring to their beds, feeling exhausted with all the dancing.

Especially Wasim, who was the most tired of all. Music was his passion, dancing was a second nature to him. Everybody was impressed with his moves; dancing the snake dance and Punjabi bhangra. Wasim had managed to get Yunus to dance with him whom everyone had thought to be a bit reserved.

Receiving lots of pats on the back for that achievement; however every body was extremely impressed when he had made Usmaan Ali to dance with him. Usmaan Ali had some really good moves that Wasim tried to copy, finding it hard to follow. After midnight Yunus put a stop to the sound of music telling everyone to get some sleep. By that time the women were also unconscious on the terrace tucked in warm blankets that Yasmin left out for them. There had been barely any space left for Yasmin. She managed to squeeze between Asma and her cousins. Grateful that at least she would not feel cold throughout the night.

Yasmin looked up to the stars and thanked God for such a beautiful evening. She didn't take a second to dose off until she heard her mother snoring who woke her up. Setting herself free from the small space, she quickly got up and tucked her mother in. This worked to help her mother to stop her snoring. Yasmin then tucked herself back in her tight space and had the best sleep ever. She tucked her head behind Asma falling to a deep sleep.

The night was colder than usual, but couldn't be felt with everyone huddled together on their beds with the sharing of the blankets. Everybody was so tired that they missed the call for the Morning Prayer; they couldn't hear it from their deep slumber.

Usually everybody was up at the crack of dawn, the cockerel croaked to wake everyone up, their sleep had missed his call as well. They all were in a deep slumber; unconscious like the castle of sleeping beauty.

Yasmin was still the first to wake up, however it was nearly 9 am by then. It was a cloudy morning so the sunlight hid behind the clouds not managing to do its morning duty. Yasmin woke up yawning and stretching her arms in the air. Feeling amazingly well rested. Touching the back of her neck believing it was just after dawn worried that she would be late to serve breakfast. Looking around she saw everyone was still tucked in their beds.

Tip toeing down the stairs to get washed, her gaze fell upon the clock, her jaw dropped in shock. It was 9AM!! Having slept in four hours put her in utter shock. She was surprised that her mother hadn't even woken up. Her father came out of the bathroom greeting her. Instructing her to wake her mother to get breakfast ready, there was a busy day ahead. Yasmin quickly got herself cleaned up and went to wake her mother. Afraid she will get in trouble, she took her chance anyway.

Fortunately Safia was still in a daze from smoking so much the night before. Safia's eyes opened all of a sudden when Yasmin told her it was nearly 9.30am. Safia got up instantly rushing to the bathroom to wash up. While she went Yasmin woke up her sisters and kneaded the flour for the *parathe*.

Safia placed a big pot of water on the stove and let it boil to make tea. Yasmin handed her the kneaded flour. Asma and Bushra went to milk the cows. They brought the milk in time for their mother, the tea was brewing nicely, had it been brewed any longer it would have been ruined.

Yasmin helped her mother with the so many parathas, using her wit she had kneaded two trays of dough. This was the first morning their mother had not shouted, she was so busy helping out with the cooking she didn't have time to pick on anyone. Bushra and Asma got a big cloth on the floor for every body to fit, making enough space for everyone.

Yunus and Wasim had the water ready in jugs and there were so many plates and glasses all around the cloth. The biggest dining area that they had ever arranged in their home; Yasmin warmed up the curry that was left over from the henna meal yesterday. Fortunately there was enough, also bringing out the left over sweet rice.

The latest breakfast that ever took place in their household. Surprisingly nobody complained at all. A lovely atmosphere, all of a sudden everyone was on the big table cloth talking and laughing. There were thirty five people in total including the Yunus household. One or two of the families had gone to their other families in the morning in the same village invited to eat their breakfast.

Eventually breakfast was served at 11 am. Yunus reminded them to eat as much as they could for this was the only meal they would be getting until dinner at Sheraz's house. In a way it was a good thing that it was brunch. Everybody complimented that they felt like they were on a vacation, having such a relaxing time. No running around after chores or waking up early. An extra blessing that the weather was lovely and cool; unusual for that time of the year. The rain clouds had made it cooler, with a little humidity.

When everyone had finished their meal, the men relaxed while the women ran around arranging their clothes and pressing them. Yasmin and her sisters finished the housework and gave the house a good clean.

They then helped to get their outfits ready. Javed would stay home alone again while Mehnaz's henna night took place another night of singing and rejoicing. This time the men would only go there to say a prayer and eat dinner. The women will apply henna and oil to Mehnaz tonight.

Javed could barely be recognized with his stubble grown. He hadn't shaved or slept properly, half due to his excitement, the ceremonies weren't helping either. His father told him to rest that day another day was ahead with all the wedding traditions. Javed tried to get some rest and to keep watch on the house while his family took their leave. Safia wore a pale green salwar kameez. The same colour as the henna. Yasmin and her sisters wore the same outfit of red and yellow; the three sisters looked stunning in their outfits. They wore a yellow kameez with a red salwar. Their kameez had a red and a silver design going along it. Their scarves were yellow with red borders.

They got permission to wear make up for the first time. Safia permitted them so long as they didn't put on too much. The girls were very careful in applying the make-up. They just applied kohl to their eyes, a hint of pink blusher to their cheeks, styling their hair in french plaits with a plait coming to their front.

Upon arriving at Mehnaz's house all the family and friends looked at them in amazement. They stood out from the crowd. The other girls had piled on make up with red blusher, red eyeshadow and red lipstick. Even little girls! Safia frowned upon their overuse. Feeling proud that her daughters respected her wishes; comparing them to the other girls who didn't look as natural or beautiful as her own.

Safia couldn't help looking at Yasmin when they were sat with the other women. Her daughter was so beautiful. She had grown up and matured elegantly.

CHAPTER 11

Safia realized that her daughter will be turning sixteen soon maturing quite rapidly. Nearly the age for marriage. *When she turns sixteen she should be married. She is now such a responsible girl. Mashallah, my daughter is turning into a beautiful woman. I bet she will have lots of suitors for her marriage soon.* Safia's mind began to wonder. Her thoughts were interrupted when the ladies brought out the bride to be.

Mehnaz was wearing a yellow and a green outfit. She had white flowers in her hair with a long plait, with matching white flower earrings. Looking elegant, brought out by her aunts and friends holding her mother's wedding scarf above her head like a flag.

Resembling a floating angel, the women sat together around, gently sitting her down on the arranged mats on the floor. The terrace was decorated especially, with lanterns to light up the evening and yellow flowers. There was a small drum in the middle near where Mehnaz sat. All the women giggled and sat down around her starting to sing. They gestured Yasmin and her sisters to join in. The three girls looked at their mother for silent permission, Safia smiled and nodded.

Hurriedly they went to sit down to join the circle. They sang lots of songs while the older women went to Mehnaz to apply the henna and oil. Once the henna ceremony had taken place, the singing began to get warmer and warmer. The girls were playing song games where they played in teams, the groom's side against the bride's.

The game was to sing the next lettered song that the other person finished off; singing a song beginning with the letter that was at the end. While all this fun was going on, Mehnaz sat getting the henna painted on her hands in a beautiful design. Her mother looked at her from a distance crying to herself, the darkness concealed her tears. Her daughter was leaving her the next day, her only daughter. She had brought her up with so much love and care now after sixteen years of up brining she was going to belong to someone else. Praying in her heart that she will be well looked after and cared for. Some women had come to Safia to compliment her that she had such beautiful children, especially her daughter Yasmin.

Also mentioning it was the first time they had seen Yasmin looking so beautiful, they couldn't believe she had grown up so quickly, trying their luck to ask if she was available or taken. Safia kindly refused, they weren't looking for a suitor as yet. Her father wasn't eager to let her go yet. They said to inform them when she was ready. Safia nodded in agreement. Safia's thoughts were coming true. Women were bugging her all night. Realizing it wasn't just her motherhood that found her daughter stunning. She would have to talk to Yunus to find her suitor soon. You couldn't let a beautiful daughter sit at home too long. The quicker to get her married would be the best thing. Yunus and Wasim came to pick them up by just after 9pm; they had a busy morning ahead. They couldn't stay up late another night there was too much to do to prepare for the wedding the following morning, even though the guests were arriving at 10 am.

They said their goodbyes lighting the way with a lantern. Another night consisted of sleeping on the roof huddled together. Everyone retired to bed at 10pm, chatting away until 12am. Nobody could sleep due to the long sleep they all had the night before. This time there was a little more room to sleep.

One couple had left to stay with another family member that night. Everyone eventually fell asleep apart from Javed. Feelings of excitement and anxiety churned about his wedding. Fantasizing how he would approach Mehnaz for the very first time. What will he say to her? How will he express his love for her? Dreaming about his future he didn't realize when he fell asleep.

The morning for the wedding arrived. The cockerel was not misheard by Safia and Yasmin; they instantly woke up proceeding with the preparations. Yunus woke the men up. It was another morning of cheerfulness the final day of arrangements. Javed was teased left right and centre that he stank. Javed laughed with them. His father informed him that when everyone arrived he would have to sit on a stool; oil mixed with milk would be applied to his hair by the guests.

After breakfast the women began to get prepared for the the wedding customs. Yasmin packed Mehnaz's wedding dress carefully. She would get ready after *nikkah* ceremony. Everybody began rushing around like headless chickens. Yasmin arranged everybody's outfits handing them out to everyone. The drummers arrived on time. Yasmin and her sisters had the same colour outfits again. They all wore sky blue with white hemming. Being a day function Yasmin designed simple outfits using cotton material. It was too hot to wear silk or polyester. She had chosen a lovely colour which brought out her natural beauty. Yasmin again looking beautiful; her brothers complimented her, blushing bright red when Wasim said he didn't know his sister was so pretty, telling her to save herself from the evil eyes. Shying at his compliment, she felt overwhelmed.

When they were at college and busy playing cricket they didn't pay much attention to her. This was the first time that her brothers took notice of her work. They thought she was just learning to sew, however they did not know that she had gained such an articular skill, becoming a professional designer. Taking lessons from Fatima had taught her well.

Constantly praised for her skills she was getting requests from her aunts to sew for them. They loved her way of design, she had a creative imagination. Even offering to pay her; she couldn't say yes or no until she spoke to her mother. The wedding procession began playing melodious wedding music. Yasmin brought out the tray of milk and oil mixed together and a towel for her brother. It was a very hot morning. Yasmin glad she had made use of cotton and not silk like the others. Cotton was the best breathable fabric to wear in the scorching heat, silk or polyester meant asking for a death wish.

Usmaan Ali stood with the men around Javed, holding out their hands to say a prayer. The music stopped instantly in due respect. When the prayer was complete, the music began again. Then one by one every one came to grease Javeds hair, sitting in a squatted position. His face was dripping with the milk and oil in his hair. When it was Wasim's turn he got his two hands together cupping the mixture in his hands. Then letting the contents spill over his brother's head, he massaged his brother's head like he was in a parlour.

The guests watching were couldn't stop laughing. He also stroked his cheeks that had his beard growing. In the mean time the women had brought the water from the well and then Wasim poured it over his head. The cold water soothed him in the scorching heat.

Safia's brother picked him up to take him to the bathroom. It was a tradition that the maternal uncle would pick up the groom and take him to the bathroom where he would bathe and dress as a groom; all of his things were laid out in the bathroom already for him.

Javed came out within half an hour later all ready in his groom outfit. He wore the beige suit that Yunus picked out for him, rather than a normal salwar he had a wrapped *dhoti* where the ends came to his shoulder, wearing a red turban. You could see his face again from shaving, his skinned glowed in the light.

His father put a *sehra* above his turban, to cover his face. The *sehra* was lika a veil to cover the grooms face. No body else was allowed to see him until after the nikkah ceremony. This was to protect him from any evil eyes. Feeling rejuvenated to be using soap and water again; not bathing in that heat had not been an easy task for him. Feeling as light as a feather from washing all the dirt away.

Ushered by Yunus, Javed was asked to sit on a chair while everyone gave him paper money necklaces as a gift. Nearly drowning in them they had to be taken off. Yunus called the horseman over into the yard.

Javed rode on a white decorated horse to Mehnaz's house: being only a five minute walk. The men followed behind Yunus with the horseman leading Javed's horse. Javed worried a little that he would fall off any minute when the horse walked over hilly parts of surface. He held really tight on to the reins. The men followed with the music procession, the women far behind.

Reaching Mehnaz's house by 11am, the men were led to another part of the house and the women to another. Usman Ali was greeted most respectively and then the men sat down to start the registry ceremony, two men volunteered to be witnesses.

Usmaan Ali started the paper work and began to recite verses from the Quran. Everyone sat around listening contently; Usmaan kindly asked Sheraz to go and seek Mehnaz's consent for marriage first for the *nikkah* then Javed will be asked. Sheraz obediently headed out with Mehnaz's brothers following behind.

"On the dowry of 100 rupees my dear daughter do you take Javed Hussain to be your husband?" she nodded. He asked again, "On the dowry of 100 rupees my dear daughter do you take Javed Husaain to be your husband?" repeating her acceptance with a nod, her face well hidden behind scarf. Tears streamed down her cheeks upon hearing her father's trembling voice. He asked her one more time, her emotions over rode her ability to talk, a final nod of acceptance half sealed the contract.

Laying out the paper work in front of her he asked her to dip her thumb into the ink pot and to leave the imprint of her thumb onto the signature area. Mehnaaz was illiterate; she could just about read the Quran. Soon as her father left the room, she burst into uncontrollable tears.

Her friends and aunts huddled around, giving her cuddles of reassurance. They couldn't believe Mehnaz was leaving them; having to grow up in one day embracing the responsibilities of a grown woman.

Kausar walked in soon after she saw Sheraz leave the room, finding it unbearable to attend the *nikkah* seeing her only daughter married was too much for her to handle. Upon entering seeing Mehnaz in the state of distraught, Kausar rushed to hold her daughter both squeezing each other so tight crying uncontrollably barely being able to breathe.

Sheraz briskly walked back to Usmaan Ali trying really hard to hold his tears back. He handed Usmaan Ali the *nikkahnama* back with trembling hands. Usmaan Ali realizing his dismay patted his shoulders for reassurance proceeded with the marriage ceremony. Turning to Javed he asked him the *three kalmas*. Javed recited them fluently. He then asked him three times if he accepted Mehnaz to be his wife. Javed said *qabool hai* each time he was asked. Usmaan Ali pointed to him to sign his name next to Mehnaz's thumb print.

His next task was to stand up and say *Aslaam aleikum* to everyone in the room. Which was the greeting of *peace be upon you*. The marriage was sealed, a new life had begun. Everyone got up congratulating Yunus and his family with hugs and handshakes.

Soon after the marriage ceremony lunch was served. Javed and his immediate family in the room got special treatment. They were immediately served. Everybody else had to go to the lunch tables that were set up outside. In the mean time Mehnaz got ready in her wedding dress. Safia showed off the clothes that she was giving to

Mehnaz outside to the guests. Proudly laying out the wedding dress and showing off the outfits she was giving alongside. Safia had gifted two purses, one to match the wedding dress and one to use for everyday use, gold and black.

There was an outfit for each member of the family. Safia also gifted a pair of golden earrings and four golden bangles. The women around whispered to each other about the presents, discussing how fortunate Mehnaz was.

Kausar felt overwhelmed with the gifts. They had only managed to give their daughter two outfits with no gold. They had also managed to arrange an outfit for each member of their family. They weren't as expensive or elegant as the ones that Safia had arranged but they were better than nothing.

When it was Kausar's turn she was internally feeling a little embarrassed after seeing the gifts Safia had bought. Safia swallowed her comments to herself, she knew better than to make a mockery of them in public. When the show was over of the outfits, everything was packed again so Mehnaz could get ready as a bride.

Mehnaz was amazed upon seeing her wedding dress. It was the most beautiful dress that she had ever seen. Normal ones were usually plain. This sort of wedding dress would have cost a lot in the shops. Yasmin had spent weeks on the dress for its unique outcome. Mehnaz was even more amazed when Yasmin told her that she designed and made it herself.

Mehnaz was brought out wearing the jewelry from Javeds family with kohl applied to her eyes, light blusher and a red lipstick to match her outfit. The outfit brought out her beauty even further. Her friends obeyed Asma's instruction to not to smother her in too much make-up, making sure she looked accordingly to Javed's taste.

On top of her bridal scarf she had another plain white scarf covering her as a veil. She was to unveil herself when she reached Javed's home; no one was allowed to lay their first eyes on her apart from Javed.

In the meantime Mehnaz's bridesmaids and aunts went to Javed to give him sweet ghee chupati, also known as *choori*. Javed had to make small balls of *choori*, handing them to her friends as a treat. Eating the remaining himself, he handed the balls out to five of them. His father handed out 5 rupees to each of them, they didn't argue and accepted it happily.

Half an hour later Yunus seeked Sheraz's permission to take their leave; Sheraz's eyes welled up with tears when Yunus mentioned taking his daughter away, he put his hand on Javed's shoulder while they got up to stand. "Please take care of my daughter, she is all that I have that is dearest to me, I appreciate you taking the burden of a good son in law off me. I hope she fulfils her duties like a good wife and daughter." He sobbed on his shoulder. Javed took his hand and kissed it gently.

"She is a part of our family now, I promise I will always keep her happy and keep her with me wherever I go. She is a respectable mans daughter, I am sure I will not have any complaints." Sheraz's chest burst with pride upon hearing such lovely words he embraced Javed tightly.

Yunus couldn't believe how much his son had grown. "My son is right. She is our daughter now. You have nothing to fear. We live close, you are more than welcome to come and see her whenever you wish." Sheraz nodded in appreciation wiping his tears leading them out of the house.

A hand held carriage had been arranged for Mehnaz to travel to her new home in. It was covered in bright pink material and golden tinsel. Mehnaz embraced all of her family and friends one by one, sobbing through her veil. By the time she reached her mother she could not control herself at all. Both mother and daughter sobbed once again, fresh tears had been rekindled. Observing this made Javed feel a tinge of guilt. I have hurt Mehnaz he thought, maybe getting married wasn't such a good idea. He didn't realise that she was crying because she was leaving her family not because she didn't want to marry him.

Javed returned on his horse after parting with Mehnaz's parents. Mehnaz touched her father's feet for respect after he hugged and kissed her forehead. Mehnaz's tears had moved all the women around her. The heartless Safia also broke down in tears.

One of her aunts brought out a small plate of uncooked rice that Mehnaz dipped her hands into and threw over her head behind her, she did this three times. Walking slowly towards her mini carriage, everybody else followed Javed's horse and Mehnaz's carriage out of the gates.

Within five minutes they were back home, Safia welcomed the mini carriage through. Javed being helped down his horse, he walked along with the mini carriage. Yasmin handed her mother a small jug of water, Safia rotated the jug around the mini carriage in a teasing way while Javed had to try to stop her drinking it.

He pulled the jug away several times, everyone watching laughed. Mehnaz was led out by Safia and escorted into Javed's room. Safia pulled up her veil placing the Holy Quraan in her hands. Opening it to a certain page she asked Mehnaz to put in a little money for charity as a blessing. Mehnaaz took out 5 rupees that was in single one rupee notes that she was given as a gift from some of the guests upon congratulating her after the nikah.

Safia called in Yasmin to take over while she handled the guests. Reminding Yasmin to adjust her make up which was now smudged with the crying. Yasmin nodded and brought a handkerchief. Sitting down next to her they exchanged smiles.

"Are you ok bhabbie?" Mehnaz nodded. "Is it ok if I help you abit?" Yasmin applying a little spit to her handkerchief she cleaned the smudged kohl gently, then reapplied more onto the spaces that it had ran down from. She then powdered her face giving her a clean complexion; adding a hint of pink blush to her cheeks, she reapplied a little of the lipstick that was in her purse.

Mehnaz looked descent, even better than when she had first got ready. "Thank you" she spoke eventually.

"My pleasure, aren't you scared?" Yasmin asked curiosly all of a sudden. "A little . . ." Mehnaz expressed her uneasiness. "Well don't worry my brother is really nice and caring. You are really lucky to be marrying him. He will always put your needs first." Upon hearing that made Mehnaz feel a sense of ease.

"It's just that you know how it is . . . I haven't ever spoken to a man, other than to my father and my brothers. So it feels a bit weird."

"Well you know now he will be the only important man in your life. He will be your life partner. Belonging to each other till you die. This is the most beautiful relationship on earth. I promise that when you finally see and speak to him you will instantly feel different." .

Mehnaz didn't know that her sister in law was so mature. Just then Javed came in to see his bride he was sat down next to her by his maternal aunts. He took off his sehra and turban, they saw each other properly for the first time; Mehnaz suddenly looked away. Both were asked to open each others bracelets.

He tried his best to not to look at her in front of his family. His aunts complemented them saying they made a lovely couple. Safia kissed them both and left the room telling the others to leave them alone. When everyone left, Mehnaz's nerves began to race. Javed sat up properly on his bed raising his legs onto the bed.

Mehnaaz looked down the whole time. Starting to tremble with fear "I'm not going to eat you." Javed teased her, leaning close to her face expecting a reaction. Mehnaz forced a smile hoping what he said was true.

"You know I fell in love with you as soon as I saw you? I thought I want to marry this woman and make her mine." He continued leaning back, keeping his gaze on her face. Mehnaz's heart softened, butterflies fluttered in the pit of her stomach. She looked at him for a glimpse, turning her gaze back down again. "You look beautiful, you are beautiful. I can't believe you are finally mine . . . ." He said in a low voice. "Is there anything you would like to ask me? Can I hear your voice at least?"

He smiled at her. "What is there to ask?" finally responding.

"Anything . . . you like" she tried to think of something smart but her mind went blank. "Well . . . erm . . . tell me about yourself . . . ." She muttered. He told her his life story from as much as he could remember from his childhood to his eighteenth year, how he convinced his parents about marrying her. What his expectations were of his wife, he asked her her expectations from him. Intrigued at his question, she tried expressing her feelings.

"I would like you to protect and look after me the way my parents did. That's all I ask. If I ever upset you please don't hesitate to tell me, nicely at first and then you can hit me if I don't listen." Javed burst out laughing. "Why would I want to hit you? You're not a child! Personally I detest physical violence, I prefer talking thanks." Mehnaz couldn't help laughing at her silly comment. Javed looked at her lovingly, finding her laugh melodious. Suddenly there was a knock on the door, Javed got up to open it. Yasmin came to give them their dinner. Smiling at them in a teasing way she left it on the table. Javed thanked her, following her out of the door closing it behind her. He gestured asking for Mehnaz's hand and led her to the chairs beside the table. Mehnaz blushed at first, feeling a tingle when he held onto it, not wanting to let go she obediently followed. They both sat down next to each other. Javed poured the water for them in one glass and rather than using the two plates, he only used one. He broke a piece of chapatti and dipped it into the curry. He put his hand towards her lip gesturing her to open her mouth.

"No no you eat please." she blushed, feeling embarrassed at being fed by a man

"From this day forward we are one, please let me feed you. This may be my only chance to do this." He protested. She opened her mouth slightly and took in the morsel. Javed pretended to clear his throat gesturing her to feed him too. She coyly broke a piece of chapatti and fed him back keeping her gaze down, he didn't take his eyes off her for a second, Mehnaz tried really hard to not to look at his eyes that she felt were burning on her every move.

They spent the rest of the night getting to know each other sharing sweet gestures expressing their love for each other. Mehnaz overwhelmed by her husband, feeling he was an angel sent from God. All of her fears had disappeared in one night. What Yasmin had told her proved true, Javed was a lovely and a caring man.

CHAPTER 12

The following morning Mehnaz got up early as the sun rose bringing out the morning dawn. Observing her husband's face, it rested still and quiet like a content baby. She sneaked out of the room tip toeing not wanting to waken him. Joining Yasmin, who was up as usual; preparing breakfast. Everyone else was still asleep, even Safia who usually woke everyone up with her shouting after the cockerel had announced the morning dawn.

Mehnaz stepped into the kitchen quietly, Yasmin pulled out a stool gesturing Mehnaz to sit down. She welcomed her with a cheeky smile; Mehnaz coyly smiled back taking the seat next to her. Mehnaz quietly started to help Yasmin flip the parathas and stir the tea.

"Bhabie leave it, you only came yesterday." Mehnaz shook her head "Doesn't matter whether I start today or tomorrow. It still has to be done." Yasmin looked at Mehnaz in amazement wondering how she had grown up so much in just one day.

All of a sudden Safia walked into the kitchen interrupting their conversation, giving Mehnaz a tense look but forced a smile when Mehnaz turned looking up at her. Safia wasn't used to having two people make breakfast. Being used to having the other chores to be done at the same time.

Not wanting to scare away her new daughter in law yet, in case Mehnaz went running home in tears on her first day. "Did you sleep well Beta?" she asked after observing her. "I hope the bedroom wasn't too hot, however we have given you two the coolest room of the house, it has big windows on each wall of the room, so there is always a good flow of air."

Mehnaz nodded in agreement feeling embarrassed to talk about her newly wedded room, looking down to the floor not sure what to say back. "I know it's your first day my child but you need to go and get my son's clothes ready for the day. Yasmin usually takes care of this straight after breakfast but now you are his wife this is your duty now." Mehnaz nodded again keeping her gaze locked to the floor.

Her embarrassment overwhelmed her that she had to be told what to do when her mother had informed her exactly the duties of a wife in a household. Although Mehnaz knew what to do she didn't answer back, nodding in agreement she excused herself from the kitchen.

Safia liked her prompt action, feeling more powerful of being able to order around a new person without any training what so ever. Safia smiled cunningly at Yasmin reminding her to hurry up. Yasmin continued her task, feeling a little saddened that her new friend was taken away from her.

One by one the whole family awoke, Mehnaz starting a mission on her first day on an empty stomach. She didn't even manage to drink any water. She was pouring with sweat when began ironing in the heat. Occupied in her mission and feeling guilty of being told what to do. She untied the big bundle of washed clothes that she found in the spare room, she did not only iron Javed's clothes but she ironed everything. She completed the job before everyone had awoken and sat down for breakfast. She folded them in a neat pressed file, in three rows dividing the female's clothes from the males.

Yasmin came to look for her, gasped in shock when she found her. Mehnaz was working on the last salwar. "Have you gone mad?!" Yasmin exclaimed "Ironing all these clothes in this room where there are no windows or air? You could have become unconscience!" she hurried out of the room to get her a cold drink. She returned with a glass of cold water. Mehnaz drank the water as she had been thirsty for days, half spilling the water on her chest. Feeling dizzy at her dehydration, Yasmin took the iron from her and finished the last pair of trousers.

Mehnaz sat down wiping her face with her cotton shawl. "This room gets warmed up very quickly can't you see there aren't any windows in here? By ironing in here you are asking for death. What would Bhai Javed have said if he found you lying dead in this room on his first day after being married?" Breaking into laughter at the innocent joke. "Now stop this giggle this instant!" Asma mimicked her mother walking in.

"The breakfast is laid out and nearly everyone is at the breakfast mat. Come on Bhabie lets go and eat." Asma grabbed Mehnaz's hand trying to lead her out of the room. "First I need to go and give your brother his clothes. Yasmin please can you tell me which clothes are Javeds so I can go and have them ready for him as I don't know which is which from the rest of the men in the household." Yasmin took out the four outfits that were in the pile handing them to Mehnaz; adding her brother's vests and netted belts on the top.

"I will try to keep our clothes in our room so you don't have any trouble." Yasmin and Asma exchanged funny looks. Carrying them out carefully, she breathed in the fresh air that hit her face when she left the room.

Safia's eyes followed Mehnaz's movements when she walked back to her bedroom. Safia sat on the breakfast mat waiting for everyone to be seated, sitting with one hand holding her fan, the same elbow leaning on her raised knee.

Yunas watched Safia in disapproval waiting for her to look at him, feeling his glare she looked back at him; he shook his head at her. Safia stopped the staring immediately, to distract herself she shouted to call the girls.

Wasim was still asleep on the terrace; Javed went to wake him using his wet hands. Wasim awoke immediately feeling annoyed at his brother. "You have been sleeping properly and I am the one who has been running around for your wedding and when the day has arrived finally to rest you are waking me up so early!" he moaned turning over covering his face with his blanket. Javed laughed at him tugging his blanket off.

"Look you can take your revenge on me when it's your turn to marry. I will run around and do everything while you sweat in the heat." Wasim pulled his blanket back over his face pretending to be shy.

"By the time it will be for me to be married you will have five children running around asking to get married early like you did, and I will be going to ask for their hand in marriage!" he teased his brother bursting out laughing.

Javed started to have a pillow fight with him locking his head in his arm. Wasim pleaded to be let go not being able to stop laughing. Javed let him go not helping to laugh himself at his brothers silly joke.

"Hurry up and come down to breakfast it's getting cold, Ammi and Abu are waiting for everyone, you're the last one to be there." Wasim got up instantly skipping to the bathroom. He quickly splashed water over his face joining everyone for breakfast. The women sat across the men. Yunas said a small prayer asking to bless his family and the new couple. Everyone held up their hands up in the air, replying ameen to their father's words.

Yunas began breakfast by unwrapping the cloth around the parathas; Safia poured him his tea from the thermos. Everyone followed suit. Mehnaz felt shy sitting with her new family.

While they all sat in silence Javed stole glances at his new bride. They accidentally brushed hands when both reached for the buttered chapattis. Mehnaz went red in the face with embarrassment; however Javed felt quite amused at first but turned red when he saw his mother staring right at him remorsefully. He took a big gulp of his morsal and looked down for the rest of the meal.

After breakfast all the girls got up to help pick up the breakfast plates. Safia went inside to get out a new outfit for her daughter in law to wear; she was being taken to her parent's house for a blessing. The whole family had been invited for dinner by Mehnaz's parents, Javed and Mehnaz would spend the night there while everyone returned.

Safia snobbed at the meal when she got back home, glad that Mehnaz wasn't there to hear her lash out on her parent's cheapness.

"All there had been were three dishes, one rice one curry and one desert. They could have kept our respect a little bit. I still don't know what my son saw in that family, selfish people!" Yunas ignored her sitting on his bed starting to light his hookah. He knew that if he responded she will have more bad things to say which he did not desire to listen to.

His son was happy and kept to his promise of looking after his household. Nothing else mattered. He hoped that he wouldn't let his wife run orders like he had let his own wife do so. Otherwise he would be having marital problems like his own father. Safia tossed and turned crossly to sleep for being ignored.

The following morning Fatima came to visit Safia regarding a really good proposal for Yasmin. "He is in the police force and the eldest in his family, I know the mother very well she will adore Yasmin. He is handsome and very fair, most importantly he is a very practicing man. He has two brothers and two sisters, all of whom he himself got married for his father died after the youngest was born. The only issue is he is at least ten years or over slightly older than Yasmin." Safia listened contently.

Yunas came over to say hello while the two women were speaking. "Baji Fatima says she has a good proposal for Yasmin. He is in the police force and is the eldest in his family. He has married off everyone in his family already. However he may be a few years older than Yasmin." Yunas frowned. "Yasmin is only fifteen years of age. I don't feel comfortable in getting her married just yet." Safia butted in, "Theres no harm in getting her engaged, and good proposals don't come often." Yunas's face softened a little. "Alright let them come I don't mind meeting them."

CHAPTER 13

A few weeks later Abdul Aziz and Jannat came to ask for Yasmin's hand in marriage. Safia stunned at Abdul Aziz's handsomeness he did not look much older than Yasmin at all. They were extremely polite you could tell they had good manners from a good family background.

Yunas was impressed. He had not met such a man with such maturity and caliber. After getting to know each other he finally asked his age. Abdul Aziz without hesitation told Yunas he was twenty eight. Before Yunas could react, Safia brought out Yasmin to meet Jannat on purpose; her eyes were stuck to the ground, only answering when questioned. Abdul caught a glimpse and fell in love instantly. He hadn't seen such an innocent face.

Her face was full of youth and life, it sparkled with natural beauty. He made it clear to himself that this was the woman he wanted to marry. Fatima and Usmaan Ali were absolutely right about Yasmin's beauty and mannerisms, he thought to himself.

He wanted a wife with Islamic teaching and it was a bonus that she was also strikingly beautiful. Safia sent Yasmin back inside after a few minutes. Finally Yunas admitted that he was quite uncomfortable with the age gap.

He wondered it might not be a good match as his daughter may be a little immature for their son who was obviously quite mature and fast thinking. Yunas couldn't possibly tell them that they were the problem; it would be very disrespectful to treat guests in that way. Abdul instantly understood Yunas's concern he tried fighting for his case.

"Uncle ji, age does not matter in a relationship so long as there is a mutual understanding between the husband and his wife. I would like you to kindly accept my proposal as my mother and I seemed to take interest in your daughter before even meeting her. However it's still your decision, you are the father you know best." Yunas quite impressed with this. He wished he had the same confidence to stick up to his *own* wife.

"Thank you son but I think we need to think about this before we can say yes." It took at least a year for Yunas to accept this proposal. Abdul persisted until he got a yes. It even came to a point where Yunas got really angry at Abdul's pestering that he told him to find a woman of his own age.

Abdul remained patient waiting until he got a yes. Abdul's mother had already started looking for another proposal, however Abdul remained persistent that he would convince Yunas, which he did.

Yunas only accepted the proposal on the condition that the marriage will take place after Yasmin would turn seventeen because of their age gap. Abdul said he was ready to wait as long as Yunas wanted him to wait. Abdul had to go for a years training with his police force in another city anyway, the year would easily pass by for him.

They had a small engagement where Jannat came with a few gifts for Yasmin and the parents.

The year passed with Yasmin's usual work routine. Safia rather than being more compassionate to her daughter made her work even harder. Every time her father tried to take her side, Safia would argue that she needed to make her daughter perfect in everything. "Mistakes won't be allowed where she will be wedded. She is going to be the eldest daughter in law and will have all the responsibility of the whole family, shes marrying the eldest of the family. I can't let her let me down and lose face!"

Upon hearing this Yunas wouldn't bother arguing again. Knowing in a way his wife was right, he wanted to forget as much as possible that his daughter was leaving him. He stopped interfering altogether.

Yasmin would quietly cry on the rooftops every night. Not because of all the housework that she had been pushed to do but because she was going to marry a complete stranger. She compared herself to Mehnaz and her brother. At least the families knew each other before marriage. She didn't know anyone at all in Abdul's household. What kind of mother in law would she have? What kind of husband will Abdul be? Her fears haunted her everyday.

Wasim felt something was up with his sister. Maybe she wasn't happy, he thought. Every night she would head to the roof tops after everyone had gone to sleep. Wasim noticed his sister's odd behavior when his exams were near while he would stay up late revising.

One night he waited until she crept upstairs. He picked up his lantern
that was on his desk and followed after. Tiptoeing up the stairs he
reached the terrace, it was pitch black. Hearing the sound of sobbing
he looked around himself. He walked further trying to trace where
the sobbing was coming from.

Walking further he strained his eyes as much as he could into the
darkness; until he saw in the far corner his sister's white shawl
almost glowing, draped around her, her knees tucked into her chest.
Resembling a white ghost, the scene frightened Wasim abit; he
gulped and walked slowly towards her.

Placing the lantern in front of Yasmin, he sat down to her level
opposite her; he gently put a hand on her head. Startled at the feeling
of the hand, she looked up. Her face was worn out with all the crying.
He gently looked into her eyes and silently wiped them. All of a
sudden he went "BOO!" she jumped with fright.

He started laughing hysterically falling on his back. Yasmin looked at
him crossly but couldn't help laughing herself. They suddenly heard
Safia talking in her sleep both stopping to laugh at once. "Shhhhh!"
they both hissed at the same time.

"I thought you were a ghost so I thought to check by scaring you."
He whispered. "You crazy girl what are you doing up here? And that
too in the bloody dark!" almost raising his voice. "Couldn't you have
found any other place to cry than up here?" Yasmin got up to leave
Wasim stopped her. I am not used to all this emotional crap with girls,
he thought. This was usually Javeds department. Being the eldest
he somehow knew how to talk to women. He had to take over since

Javed was a love sick puppy to his wife and didn't seem to notice any one else since his marriage.

His soft voice stopped her steps, keeping her back to him. He picked up the lantern and walked over to her. "Sit down." he ordered and placed the lantern in front of them as they both sat down. The light of the lantern put a glow on their faces in the dark.

"Ok, Yasmin," he started, trying to be serious for once in his life. "Why are you doing this to yourself? Have you seen your face in the mirror? You literally look like a ghost, poor Bhai Abdul will run away if he saw you like this." He teased her trying to put a smile on her face.

Yasmin stared at the lantern lost for words, but broke a weak smile when Wasim tried to make her laugh. "Ok . . . . spill, whats up?" Yasmin looked down scrunching her shawl. She wasn't used to expressing her feelings. Not to her sisters or anyone. She found it easier to cry them out.

"Look I am not going anywhere until you tell me, and now you are being quite unfair to me, for once I have started to revise for my exams and have left my revision to talk to you." This made Yasmin feel a bit guilty, plucking up the courage to speak.

"I am worried about my future and scared to marry into an unknown family. I have only a few months left. I don't know what to expect there. It will be like going to another world."

"Hmmm, I see the dilemma. They will probably cook you up into a stew and feed you to the jinns." Tears began to roll down Yasmin's cheeks again, she didn't see the joke that her brother was trying to make. "I am joking you silly girl, I was just trying to point out that it's that bad as it seems. What is your main concern? You know that it's the ritual of every woman in Pakistan that when they marry they go to live with their husband's family."

"I know that, I am just worried about Abdul Aziz Saab I don't know him at all, will I be able to keep him happy? He might not like me." Wasim tried really hard not to laugh at his sisters naive comments. She obviously wasn't aware of how much Abdul Aziz loved her already. How much he begged her father to give her hand in marriage to him. Then it occurred to him how many times she was sent to the neighbors whenever he had arrived. He decided to let her in on the secret, hoping it will clear all of her doubts. "I don't know how you are going to take this. But I think Abdul Aziz Bhai really loves you. It feels awkward to say it but he really does. Abu ji said no to the marriage many times but he insisted he will only marry you. My dear sis you have nothing to worry about. He will take good care of you." Hearing this lovely story instantly lightened the burden on Yasmin's heart.

"You are also forgetting that he is incredibly handsome, hard working and educated. I know there is quite an age gap between you two but I promise you look older." He teased again. Yasmin's cheeks blushed in the light of the lantern when she laughed at her brother's innocent joke.

"Now go back to sleep and stop this nonsense. You are destroying your beauty. And yes before you ask me, you look like an innocent angel, to me anyway." Yasmin's face lit up even more.

Wasim's heart sank when he spoke to her. He realized his sister would be leaving permanently. From there on he decided to show her all the love and care that she was craving.

The talk that he had with her should have come from their mother. But he knew no one could change her so he decided there on to support her in anyway he could. He put his hand on her head as he got up to leave, "If you ever need to talk you know where to find me, and if there is anything that you want. I mean anything, from the shops or market, don't hesitate to ask."

Appreciating his thought she thanked him. He picked up the lantern and led her down the stairs. As Yasmin lay down back to bed she began to fantasize about her future with Abdul Aziz.

CHAPTER 14

As the wedding approached closer and closer Yunas's grew sadder and sadder. Safia seemed to be coping well. She felt her status rising now that her daughter was marrying a police officer. Safia expressed her sadness through tormenting Yasmin and making her run around on her own wedding arrangements. Poor Yasmin took all the abuse that Safia imposed upon her.

Wasim always knew how to make her feel better. He would bring her little gifts from the market on his way home, sometimes bangles, sometimes a scarf or sweets. Seeing all these little gifts made her smile. Now as the wedding was approaching Wasim's exams were over. The two of them would sit on the terrace at night to talk or play games. Each of them had found a close friend. They became so close that they both gave each other tips on how girls or guys thought.

The rituals took place and on the day of the nikkah Abdul Aziz brought his whole village to the wedding, being a well known man in his town. When the betrothal rituals began Yasmin trembled in her red veil. You could tell by looking at the flowered garlands hanging from her henna covered wrists. Bushra and Asma cried uncontrollably. All of the women surrounding had tears overflowing their eyes.

Yunas's face was expressionless. Javed and Wasim tried really hard to hold their feelings in. Yasmin met everyone one by one and said her goodbyes. Yasmin's face wet with tears, Mehnaz comforted Asma and Bushra.

Bushra held onto her waist tightly as she did her round of meeting the family. She caught a glimpse of Wasim from her veil. His face looked completely torn. Her lips began to quiver from each step that she took forward towards him. Reaching closer he looked away and did not let a tear drop from his watery eyes. He raised his hand and stroked her head with a broken smile, trying to reassure her. Javed also stroked her head with tears rolling down his cheeks. Asma pulled Bushra from Yasmin's waist.

When Yasmin came to meet her mother, Safia gave her a tight hug, possibly the first ever hug she got from her mother. Her mother finally broke down in tears. That moment Yasmin felt her mothers love. The love that she had been craving, from that moment she realized that what ever her mother tried to teach her was for her benefit. Of course her mother loved her. She gave birth to her. Her mother loved her so much that she did not want her daughter to get mistreated from her in laws or to ever fail as a woman for the rest of her life. That *was* her mother's love. Yasmin then turned to her father who looked lost, not being able to meet his daughter's gaze.

He kept looking to the ground finally embracing his daughter. They both sobbed in each others arms. Yunas walked Yasmin to her hand held carriage with a hand onto her shoulder, which would lead her to the car that had Abdul Aziz waiting. Jannat helped Yasmin into the car and sat next to her. Abdul was sitting at the front with the driver.

He sneaked a look from the side mirror and adjusted it accordingly so he could look at Yasmin throughout the journey home.

When the car reached their home, Jannat led Yasmin out of the car into their massive court yard. The extended family awaiting for her arrival, Jannat led her around to all the rituals. Finally leading her to her new bedroom, helping her to sit down, she opened her veil. "Oh dear you look terrible, look how you have ruined your lovely make up." Jannat smiled at her. She then took a corner of her own shawl and cleaned all of the smudged make up. Yasmin looked at her in a stunned manner. Was she really her mother in law? She thought. She can't be that nice. She knew mother in laws to be rude and evil. But her own mother in law was showing her love care on her first day. Surely she must hate me thought Yasmin, her son married me, mothers hated to share their sons with another woman. Jannat then fixed her hair for her that had got ruined on the journey home; she took out her kohl and reapplied it to her eyes. "Now you look like an angel for my son." She smiled. She then got up to get her a handheld mirror to look into. Yasmin couldn't help smiling at her reflection.

"My son Abdul only likes a natural look in a woman; he believes make up is unreal. It hides the real woman. So he says." She giggled. She then placed one hand on Yasmin's shoulder and the other on her hand. "From this day forward, you are my daughter, not a daughter in law. All of my daughters in laws are like daughters to me. They All show me the respect of a mother and I show them the love and respect they expect from a mother. If you ever need anything to talk about you can ask. You see all of my sons live separately. Abdul is the eldest and the last to be married, he insisted that I live with him.

Does it bother you if I live with you two? I can always stay with my other children if it ever bothers you."

Yasmin looked at her shockingly and shook her head. "This is your home, you live as you please. I will try to care for you as much as I can. Having elders in the house is never a burden but a blessing." Jannat was very pleased with her answer. She then told her to rest and went to bring her some food.

Yasmin looked around her room. It was quite plain but elegant. It had a four poster bed a wardrobe and a few chairs with a small table. The bed had a set of clothes for her and Abdul to change into, and rose petals spread on the bed. For some reason, this felt more like home than she ever felt at her parents house. She thought she had a dream when she re-winded Jannats kindness in her mind.

Jannat returned with some food and water on a tray. Beginning to feed Yasmin with her own hands and told her this might be the only time they will get to share a loving meal together as Abdul will probably take over. Yasmin blushed looking down her heart sank in appreciation. Yasmin fed Jannat back. This was a start to beautiful relationship they both thought. Yasmin had to stop Jannat to feed her feeling quite full from all the feeding.

Suddenly realizing that she had not eaten since breakfast, the guests had all eaten well. But Yasmin was forgotten, her own mother hadn't bothered to send her any meals throughout the day. This thought made her a little sad making a tear fall from her eye. She turned away from Jannat to wipe it. Jannat asked her if she was alright. Yasmin forced a smile and nodded.

"Don't worry my son wont bite." She teased. Gathering the dishes she headed to the door. "I will send Abdul in soon." She winked at the door. Yasmin trembled with fear. She had never spoken to Abdul. He was a complete stranger. The mother is nice I am sure he will be nice too. She consoled herself. The door creaked open. Abdul walked in with his white salwar kameez, rolling up his sleeves when he made his entrance into the bedroom.

He turned around and shut the two doors behind him locking them tight shut. He turned back to walk towards her. Yasmin froze in her chair gazing down. He sat on the chair next to her raising her face with his hands to face him. She finally plucked up the courage to look into his eyes. He *is* incredibly handsome like Wasim had told her she thought. "Aslaam aleikum, Yasmin." He whispered. "Walikam salam." she muttered back. "How are you? Are you comfortable?"

"Jee" she muttered. He smiled and held her hand kissing it like a gentleman. "I fell in love with you the moment I saw you, it seems as if Allah took his time in creating you, I feel extremely lucky to have gained you as a wife. I want to give you all the love and respect in the world, even more than your parents. As long as you never break my expectations as a dutiful wife, or break my heart." He placed the back of her hand on his beating chest; coyly pulling away she nodded in agreement. "You must be tired. Go and change and get some sleep." Yasmin followed obediently falling into a deep sleep on her new comfortable bed.

CHAPTER 15

It was only within two weeks of their marriage that Yasmin was given the most heartbreaking news. Her parents had sent for her through a passer by to come home immediately. It was raining the day she had received the calling. Abdul and she were just sipping hot tea and pakoras. It was 4:27pm, the exact time she saw on the clock. Her hands trembled when Abdul told her to get ready immediately to go to see her parents. Quickly picking up her white shawl she wrapped it around her face only leaving her eyes apparent. Jannat just walked in the gate holding an umbrella as they were about to leave. "Where are you two going? Yasmin why do you look so worried my child?"

"Safia Khala and Yunas Mamu have ordered us to come immediately; they sent Ditta to pass the message. We are hoping everythings ok."

Jannat knew what this kind of news meant. "I will come with you." Jannat and Abdul locked all of the doors of the house and the gate while Yasmin froze in her position, fearing the worst.

The three of them squeezed onto the motorbike, Jannat sat in the middle holding the umbrella above their heads. Abdul rode his bike carefully on the wet dirt path. The rain had made it really slippery. One slip and you were goner. Jannats huge umbrella kept them dry from the rain. Many thoughts went through Yasmin's mind.

"Ya Allah make sure everything is ok . . . Please please . . ." there was a unusual silence in Yasmins village. Every house they drove by was empty. Yasmin's fears grew worse. She was the first to jump off the motorbike rushing up the outside stairs. The courtyard was filled with the whole village wailing.

She pushed through the crowd in the heavy rain, her heartbeat pounding faster and faster blocking the noise of the crowd.

Shock, Despair overrode her. She fell on her knees looking at the sight before her. Her body shivered with fear. Wasim her lovely brother Wasim lay there wrapped in a white cocoon sheet. She looked around her. Everyone wailed uncontrollably. Abdul finally caught up with her through the crowd, his face grew pale when he looked at the sight before him. Jannat followed gasping at the sight in front of her.

Yasmin's throught swallowed her tongue making it difficult for her to speak. Safia was beating her chest wailing. Nobody had noticed Yasmin's arrival; all imensed in their sorrow. Jannat walked over to Safia and held her in her arms with tears following through. "bas, bas . . ." she cooed to Safia, like she was holding a baby in her arms. As soon as Abdul placed his hand on Yasmins shoulder squeezing it hard, not being able to control her emotions, she sobbed in her hands.

Bushra and Asma heard Yasmin's sobbing rushed to her aid. The three sisters held onto each other walking slowly closer to Wasims bedside. "Please tell me he is asleep, Bushra. Please tell me he is asleep Asma . . ." she wailed. Her mother heard her voice and said "Look at your still brother, he's gone he's left us forever!" Abdul

148

consoled Javed and Yunas. He still didn't know what had happened or more so how the death had happened.

He was ever so young only a few years older than Yasmin. It occurred to him how Yasmin had told him how he had taken such delicate care of her the year before their marriage and now he was gone . . . just like that. Abdul didn't have the courage to ask Yunas or Javed what had happened. Feeling suspicious. Wasim had no bruise whats so ever. Usmaan Ali pulled Abdul over to one corner and told him that Wasim had drowned in a lake nearby.

"He went swimming with his friends. They were messing around and dared each other for a race. He was the only one who could swim. The others dared him to swim to the other side. You probably know it's a bit of a distance from one end to the other. His friends stopped at the shallow end. He like the daredevil he was carried on to the other side, not knowing how deep it was or what dangers lurked inside, something pulled him in and he drowned."

"Oh my God . . . ." Was all Abdul could say. The police officer that he was had made him wonder how could he have drowned if he *could* swim. He plucked up the courage to ask this question, inquiring further who had swam in to get him including when did this happen. Usmaan Ali took a deep breath.

"This happened just before noon, yes I am also wondering the same thing if he could swim how he could drown. The boys claim that he was screaming and struggling as if he was being pulled into the water. The idiots didn't even try to save him, one just ran to get me for I am the only one here who knows how to swim and have first aid knowledge. The other one just froze there not even bothering to call for help around him." Usmaan Ali proceeded with the details further.

"When I got there I jumped into the lake and swam across. At first I couldn't find him the water was too deep. I had to come up for air a couple of times the water was very cold. Then I took another dive, until my foot felt his arm. I held my breath once more and tried to pull him up. When I tried pulling it was quite hard to grab him to shore." Usmaan Ali starting to well up from repeating the story, it wasn't easy having to relive the horrible tragedy.

"I then investigated what was tangling him. As I got lower I saw his foot was tangled in the weeds, so I took out my Swiss army knife and chopped him free."

"Was he still breathing when you brought him to the shore?" Usmaan Ali sighed sadly, wiping the tears that had come to surface.

"I tried to pump the water out of his chest, but only a little came out. As I was about to do a mouth to mouth the villagers had surrounded by then and told me to take him to hospital. I didn't want to interfere too much just in case they were to say you didn't let us take him to the hospital. They took him to the small local hospital, and the doctors said we were too late. Hes no more . . ." Abdul couldn't help but to cry after hearing the tragic story.

Usmaan Ali squeezed his shoulder and told him to have faith. He belonged to God and when God wants his people back he has every right to take them back when he pleases. "Yasmin is like a daughter to us, I know this goes without saying but please give her all the support you can now, you have to be strong for her. Poor thing only got married a few weeks ago and has had to return to a brother's funeral." Abdul nodded in agreement wiping his tears with the back of his hand.

He could not imagine what the family must be going through. Especially the parents who gave birth to him and brought him up into such a strong lad, all their expectations must have been shattered. Poor Yasmin he thought. He just wanted to take her to a room and hold her close. He could hear her wailing from the room where all the men were sitting. He wanted to take away all her pain, which he could not do in front of her family. If only he could have five minutes alone with her, maybe he could make her feel better.

It suddenly dawned on him maybe due to their marriage this tragedy took place. He had heard that your destiny changed when you got married. You start to share the good and the bad from one another, how it could affect the other person. For a minute he felt it was his fault that the woman he loved was going through all this pain. Then suddenly he remembered Usmaan Ali's words. Wasim belonged to God, death was a fact of life that one could not dodge, or change. We all have to die one day, how what and where it will happen, only God knew. These thoughts made him feel better instantly.

He then went over to Yunas and gave him a hug, then embraced Javed, they both cried uncontrollably in his arms.

"Its time for the Janaza now," Usmaan Ali announced. It had stopped raining. Fatima asked the women to move away and to recite the kalma, for that will ease their pain. As the men were about to carry his bed, Yasmin broke down wailing; "You said you will always be there for me! How could you do this Wasim?" Jannat held her back and told her to stop questioning Gods will, if she screamed and cried like this it will hurt his soul. Yasmin felt dizzy falling unconscious from the shock. All the women crowded her taking her inside.

After a few slaps on the cheek with water thrown on her face she was awake again, she smiled upon waking, believing it was all a dream. Jannat was at her side asking how she felt. "Oh I just had the most awful dream . . ." Jannat didn't let her finish the story.

"It's not a dream my love, this is real, Wasim is gone." She looked outside and saw that his bed was gone; the men had taken him to the grave yard.

Jannat held her close they both cried uncontrollably into each others arms. Fatima joined them and stroked Yasmin's hair. "Oh my poor child, this is Gods way, he takes those whom he loves the most."

The whole masjid was filled to the brim with men from all over at the funeral. Usmaan Ali led the prayer; Abdul helped Javed to lower Wasim's cocoon like coffin into the rectangular hole in the earth. They all recited the kalma and said their prayers.

Yunas couldn't believe his eyes of what was happening. He sobbed quietly watching each member throw a handful of earth onto his coffin. One by one each handful of soil covered his face and then eventually Wasim was gone for the world, buried into the earth.

Abdul tried to question the boys involved but the parents of the boys did not let him take his investigation further. Yunas and Safia told him to leave them and to let Wasim's soul to rest in peace. Abdul obeyed, he then asked if he could stay with Yasmin until all the funeral rituals were over. Jannat also stayed to help out. The three of them stayed for forty days.

By that time everyone was so attached to Abdul as he supported not only Yasmin but the whole family wholeheartedly. Yasmin thanked Allah and Fatima everyday for such a loving and a caring husband. He hardly knew her but he dotted on her. He took over a month off work and supported her parents like his own.

Jannat was quite proud of him the whole village spoke highly of him. He made the family laugh with his innocent jokes bringing gifts for Yasmin, as well as helping with serving the guests who came to give their condolences.

When the forty days were over Yunas found it hard to say goodbye, Abdul joked if he should move in with them. Yunas smiled agreeing he would love that but a daughter looked better in her husband's home. Jannat was relieved to be going home, including Yasmin, she wanted to be alone with her husband and thank him properly. They were unable to spend anytime alone together, she found it embarrassing to talk to him in front of her family even though now that they were married. Let alone talking she wouldn't even sit next to him where he sat, she learned this from her own parents and her older brother and sister in law.

When they reached home, Jannat purposely went to spend the night at her sister's house to give them some space. It was early evening when they came home, finally alone when they were about to retire to bed. Yasmin was eager to hold him and to say her thanks properly. The moment they were alone Abdul gave her a big hug and Yasmin sobbed again in his arms. The trauma replayed in her mind. "Shhh . . ." he cooed.

"If it weren't for you I don't know how I would have coped. Thank you so much. How can I ever repay you?" he stroked her hair and smiled looking into her eyes. "First off you can stop crying, and secondly I just want you to be a good wife to me and a good mother to my children. Please don't ever keep anything from me. I don't like secrets I feel they build distrust. I trust you with my heart and hope you do the same. I also hope for some love in return of mine. That's all I ask for . . ." He whispered lovingly, Yasmin buried her head in his chest again, both squeezing each other tightly.

CHAPTER 16

From that day forward Yasmin obeyed Abdul, not giving him any reason to lessen his love for her. His love grew deeper the day Elaynna was born when they settled in the United Kingdom, he was so proud of Yasmin for giving birth in a unknown country and coping ever so well with Elaynna's premature birth.

He had worried that they would lose Elaynna, being a very weak baby. Both husband and wife prayed day and night to Allah for her recovery. The hospital kept her in a cubicle for a month. Elaynna was the size of Abdul's hand. She recovered well with the hospitals support and her parent's prayers.

Now she was in the same position like she was born, still and lifeless the way she had been in the cubicle. Yasmin felt guilty praying that Elaynna would wake up. Yasmin ran outside upon hearing the sound of Abdul's motorcycle.

He helped the doctor with his bag both rushing towards Elaynna's bed. "How is she Ammi?" Abdul asked with a tone of worry in his voice.

"She woke up and had a sip of water but fell back to unconsciousness. I have been continuously keeping her forehead cool with cloths of water. She seems to have cooled down dramatically."

"Well done, you did the right thing." Doctor Imran interrupted. He was the family doctor whom Abdul always turned to. He always came to their aid be it day or night. He took out his stethoscope and checked her heartbeat.

Her skin felt hot to the touch. Further checking her pulse and temperature her temperature had raised much above the normal range. Her lips had cracked up dry even with Jannats continuous wetting. "Hmmm," Dr Imran finally mumbled, trying to diagnose her ailment. "She has a case of really bad dehydration. Has she not been drinking enough water and maybe playing or working too hard?" he asked taking out a glucose drip. Jannat shook her head keeping her gaze locked at Yasmin with angered eyes.

Abdul sensed the tension; he tried to figure out what was hotting up between his mother and wife. He also noticed Yasmin look away from Jannat not being able to look back at her, while she patted Qasim on her shoulders. He knew something fishy was going on. His concentration was disturbed when Dr Imran injected Elaynna on her wrist setting up the drip. He hung the glucose drip on the small branch above so that gravity would pull the contents into her veins.

He gave her an injection to reduce to her temperature. "She will be OK? Right?" asked Abdul anxiously the worst going through his mind. "Yes, yes don't worry brother Abdul. She will be fine. I have given her an injection. The rest the glucose drip will do its job. It will replace all the fluids that her body has lost. Hence why she was dangerously unconscious, you called me at the right time." He patted Abdul on the back for support. "What do you mean *exactly* by right time?" Jannat queried further purposely trying to teach Yasmin a lesson.

"Dehydration can be very dangerous especially if accompanied by a temperature. If you lose all of your body fluids it can cause other medical complications. So don't worry she will be fine."

"Hmmm, so can it also KILL a person?" emphasized Jannat further. "Yes, it can" answered Dr Imran turning his gaze curiously at Jannat.

"Just let her rest and feed her well as well as plenty to drink of course, In shaa Allah she will be fine."

Abdul offered him to stay for lunch the sun was getting really hot. They all picked up Elaynna's bed and placed it carefully in the veranda. Jannat carried the glucose drip following behind; they placed the bed next to the window outside of Abdul's room. It was the perfect place to hang the glucose drip on the netted windows and patterned bars, staying firmly in place.

Dr Imran accepted the invitation for lunch. Elaynna finally gained consciousness within an hour of the glucose drip being emptied. She still had a slight temperature. Jannat and Abdul rushed to her side.

"How are you feeling beta?" asked Jannat lovingly. Abdul stroked her hair and checked her temperature. She was still hot. "Im OK . . ." mumbled Elaynna. "I am just feeling a bit weak." Abdul helped her sit up and Jannat went to fetch her something to eat. She brought the chapatti that she saved for her and the lentils. The hot weather kept the food a good temperature, it did not need reheating. Jannat fed her, it had been a long time since anyone had fed her so lovingly.

Yasmin joined them after hearing Jannat and Elaynna's voices. She sat next to Elaynna and stroked her hair. "You OK beta?"

"Yes Ammi I am alright, hows Qasim?" Elaynna innocently asked.

"Don't worry about Qasim hes OK, you get better my child." Elaynna wondered whether she was dreaming, her mother was being unbelievably nice to her. Qasim awoke from his nap crying for his feed.

Rahim and Kareem were taking a siesta. Abdul tossed and turned in the shade, finding it difficult to sleep, thoughts running through his mind, why Yasmin had been acting unusual, any normal mother would have been by her daughter's side but Yasmin was keeping a distance from Jannat as well as Elaynna. Is she hiding something? He wondered. No. She told him everything; not a single secret between them. Why was Ammi also acting so odd and crossly at Yasmin like it was her fault if she wasn't? Ammi knew everything about how Elaynna was born, he tried to fit two and two together.

Only one way to find out, he began his investigation. Yasmin had just finished feeding Qasim when Abdul walked in on her. Believing it would be best to get straight to the point.

"Is everything ok? Why was Ammi brushing you off today?" Yasmin did well in keeping her face straight. Avoiding eye contact, pretending to be busy with Qasim. "Maybe because I gave Qasim a bad stomach ache, Ammi was quite cross about that. Perhaps she has to do everything herself and now Elaynna is not well . . . ."

"Hmmm . . . ." he answered back without letting her finish Abdul left the room. Yasmin felt relieved that she did not have to make any more excuses, believing that Abdul had been satisfied with her answer.

Jannat remained sitting by Elaynna's side. Fanning her to keep her cool while she slept. Abdul sat on a bed nearby, not helping to smile when he observed the love between them.

"Ammi is everything OK? Why were you unusual with Yasmin earlier? I know she can be quite stubborn at times. But in a situation like this you were being quite harsh don't you think?" Jannat remained quiet at first. With a bit of stern in her voice, she thought it was about time Abdul heard the reality of his wife's nature.

"Your lovely wife thinks she's always right no matter what happens. She doesn't ever think of the consequences that could take affect. She can be so careless and even . . . . heartless." Abdul thought for a second how could she be heartless? What by eating rice and giving Qasim colic? He began to wonder. "Ammi are you sure that you are not hiding something from me? How can my beloved Yasmin ever be heartless by giving Qasim colic? Ammi, why are you making a fuss over such a small thing?" Jannat couldn't keep quiet any longer.

159

"Do you even know why Elaynna is in this state? It's all Yasmins fault." His face dropped in shock.

"What do you mean by that?" Jannat told him everything, she told him word for word of the whole incident that took place a few days earlier, and how Qasim had been born. Abdul's heart shattered to pieces. Stunned at how evil his wife could be to their daughter. "Look I didn't say anything earlier because I didn't want you to think badly of Yasmin, but now that Elaynna is ill I couldn't hold my emotions any longer."

A lot of rage began building inside Abdul; Jannat noticed how his face went from pale to red. "Please don't go shouting at her now, or arguing with her. Especially in the state she is in now, there won't be any use. I have had words with her already. When you went to get Imran I did say a few things that I am now feeling guilty for, but at the time she deserved to hear them. I know I shouldn't be making her emotional at this time." Abdul's temper calmed down upon hearing that his wife didn't get away from her act completely he then left without saying a word more.

He walked back into his bedroom to have a lie down. His wife had broken his trust. His beloved Yasmin had broken his trust, not just his trust she lied to him. Punishing their daughter so terribly for being caught washing dishes at school. Why was Elaynna doing this in the first place when she should have been in class? Many questions went through his mind. He wanted to talk to Yasmin. Actually he wanted to punish Yasmin for being so cruel to her only daughter. Had she forgotten the days she was in a cubicle finding it difficult to breathe? What if she had died? Who would have been to blame?

He was in complete shock and disturbed that his love would betray him in this way.

He would need to talk to her and question her when the time was right. Now was not a good time as she had just given birth and Elaynna being unwell.

CHAPTER 17

Abdul's behavior towards Yasmin changed dramatically. He would hardly talk to her or show her the same affection he used to. He transferred that affection to Elaynna and the boys. Yasmin found his behavior odd. Whenever she would try to meet his gaze he didn't bother to look back or smile like he used to. All of a sudden he would just smile at Elaynna or his mother pretending he didn't see her.

Elaynna recovered within a week, back to her usual self taking care of the house chores. Yasmin tried to teach her Arabic. She was very slow at learning. It took her three years to complete reading the Holy Quran. Rahim and Kareem completed the Quran much earlier than she did. Her mother would taunt her that she was so lazy and stupid that she was just making excuses to not to learn on purpose.

Dismissing the fact that maybe Elaynna might have a learning difficulty. Jannat would give her extra lessons to sharpen her pronunciation. But they were no use. Even though she somehow learned to read the whole Quran by reading a little bit each day, she soon enough forgot. She felt relieved when she had finally completed reading all of it. Yasmin held a feast for when Rahim and Kareem finished their Quran but she didn't bother celebrating anything for Elaynna. "Shes a teenager now, it will be an embarrassment to hold a feast for her what will the neighbors think?" She told Abdul and

Jannat on day. That night Elaynna cried all night. She felt her parents didn't love her at all. When she had finally achieved something, it didn't seem important at all to anyone. She was just a piece of old furniture. At least the furniture occasionally got polished but Elaynna didn't get a single applause. Waking up in the morning no one noticed her swollen eyes.

Being at the age of thirteen, she was burdened with more responsibilities. Yasmin was happy that now she didn't need to teach her the Quran any longer, instead she would focus on making her sharp in the housework. Elaynna knew how to do most of the housework from the back of her hand; she was still an amateur to cooking. She knew the simple stuff of making chapattis and boiling rice.

Jannat taught her how to read the five daily prayers as well as the required verses of the Quran to learn to memory. When it was time to pray Elaynna would rush her bows and speed through the verses. Rahim would make fun of her and ask her to recite the verses out loud and when she did recite them loudly she would read them really fast, making constant fun of her that they would end up fighting. Kareem would scold him to stop, it was not a nice thing to do to their older sister.

"She will always be stupid, she doesn't understand common sense." Rahim would protest, teaching Qasim to make fun of her.

"Baji can't even read!" Qasim would tease. When Qasim would be doing his homework or revising for his exams he would call Elaynna asking her to read the first lines for him. When she would try and struggle to read the word, Qasim would hold his stomach and laugh at her uncontrollably. Rahim would always come and join in making her feel worse.

Elaynna would pretend that their words didn't hurt her feelings. She would walk off and act like she didn't care. At first whenever she was alone she would sit and cry. Getting used to all the taunting she let it be a part of her life, believing it was something she couldn't change, beginning to wish that she still went to school like her siblings.

If she could at least read then no one could make fun of her. All her friends of her age were now literate and spoke sensibly. Elaynna kept quiet worrying she would embarrass herself if she ever spoke too much. Elaynna was quite slow at understanding things. When things were done routinely she would do them well but if she was given an instant order for something out of the ordinary she forgot or messed up the task. When ever she was taught something new she instantly forgot.

If it was something physical to do with house work she would master that task quite in no time. Because of her swift ability for housework her mother and Jannat were quite proud of her. She didn't give them a chance to complain. By the time she turned fifteen she began to get proposals, Abdul Aziz had other plans. Now that things were in order again he wanted to move back to England and start a new life with the children. He was still distant with Yasmin. Yasmin didn't notice too much of this distance believing it was due to the growing responsibilities. With three boys growing up, they needed their father more than she did. Believing it was her responsibility to bring up

Elaynna in the same way her mother had brought her up teaching her everything.

Yasmin couldn't see her daughter's confidence deteriorating making the same mistakes that her own mother did, in fact she was worse, she couldn't remember the necessities of the importance an education, and how lucky she had been in having Fatima's support in teaching her to read and live the life that she was leading.

"Ammi, I want to move back to England now, if I have your permission?" Abdul started to ask randomly one evening. Jannat listened contently, her eyes blurred with tears in an instant. It was getting dark the power had gone Abdul couldn't see the despair in his mother's eyes.

"I think it will be better for our children to grow and make an income there, as you know how hard it is to build a life here in the village."

"Hmmm . . ." mumbled Jannat. She couldn't bare the thought of having Elaynna separated from her, but she knew it was coming.

"We will only go Ammi if you are comfortable with us going. I will send you a money order each month so you don't have to ask anyone for money." Jannat took a deep breath, trying to sound supportive. "So when are you thinking of going?"

"I have applied for the visas, the immigration lawyers said it shouldn't take too long. Since I have already been there and have a good work record. Plus my visa is still valid. I just need to get the children's visas ready. I have been putting a little money aside and the remaining money I can borrow from a friend over there that will let us stay with him until we become stable."

Jannat nodded in agreement, but couldn't help being a little upset; a tear out of nowhere ran down her cheek. Her son was asking her permission after he had got everything sorted and decided to go already.

"You have my permission." All of a sudden the electricity power returned with her consent. Abdul smiled at Jannat.

"Go and live the life of your dreams my son." She returned his smile without letting him see the tears in her eyes. She got up to give him a kiss on his forehead and called Elaynna to lay the beds out in the courtyard for it was getting late. Abdul was so happy with his mother's permission, falling asleep instantly feeling light as a feather. Jannat couldn't sleep at all that night. Crying silently all night, the mere thought of Elaynna leaving her made her feel distraught.

She had got so used to her grand daughters company; Jannat the only one who knew and understood Elaynna's difficulties. It haunted her that by going into an unknown country the little confidence that Elaynna had would be crushed.

The following morning Elaynna could see that her grandmother didn't look right. "Dadi, are you feeling alright? Shall I go get your medicine?" Jannat smiled at her curiosity. Her own son or daughter in law couldn't see the sadness or unusual behavior in their mother but her granddaughter saw right through her. She sat her down beside her in the kitchen. Holding her face she looked deep into her eyes.

"My child whoever says that you know nothing or try to act smarter than you, remember you are better than they ever can be; your heart is clean as gold. What you see in others, others can never see. Doesn't matter if you know how to read or write. You will always be better than them." Elaynna warmed to the compliment. For once feeling useful to the world, her grandmother knew how to make her feel special.

"Are you upset Dadi because we will be moving to England?" she asked innocently.

"Just a little bit beta, you wont forget me will you?" Jannat sobbed with tears starting all over again. Elaynna hugged her tightly starting to cry as well.

"Bas bas beta, we will end up making the tea salty if we carry on crying like this." They both giggled at the innocent joke.

"Any chance of breakfast served today?" Rahim walked in interrupting.

"Don't you try acting like you are my father you donkey, you have no manners I tell you!" Jannat snapped at him.

"Sorry Dadi." Rahim feeling a little embarrassed.

"Go and lay the mat and the dishes, we will bring the rest."

"Jee Dadi . . ." rushing out to do the task. Elaynna couldn't help giggling at her brothers quickness. Jannat lovingly stroked her head.

"I know how much he can hurt your feelings sometimes. The little scroundrel deserves it!" Elaynna felt sorry for him for a minute, but tried to savor the moment of Rahim getting in trouble.

CHAPTER 18

Abdul was checking all the last bits of paper work the night before they were flying out to England. He had all their passports and visas ready. The women of the household were busy packing their belongings. Abdul had brought them lots of winter wear in the month of September London was a pretty cold city compared to Pakistan.

"I am so excited!" Rahim told Kareem taking their last stroll around the village.

"Aren't you afraid? Starting a new life in a whole new environment? They speak English there. We can just about read it." Rahim gave him a funny look, trying to show off his braveness.

"We *will* go to school you know. And see all the gauri girls. I hear they don't wear dubattas or salwar kameez there!" Kareem returned his funny look with a disgusted one.

"Tauba tauba, you are disgusting. Have some shame. Every woman is like a sister." Kareem even at the age of thirteen had great morals. Rahim instantly changed the subject.

"Well I am sure Abu has everything planned out for us. We will live like princes over there." Qasim squealed with excitement upon hearing how luxuriantly they would be living. When they took a last look at their village in the moonlight, they took a deep sigh at the same time, internally feeling saddened that this will be the last moonlight of their homeland.

Upon entering their courtyard it was filled with the villagers who had come to say their farewell. Elaynna ran around serving tea and water. Yasmin's family had come to say good bye. Safia and Yunas came to give their blessings to the children and their daughter. They gave them gifts of new clothes to take with them. Yasmin really appreciated their lovely gesture.

"See how clever my daughter is? She is now going to be living like a queen. If it weren't for my taunting she wouldn't have been able to handle such a big household." Safia said proudly to Yunas and Jannat.

"In today's time if you don't put pressure on the youngsters they never learn." She spat out her red paan, showing her red teeth and shook her head gesturing to Elaynna.

"Well in our village we believe in bringing our children up with as much as love as we can shower them with." Jannat answered sternly also gesturing to Elaynna.

Elaynna noticed and smiled appreciating her grandmother for standing up for her.

"Ammi is right, the better the children understand their parent's pressure the more they will be able to handle challenging situations." Yasmin interrupted. Jannat wasn't in the mood to make a scene. She walked off to check if all was packed properly saying good bye to all of the guests. When everyone had left, Jannat led Elaynna inside alone to talk to her.

"Beta I want you to always listen to your heart where ever you go, don't let anyone push you around. This is your only chance to educate yourself and grow independent. What ever you do don't forget our culture." They embraced each other crying their heart out. Jannat took out a black threaded necklace which had a sterling silver square pendant on it. She untied it and put it around Elaynna's neck.

"Whats is it Dadi?" Elaynna held the pendant in her hand curiously.

"This is a blessing from Peer Saab. It has special verses of the Quran written in it for your protection. This will always give you victory in what ever you do. It will also give you confidence. When ever you are lost just think of Allah he will always guide you on the right path. Just remember what ever he does he does for the best." Elaynna clutched the pendant tight with her fist, feeling special. "What ever happens always look for the good in the situation. In life we all go through a bad time, Allah will bless you with something good in return for your patience. Allah is always with those who are patient and grateful."

The hired van beeped its horn arriving on time to take them to the airport the following morning. Jannat and Imtiaz walked them out on to the main gate.

"All the best Yasmin, please don't be too hard on Elaynna. She is just a child, the more love and care you show her the better the daughter she will be." Yasmin nodded hugging her back, both breaking into tears.

"Look after Ammi. I will always write to you." Abdul requested Imtiaz. "Of course I will take good care of her, shes everything to me." She kissed his forehead and bid him farewell. Abdul's brothers and Javed accompanied the driver to the airport. Elaynna sat by the last edge window wearing a white shawl. She locked eyes with Jannat as the vehicle drove on. They both stared at each other until they could no longer see each other. When the vehicle was out of sight, Jannat put her shawl to her mouth and sobbed into it. Imtiaz comforted her and walked her home shutting the gates behind them. "Bas bas, time will heal." holding her hand squeezing it tight.

"My Elaynna, Oh my Elaynna . . ." sobbed Jannat. "How will I survive without her? Her witch of a mother will continuously taunt her; at least when I was around Yasmin would stop because she feared me." Imtiaz stroked her head.

"Don't worry all will be well, you will make yourself sick if you carry on like this." She sobbed uncontrollably.

"I won't let you stay alone in this house; God knows what you will do to yourself." She blew her nose into her scarf. Jannat catching her breath, "I will be OK, I want to be alone. Who will look after this house?" Imtiaz looked at her crossly, "I am your sister you have my *kasam* you will live with me from now on. I can't bear to see you like this. I will send Sakina later to finish the tidying up. Now let's pack your clothes. Tomorrow we can come together and pack stuff away properly." Jannat let out a long sigh. Maybe it would do her good to be kept busy and to be around people she thought.

"I don't want to be a burden on you, sister." Before Imtiaz could tell her off, she got up and packed two outfits. They then locked up all the doors and windows. They both strolled slowly to Imtiaz's house.

Imtiaz took out a bed for her from inside and put it under the shade. She told her to have a nap until lunch was ready. Before she knew it she fell asleep like a baby. She hadn't slept ever since Abdul had announced their departure.

Elaynna could no longer see her grandmother; she buried her face in her hands and cried until she reached the airport. Rahim, Kareem, and Qasim excitedly looked out of the window. This was the first time that they had left their village and drove through the main city. It felt like a new world. Abdul laughed at their behavior.

"This is nothing my boys, wait till you reach London. There are many many big buildings there; your school would be the same size as these buildings." They got even more excited. Elaynna couldn't bear to look out of the window, not even once; she was too consumed in her sorrow for leaving her grandmother. Her only support of life, the only one she could ever talk to and who understood her.

Without realizing it she cried herself to sleep. She stumbled awake when they reached the airport. Her uncles got the carts to put the suitcases in. Elaynna's jaw opened when she saw the aiport. It looked like a dusty palace. There were crowds and crowds of people rushing left right and center. Each and everyone bumping into each other, some were there to collect their loved ones, and some were there to bid farewell. You could tell who was who by their facial expressions. The ones that were bidding farewell were in tears with sad faces. The ones who were on the receiving end were smiling from ear to ear. Elaynna felt uneasy saying her last good byes to her uncles. Walking down the departure hallway she wanted to find a place to hide. There were lots of boys gaping at her and licking their lips at her like hungry wolves. She realized suddenly she was almost a woman now, a fifteen year old.

They pushed through the crowd, all clutching their own suitcases. Abdul held Elaynna's hand, Elaynna held Qasim's. Yasmin held onto Rahim and Kareems. If they let go they could be lost. Finally past the crowd it was all calm in the departure area. There was a long line through the security check up. Abdul being in the police force, was able to go straight to the departure desk of PIA.

"Tickets and passports please." A lady in the PIA uniform asked politely. She wore a green and white salwar kameez. Her hair was tied in a high bun, with a small rounded hat and a dubatta hanging from it. Her make up was elegant with red lipstick. Elaynna thought she looked like a bride. She smiled at Elaynna, when she noticed she was staring right at her, Elaynna smiled back shyly. After checking their passports and tickets she guided them through immigration. Their entire luggage was booked, Abdul carried his little leather bag which had all of their important paperwork.

Feeling lighter for not having anything to carry they followed obediently, it wasn't so crowded anymore. They lined up at immigration having all their paperwork checked. One by one they went through security, a gent's side to check the gents and a lady officer to check the females. When Elaynna went in the lady gave her a curious look. "Arms up." Elaynna followed instructions obediently. The female security guard was a short plump woman who had a big wart on her forehead; it had hair growing out from it.

"Oh aren't you a pretty little thing? Where are you off to eh?" Elaynna shrugged her shoulders.

"Oh so you must just be mute, poor thing. Off you go." She walked straight to her mother who was waiting for her outside the cubicle.

"Come on, hurry up your father is waiting." Abdul had all the boys in a line behind him waiting at the bottom of the stairs. Abdul led them up the stairs to the departure floor. It looked even more beautiful upstairs. It had a white tiled floor with small shops that had clean items to be sold. Unlike the ones in the village town, they were bright and full of life. The shop keepers were classy they didn't shout their heads off to get items sold. Each item looked really valuable, even if it were a pack of cigarettes.

The four of them walked through the departure with their mouths open in astonishment. Elaynna began to feel really excited. The hall was filled with all sorts of passengers. There were lots of people well dressed and in western clothing. The well dressed people were going to these small shops and buying items without bargaining.

Abdul made the five of them settle on the chairs and wait while he had seen an old friend in a distance that he went to catch up with. They all gaped at the behavior of the passengers nearby. They were amazed at seeing the exchange of goods so easily and pleasantly. There was no question of this is too much bring the price down. The customers took out wads of cash buying these small high priced items. Suddenly there was a calling for their flight.

Abdul returned to them in time. He handed them each their passports but held on to the boarding passes. For a moment he wanted to hug Yasmin for the excitement he was feeling, but when he looked at Elaynna, the incident replayed in his mind fading away the affection.

Whilst lining up Yasmin began to feel upset for leaving her country when she had just got so used to everything again.

"Passports please." the steward interrupted their thoughts. They each handed their passports one by one. The steward returned them after checking their visas and identities. They all quickly returned their passports back to Abdul worried in case they would lose them. Upon walking down the ramp to go outside to the planes the crowd increased while they waited for their bus to take them to the plane.

"Be careful here boys, it will be difficult to get on to the bus." Soon as the bus arrived all of the passengers rushed to climb on like monkeys climbing a tree. Abdul held onto Elaynna and Qasim's hand helping them to climb on, Yasmin climbed on using Rahim's and Kareem's help. It was extremely hot in the bus. Feeling they would suffocate any moment. The bus stopped within 5 minutes releasing its doors, they jumped off as quickly as they could, stepping onto the hot concrete. The airwaves of the plane were blasting hot air on to the surface; the thirty degree weather wasn't helping either. A sweating steward waited at the bottom of the plane by the staircase. He forced a smile handling the heat with his thick uniform. The passengers staggered up the long metal staircase.

Upon reaching the top of the staircase Abdul took out their boarding passes he showed the awaiting steward who welcomed him with a smile.

"Ok so your seats are 16 B and C the last four, 14 E, F, G, H." Abdul led the way to their seats.

"12 . . . 13 . . . . ah 14 . . . ." he mumbled to himself. He looked down at the tickets telling his children that the four middle seats were theirs.

"Elaynna you sit in the middle, being the eldest you can look after everyone." Rahim started to laugh.

"Whats so funny; why are you laughing Rahim? Don't embarrass me on the plane." Abdul snapped. Rahim hid his face in his shirt collar out of shame. Kareem and Qasim laughed at him for getting in trouble. Elaynna joined in. Rahim gave her a threatening look. She stopped immediately and looked down. It was so nice and cool in the plane with the air conditioner. They hadn't seen a television before, they were amazed at the little screens in front of them, they had only seen a television once at their grandparent's house, their Uncle Javed had one in his bedroom. Only seeing a glimpse of it, it confused them that their uncle's one had sound and these were without.

Abdul and Yasmin sat two rows up by a window seat. Abdul sat down trying to relax. The hard part of the journey was over now, just an eight hour flight left to go.

"Go and check on the children, they might be worried." Yasmin ordered, without making any eye contact he looked away and closed his eyes.

"I can see them from here; get some rest there's a long journey ahead of us." Yasmin leaned back in her seat and gazed lovingly at Abdul. After such a long time she had him all to herself, without housework or the children getting in the way, falling in love with him all over again.

The stewards came around to hand them head phones reminding them to fasten their seat belts.

"Can I have two blankets please, two for here and can you give 4 blankets to my children in 14 please." Abdul asked the stewardess in English. She nodded in agreement rushing back immediately handing them to him with a flirty smile. Yasmin looked at him surprisingly, he still remembered how to speak English, but also wondered why had he asked in English when they were still in Pakistan. She gave the stewardess a tense look, who was obviously flaunting herself in front of Abdul.

"Why did you speak to her in English? What doesn't she understand Urdu?" Abdul laughed at her.

"When you speak in English they respect you more. See how quickly she handed the blankets?" She looked at him sternly,

"Yes and gave you an inviting look too." He laughed again.

"You know me, I can't help being handsome, I didn't even notice. But I will prove it to you that when you speak in English they will serve you instantly."

"Yeah right, you were just trying to impress her." Yasmin huffed.

"Oh you don't believe me? OK when you need something, you ask in Urdu when I need something I will ask in English. I bet you whatever you want to place a bet on that I will win." Yasmin knowing she would lose; ignored him.

As the plane was getting ready to take off, Elaynna's nerves were racing at the speed of the plane. She started to read the Kalima when she felt her stomach sink into her pelvis, the sensation felt like it rose and fell into place again. Rahim remained quiet. He tried to make fun of his sister, but the same pit feeling in his stomach made him nervous. When the plane reached the air floating at a stable pace, they all relaxed.

"Oh we survived . . ." gasped Elaynna.

"I have never been so afraid in my life. I thought we would fall out any minute." Rahim couldn't help but to agree, when he saw other passengers release their seat belts and leave their seats. He copied them, feeling a bit dizzy when he got up to look for his father, recognizing his hat he walked over and kneeled down beside him, Abdul got up at once from his snooze.

"Whats wrong Rahim go and sit down." this was the first time he saw his cheeky son so worried.

"I am scared Abu jee, are we gonna fall out and die. I am feeling sick." Abdul put his hand on his head, laughing at his innocence.

"Don't be silly, this is your first time on a plane. I felt the same when it was my first time." He opened the window to show him the beautiful scenery above the clouds.

"Oh my Allah we are so high!" he panicked.

"Shhh . . . don't create a scene. Now go back to your seat they will be serving us lunch soon." Rahim stumbled back to his seat. Trying to take deep breaths to calm himself down.

"Where did you go?" asked Elaynna.

"I, I, I er just went to see Abu . . ." Elaynna was surprised to see her brother stuttering for the first time. Kareem showed him how to use the head phones.

"This helps us to listen to the television. There are so many different things to watch! Isn't that cool!" Rahim copied Kareem trying to distract the nausea in his stomach. The four of them were engrossed in the entertainment in front of them. They had never seen anything like it.

Elaynna got to sit and relax for the first time in her fifteen years of age. She was feeling excited for herself, she was getting to enjoy a whole new experience.

Yasmin stared at Abdul feeling an urge to kiss him. Abdul always kissed her or held her hand the first time they travelled to England when they were younger and newly married. He told her it was more romantic sneaking kisses or holding hands when in public transport.

Yasmin would tell him to stop and shy away. But this time he was totally different he had changed so much, he was more concerned with his sleep than giving her any attention. This confused her; she kept herself pretty in front of him. Yes they made love, but he stopped showing her the affection that he used to. She took it down to maybe he was over worked and tired. While he tried to sleep beside her, she held his hand under the blanket and quickly planted a kiss on his cheek. He squeezed back for a brief moment but then instantly let go when he opened his eyes. "Don't do such things in public, people are watching." He whispered sternly.

"But you used to always use these times to be romantic, whats changed?" Yasmin asked sounding like she was about to cry, feeling neglected.

"Am I not beautiful and young anymore as you used to say? Just because I have had four children I am no longer the love you desired and waited for?" Abdul shook his head.

"I will tell you whats changed, we have four children, I don't want them to see us like this. They will ask weird questions that I would not be able to answer, don't shame me in front of them." Yasmin didn't bother arguing or asked more questions. Maybe that was their time then, a lot had changed now.

The stewardess came around to give them their lunch on neat trays.

"This is the life of royalty. I didn't expect this much royalty just on the plane." whispered Qasim excitedly. Elaynna smiled at him looking away from their mini screens to start to eat. Elaynna's eyes overwhelmed with joy, she couldn't believe she was being served and asked so kindly what she wanted to drink. "Pani . . ." *water* was all she could croak, without saying please the stewardess still smiled at her, and handed her her tray of food. They all licked their lips as they tuck in to the tandoori chicken and pilaf rice, which was accompanied with a mini salad and Greek yoghurt. A sweet kheer served for pudding. The four of them didn't leave a single morsel of food. They had cleaned their plates like new, wishing for seconds. It excited them when the stewardess arrived with tea and biscuits. They all said yes please at once when they were offered the bevearage.

Rahim started to feel better, he began to enjoy himself. They all snuggled under their blankets trying to get some sleep while they watched their little screens.

Towards bed time the pilot turned the lights off to create a cool dark atmosphere. While Elaynna and the others slept, Rahim was feeling quesy. The plane started to shake a little due to the weather conditions. It was raining hard with thunder and lightening.

Rahim started to break out in a sweat, his cheeks turning pale, his stomach was churning. Elaynna woke up all of a sudden feeling his heavy breathing.

"Whats wrong? Are you alright?" she asked anxiously.

"Yyyesss I am am fine . . ." he answered swallowing down his dinner that seemed to be coming up in his throat.

"You don't look fine, I know you don't like me much but let me help you." She took out some tissue that she kept behind from the dinner trays and wiped his forehead.

"You look so pale; let me get you some water." Not knowing that all she had to do was press the stewardess button, she went to the back where she had watched them come and go with their trolleys.

"Madam Ji please can I have a glass of water for my brother he doesn't seem to look well." The lady nodded and handed her some water in a plastic white cup and a paper bag in case he needed to be sick.

"If you need anything please push the button next to your arm rest and one of us would come to you." The stewardess answered nicely when she turned around returning back to her seat. Rahim was paler than when she had left him, she handed him the cold water; soon as he took a sip he told her he was going to vomit. Quickly handing the paper bag he poured out all of his food in an instant. She rubbed the back of his head for comfort until he had stopped.

"Ahh now I feel better, this had been making me feel awful. Thank you Elaynna . . ." he gasped, she tucked him in with the blanket reminding him to get some rest. She stroked his hair until he drifted to sleep like a baby. She remembered her father's orders to look after her brothers. Her father knew that she was responsible that's why he left her alone with them. Their parents hadn't come once to check on them.

Only two hours left for landing time, Yasmin came over to remind Elaynna to comb her hair, asking her to freshen up in the bathroom. Rahim remained asleep the whole time.

"Tell your brothers to wash their faces and to look decent." Before Elaynna could tell her about Rahim not being well, her mother quickly retuned to her seat. Elaynna went into the bathroom toilet, a little surprised to see the toilet like a chair with a hole in the middle. She saw a few illustrations with a stick man on the toilet. Gathering the drawn instructions, she realized she had to sit on it like a normal seat and not in a squat position the way she was used to in the village.

After figuring out the toilet and the tap she felt she was in another world. Everything felt so much easier. To her surprise there was hot water coming out of the tap! This never happened in her village. You had to always boil the water in the winter to take a hot bath. Now everything was feeling a bit too good. She looked at her reflection in the mirror, remembering the boys that were staring at her and making her feel uncomfortable.

Untying her hair she began combing it gently, her plait had become very messy from the odd positioning of sleeping. She looked at her reflection in the mirror admiring her long thick hair; looking like a woman with her brunette locks in front of her. I must be quite beautiful for those boys to be drooling at me, she thought. Her friends always told her that she was attractive; she didn't need to do anything to her appearance to make it more attractive. Her grandmother proudly told her that she would grow into a beautiful woman. Combing her hair slowly, she thought she looked more and more attractive every time she settled her hair more neatly. She copied a few poses of the women she had saw in the little screens.

A smile took over her face, feeling like the prettiest girl in the world. Maybe I am prettier than those plane ladies, she thought. That's why the boys were looking at me and not them. I am a natural beauty; they have cake like faces, giggling at her innocent thoughts. Suddenly there was a hard knock on the door.

"Oi! Who is taking so long in there!" someone asked in a loud voice. Elaynna startled at the noise quickly plaited her hair and splashed her face with cold water. Wiped her face with her scarf and then placed it on her head, making sure to cover her chest and neck. She opened the door and there was a long line of women wanting to use the bathroom. In her face of just two inches distance was a forty year old plump woman who looked a lot older than she actually was, had her eyebrows twitching with anger.

"When I was your age I never took so long to use a mirror, who are you trying to impress eh?" snapping crossly with her onion breath pushing past her.

Elaynna quickend her steps to her seat, waiting for the stewardess to give her their breakfast. Rahim was up by then feeling a lot better.

"What took you so long in the toilet? Are you feeling sick as well?" Elaynna smiled at him and shook her head.

"You are looking better, actually much better. Would you like me to get you anything?" Rahim looked at her with watery eyes.

"No I am OK now thanks, sorry for being such a pain to you when Abu said you were the eldest asking you to look after us. You proved him right. I think I have misunderstood you . . . I, I am, am . . ." he stuttered.

"Its OK you don't have to apologize, maybe moving to England is a new beginning for us." He nodded in agreement breaking a smile. This was their first proper conversation. The longest they had to sit next to each other in their entire lives. After breakfast nearing to landing, Abdul came over to remind them it would be scary to land confirming the scary part would only last a minute.

"Thank you for the warning." Rahim answered back when Abdul quickly returned to his seat. Elaynna again didn't get a chance to tell her father how responsible she had been. He was taken back to his seat by a stewardess when Elaynna tried to speak to him.

When they reached London Heathrow Airport they began to shiver because of the climate change. After the immigration check they went to collect their luggage, growing really tired from their long walk, their jaws opened when they saw rows and rows of moving luggage. Since Abdul had traveled many times before he just moved towards the numerous screens before him to read which aisle their luggage was in.

"This way." they obediently followed his voice.

Along the way he picked up a trolly. Upon reaching their aisle there was a big crowd of people from their flight waiting beside the moving luggage. All rushing to pick their luggage, Elaynna scratched her head wondering how they would find their bags. Would they have to follow each bag and check individually? Biting her nails in worry, their luggage had been lost. "Rahim come here, wait beside me and this trolly, when I see our bags I will quickly unload them you pick them up and place them in the trolly quickly. Got it?" Rahim nodded obediently waiting next to him.

The rest of them watched the entertainment before them. Some people had so many suitcases that they were finding it extremely hard to push their trolleys. There were piles of wooden boxes that people had brought with them, these boxes contained sweet mangoes. Almost everyone had brought mangoes with them. Qasim licked his lips when the fragrance of mango reach his nostrils, a lady walked by pushing a trolley with her mango chest right at the top. Wishing they had brought a mango chest, only if the lady would give him just one. It tempted him to ask, but he knew his mother would kill him if he did. All of a sudden he had an idea. He asked his mother where the toilets were.

"You see that man sign it leads you to the toilets, make sure you go inside the sign that looks like a man not like a woman, will you be OK alone or shall I send Kareem with you?" Qasim shook his head in confidence.

"No I will be alright; I will be back in a flash." Running fast he caught up with the lady who seemed to be alone pushing her trolley.

"Baji ji, your mangoes seem very ripe where did you get them from?" Startled by a seven year old asking her such a question..

"I bought them from Gujar khan, why are you so curious?" bending down to his level. "Oh just that they smell really nice. That's all." He huffed from the running. "I tell you what, you watch my luggage while I quickly use the bathroom then I will give you one as a reward, how does that sound?" she asked ruffling his hair.

"Yes please!" Qasim jumped excitedly. She headed into the ladies toilets, leaving him alone with the luggage. She came back within five minutes, opened her mango chest and handed him one.

"Make sure you wash it now." He thanked her sneaking into the men's toilets and rinsed the mango. The other passengers looked at him in an unusual way. He walked out biting a hole on the top of the mango and began to suck out its contents.

"Mmmmm . . . ." he hummed to himself. His mother came looking for him wondering what had taken him such a long time. Yasmins face was pale as white with worry when she reached outside the toilets, her eyes searching through the crowd of people passing by, her eyes fell upon Qasim sitting on the chair opposite sucking on a mango like he had never tasted a mango before. His hands dripping with mango juice, the passengers walking by laughing at him, saying he looked like a monkey.

Qasim was enjoying his mango too much to care about their comments. He felt a shadow in front of him while his eyes were closed. He recognized that perfumed smell very well. He gulped down the last of his juice that was in his mouth and opened his eyes to his angered mother. Her face was bright red, breathing heavily; looking like smoke would puff out any minute from her ears. Qasim was fortunate that he was in a public space or he would have got a thrashing. She grabbed him by the collar firmly and asked where he had got that mango from. He looked at her with innocent eyes.

"I helped out a lady by watching her luggage and she rewarded me by giving me a mango, that's all Ammi, I would never dare to ask for one."

"Oh really . . . I am sure that wherever there are mangoes you will be there somehow, don't play innocent with me you little rascal." pulling the soggy mango off his hands she took him by the wrists to the ladies bathroom. She pushed him in front of the sinks opening the taps in front of him. He quickly washed his hands and face while she used the ladies toilets. After washing her hands she handed him a paper hand towel.

"No hurry up your father is waiting for us. I will deal with you when we get home." she slapped his head walking out.

"Ouch!" he moaned rubbing his sore head. Sneakily smiling when his mother wasn't looking, it was a small price to pay for a free mango he thought. He knew his mother would forget by the time they got home.

"Where have you been?" Abdul asked when they went back to the luggage pick up. "Nothing Abu ji I just went to the toilet." Yasmin gave him a tense look, but didn't tell Abdul where she found him knowing he would hit the roof. Feeling too tired to create a scene.

"Come on, my friend Mushtaaq will be waiting for us, Allah knows how long hes been waiting." He snapped crossly.

They all followed behind their father. Looking around them trying to absorb the new environment, everything so clean and neat. The air felt clean with no dust in the air. When they walked out to departure with the other passengers, they saw the similar shiny shops again that they had seen at Islamabad Airport but these were bigger with much more items on show.

They walked through gaping and awing. When they got outside there were crowds of people who had come to collect their family. Their father paced his steps when he saw his friend Mushtaq; they embraced each other tightly slapping each others backs.

"Aslaam aleikum my friend! How are you?! Thank you for your coming." Mushtaq's face broadened with a smile upon seeing the extended family.

"Don't embarrass me Abdul. I can never help you enough you are like a brother to me. If it weren't for you I wouldn't be where I am now." The children greeted Mushtaq with a blushed smile.

"Mashallah, is this Elaynna? Elaynna you were so little when you left. You were this tiny, and now you are a beautiful woman almost." Elaynna shied away. Yasmin couldn't help feeling jealous.

"Looks aren't the most important thing brother Mushtaq; a girl should know how to look after her house." Mushtaq laughed at her telling Yasmin she was growing too old. He grabbed the trolley off of Abdul and showed him the way to the car. The adults walked alongside each other while the four of them trotted behind. By the time they reached the car park they were freezing in their cotton outfits. It was a windy and cloudy day. Mushtaq put their luggage in the boot, opening the doors for the let them in. It was mid afternoon in England, an autumn September day. Mushtaq realizing how he had felt when he came to England for the first time put the heating on in the car for the children. The warmer the car became the more their eyelids closed upon them. Apart from Elaynna and Abdul, it would have been rude for Abdul to fall asleep while his friend was driving them and taking them to his home.

"How are the children? And your stubborn wife, Shabnam?" Abdul teased.

"Oh shes well, shes not so stubborn any more. She has grown quite mature for the past 10 years. She has a job in a factory and is managing well." Abdul looked at him surprisingly.

"You are letting her work? Have you gone mad?" Mushtaq laughed at him.

"Brother when a woman goes out to work she realizes the value of money, when you lay everything on the table for them they don't appreciate it or understand when you are falling short. It's actually been quite helpful having her help me with the finances. She brings in an OK salary that we keep aside for short comings and she doesn't ask for an allowance. To be honest she has become more aware cautious with money now that she earns it herself!" Abdul couldn't help but to laugh. He looked to the back to make sure Yasmin was asleep.

"I doubt it if Yasmin would be able to work even a day outside, she works so hard in keeping the house in order." Mushtaq nodded sympathetically.

"Well brother you do what you feel is best for your family. I have found it to be easier with two people bringing in an income. There is always enough for us now and we keep a little on the side in case we have to go to Pakistan or keep saving it for the children's education." Abdul looked to the back again, this time he noticed Elaynna wide awake.

"What are you looking at beta? You should get some rest. I bet all this is new and exciting huh? Hard to sleep?" he teased. Responding with a smile she continued looking at the clean city they were driving through.

A yawn came to her lips; she leaned back in her seat next to Qasim, who for some reason smelt like mangoes. She didn't mind the smell, it reminded her of the times how her and her Grandmother would sit and eat mangoes in the warm sun. The thought of her grandmother made her feel guilty. Dadi, she thought, I wonder how she is, I haven't thought about her once throughout the whole journey. Her grandmother's words echoed in her ears,

"You won't forget me will you?" She looked down at the pendant that her grandmother gave her and squeezed it tight closing her eyes next to Qasim.

Before she knew it they had arrived home. His wife Shabnam and their boys Hassan and Hussien welcomed them into the house. The smell of home cooked food made their tummies rumble. Mushtaq and his sons helped them with the luggage; Shabnam led them into the living room. The living room was quite small compared to their living space in Pakistan. It had a floral red carpet, with beige walls. Beige leather sofas and a small beige rug mixed with red that had a similar pattern to the floral carpet. The curtains were also red with similar flowers matching the flooring. One corner had a small glass coffee table. Although the room was not as big as their living room back home it was decorated elegantly. Yasmin was quite impressed.

She hadn't been to England since Elaynna was born. Even their home at that time was not as elegant as this. The room was decorated with frames of beautiful Arabic calligraphy of verses from the Quran. There were two four seated sofas and a one three seater sofa.

Elaynna, Qasim, Rahim and Kareem easily fitted on the three seated sofa. They were thin enough to sit side by side leaving enough space between them. Hassan and Hussein were the same age as Elaynna and Rahim; with a year between them. However they were much bigger and taller. Elaynna and Rahim looked malnourished next to them.

"Wow, haven't you boys grown up?" Abdul boasted to Hassan and Hussein when they sat down next to their parents. Smiling shyly looking down at their feet.

"How was your journey brother?" Shabnam asked drying her hands on her dupatta.

"It was good, thank you, just quite tired really; you know what it's like, the long journey to the airport and the long flight." They all nodded in agreement. Shabnam was quite thin, with small sharp features. Her hair was light brown and her skin was fair. She looked attractive in her own way. Her parents were from Kashmir so she inherited the fair skin, chestnut eyes and hair.

"You all must be very hungry and tired, I will lay out the food, come on Hassan and Hussein please lay the mat on the floor and bring in the food."

Abdul teased her. "Oh you mean you must be hungry and tired preparing all this delicious food that I smelt when I came through the door." Everyone laughed with him.

"Shabnam looks like she doesn't eat at all. Brother Mushtaq I think you have overworked my sister, she was never this thin." Yasmin giggled along.

"Believe me she eats more than me the way she runs around doing everything." Shabnam left them to chit chat sending Hassan to lay the mat on the floor, Hussein followed behind him with the glasses and plates. When all the dishes were there, it looked like a wedding feast.

"Why did you go through all this trouble? This is too much." Abdul protested seeing all of the dishes on display. It looked like a seven course meal.

"Brother just eat and enjoy, even this is nothing." Shabnam smiled sitting down to join them. Qasim licked his lips when he saw the tandoori chicken, lamb curry, pilaf rice, raita, chapattis, daal, okra curry, gourd curry, salad and chicken tikka as well as kheer for desert.

They were all confused where to start, Mushtaq ushered Abdul to start, being the eldest in the room. Abdul suggested that first they should all say a prayer in order to say thanks for the safe journey and being welcomed so lovingly. After the short prayer of verses from the Quran that Abdul knew, he thanked Allah for everything and asked Allah to bless Shabnam and Mushtaq with all the happiness in the world. Abdul wiped his hands over his face beginning with the tandoori chicken and chutney. The rest followed taking their favorite choices.

They all ate in silence. It felt quite odd being able to eat such tasty food without having mini beetles or mosquitoes hovering over the light or eating in the dark when the electricity came and went. The air was clean, almost too clean. They couldn't see any specks of dust in the light. When they had finished eating Yasmin offered to help to wash the dishes, Elaynna instantly offered to help, usually that was her cue to do the dishes when she was home.

She followed her mother and Shabnam through to the kitchen. Shabnam said it was enough she didn't need to help.

"You have grown up so much haven't you? I can't believe how helpful you have become. You were this tiny the last time we saw you." Elaynna smiled at her. She didn't remember Shabnam or Mushtaq at all. But whoever they were she was really starting to warm to them. Their kitchen was bigger than their kitchen in Pakistan, Yasmin and

Elaynna thought at the same time. It was very modern. This had many cupboards and a dining table. Just like the one she had seen in the films on the mini screens on the plane.

"Thank you for all the hospitality, you have been ever so kind. I hope we won't be too much of a burden on you Shabnam; we will leave as soon as Abdul settles with a job and we will probably find a small place to rent. Until then we will help you as much as we can." Shabnam shook her head in disapproval.

"You haven't changed Yasmin; you can never be a burden on us. To be honest we were so excited when Abdul called Mushtaq that you were coming back to settle here. It will be like having our own family to visit. You can't imagine how happy we are. Living in crystal palace is so quiet and we only know a few of Pakistani families and you can't trust anyone these days. It's so nice to have someone close that you know well."

Yasmin nodded in agreement. "I know what you mean." Shabnam then sent Elaynna to the living room to go and rest so she could chat to Yasmin; they had fifteen years to catch up with. Elaynna was enjoying all the rest; she had not ever just sat and ate before in such many hours. Following the orders obediently she sat down in the living room next to her brothers who had now started to get to know Hassan and Hussein. Leaning on the arm rest watching the boys laugh and joke, she began wishing that Shabnam and Mushtaq had a daughter she could have spoken to and made a new friend of.

Without realizing she drifted into a deep sleep. She was woken after a few hours when all of the boys had left the room to change, it was dark outside; she had been asleep for three hours. Yasmin helped Shabnam lay out the rolling mattresses and blankets on the floor.

"Elaynna go and change, while we arrange the beds, this will be our new room from today. All of us will sleep in here together." Elaynna surprised that she wasn't taking out any beds for anyone for the first time. She usually had every one's bed ready out in the court yard every night. Whenever she put them in the wrong place she would get abused by her mother. Once she accidentally mixed her mothers bed with her grandmothers, Yasmin went so mad that she slapped her so hard on her ear that she thought she would go deaf, grabbing her ear so hard and pointed to her how to identify whose bed belonged to whom. She didn't cry or shout in pain. Believing it was her mistake; she should have learned or asked her grandmother for advice.

She didn't like upsetting her mother; being only eleven years old then. From then on she didn't make the mistake of putting the beds in the wrong place, once or twice she put the blankets on the wrong beds, for that she didn't get any physical abuse but was cursed by her mother for being so stupid.

Elaynna got up to find her suitcase; she walked out onto the hallway. A little lost to where to go to change, Shabnam came out to show her around.

"Your mother has gone to lie down, I showed her around earlier, let me show you where everything is." She showed her the toilet and shower downstairs. Upstairs there were three bedrooms. Two were a normal size and one was too small, the third room was just used for storage. There was a main bathroom and a room each where one was for the two brothers and the other for Shabnam and Mushtaq. Shabnam told Elaynna she could change in the bathroom. Rahim and Kareem were snoring in Hassan and Hussein's bedroom already.

Qasim, Abdul, Yasmin and Elaynna's beds were laid out in the living room. Elaynna came down after getting changed, still feeling drowsy. All of the lights were switched off apart from the hallway light. Elaynna quietly walked down to the darkened living room. Her mother was snoring next to her father with Qasim on her side. The last mattress empty left for her. A soft fleeced lined quilt laid out with a flat pillow. She lay down on the mattress trying to get comfortable in her new bed, it felt a little hard but she didn't care. It was perfect; she cuddled up under the blanket letting the softness envelope her thin body, the soft texture felt soothing on the soles of her feet.

Curling to her right side, she rested her cheek on her right palm. Even though everything felt perfect for once in her life, something churned her in her chest making her feel at unease. As hard she had worked back, she almost always drifted to a deep sleep. The once when she had felt in a similar way, that following morning, Qasim had been collecting some rocks around the well, Qasim playfully began walking backwards, losing his grip he fell in.

Fortunately that day Abdul was home, Elaynna witnessed the incident. She went running home to tell her father who climbed down the well and grabbed Qasim in time, Qasim was unconscious, Abdul swiftly did mouth to mouth with him pumping his chest, he survived. Yasmin fainted upon hearing the news. Since her brother's death, going anywhere near water was out of the question for her.

They held special prayers that night to thank Allah for saving Qasim and taking the calamity away.

Elaynna wondered for a second whether her feeling this nervousness was the sign of bad news. Until her body warmed up under the blanket she finally fell asleep.

CHAPTER 19

The morning was bright with the sun playing hide and seek behind the clouds, it felt unusual waking up so late without a cockerel announcing the morning dawn in your ears. Elaynna looked at the time, which was all she could read, Jannat had taught her. It was 9 o'clock. She found it unusual how her mother was so relaxed for waking up late. It had been over twenty four hours that her mother hadn't shouted at her. Did she swap her mother on the aeroplane or something, she thought.

Her mother hadn't even woken up herself. Elaynna was the first to wake up, she wanted to make herself scarce before her mother scolded her or abused her. She went to her bag to collect the miswak to clean her teeth, she washed her face and rinsed her mouth. There was a comb in front of the mirror, Elaynna combed her hair and used some of the cream that she found in the cabinet. She hadn't moisterised since she left the village. A guilty feeling overcame her, she felt she should have asked. Hoping Shabnam wouldn't mind. Had she been awake she would have definitely asked her permission. Elaynna assured herself.

Returning to her bed, she sat back, feeling the urge to do something useful. Finally deciding to lie down, snuggling back under the blanket. It would have been so easy to go back to sleep, she was just closing her eyes until she saw Shabnam walk down the stairs putting her hair up in a bun heading towards the kitchen. Elaynna got up quickly following after her.

Shabnam didn't realize she was behind her until Elaynna quietly said hello. Shabnam gestured her to sit down.

"Did you sleep alright? I hope that you aren't too hungry, I will make breakfast when everyone wakes up." She assured her with a smile. Elaynna wanted to help her but Shabnam wouldn't have it.

"I wish I had a daughter like you. Girls are so swift in doing house work. Your mother says that you have learnt how to do everything. And not only learnt but that you are very swift and perfect in all the house chores. Your mother told me last night that you have mastered all the cooking as well." Elaynna quite starteld to hear her mother had complimented her and that too behind her back.

"Would you like any help? I don't mind making the tea and the chapattis." Shabnam laughed at her persistence, ordering her to wash some of last night's dishes if she couldn't sit still.

While Shabnam showed her what to do, Elaynna did the dishes in no time. It's so easy to wash the dishes here thought Elaynna, the water is warm and the soap is a funny liquid. Tracing back her mind how she had to wash the dishes using a bucket of water and detergent powder in Pakistan, usually that would take ages and your hands were left feeling sore at the roughness of detergent powder and cold water.

Yasmin joined them pulling out a chair of the dining table, yawning and stretching out her arms.

"You have trained your daughter well Yasmin, she doesn't know the word of 'sit down.' She insisted to help." Yasmin changed the subject without adding any praise.

"I can't believe we are back in England after such a long time. So much has changed. We all slept so well last night, I forgot how hard the journey was."

Oh no I didn't read the Morning Prayer; thought Elaynna, back home the cockerel woke her up in time for the Morning Prayer. Dadi and I would pray together she remembered, realising Ammi didn't wake up for prayer either, who usually read all.

"I am glad you slept well, I was so tired with work and housework. So glad it's the weekend." Yasmin started to help with the breakfast, ordering Elaynna to wake everyone up and to tidy up.

Elaynna took the orders, heading to the living room. Abdul was out of his bed. Qasim lay asleep with his mouth wide open, morning drool coming out of his mouth. He was sleeping on his stomach with one leg curled up; his pajama bottoms were stretched up to his knee. You could see his skinny legs, which barely had any meat on them. Elaynna smiled to herself, he still looked like a baby.

She went over to wake him; he didn't budge, so she left him to wake up the others. However when she got to the boys room she was too late they were already woken up by her father. All lining up to go to the bathroom; they were sitting chatting away in their room.

Elaynna felt shy in front of Hassan and Hussein, she was already having a hard time living with three boys, now she had to live with five! They didn't see her, she decided to go downstairs to sort out the living room and to try wake up Qasim again. Soon as she opened the curtains and began folding away the blankets Qasim started to wake up,

"Go and get washed breakfast is almost ready." Qasim rubbed his eyes and let out a big yawn with his mouth opened wide like a lion cub.

Elaynna began to fold away the blankets and rolled back the mattresses, hiding them behind the sofas. Hunger was creeping up on Elaynna; her stomach began making funny noises. She wasn't sure how to clean the floor but generally the whole room was looking the way it did the day before. Going back to the kitchen to ask for the next task, Shabnam handed her the floor mat.

"Oh dear you are very quick aren't you? My boys usually take ages!" Elaynna blushed taking the rest of the things in for breakfast. Everyone joined in to eat and asked what the little square breaded things were. They hadn't eaten seen English bread before.

"This is English peoples chapatti." Abdul told his children, "Taste it with the butter and jam, it's like a sweet treat." He then showed them how to spread the butter and raspberry jam; he also showed them the marmalade. "Yummy!" exclaimed Qasim, everyone laughed at his outburst.

The weekend followed with lots of old friends coming to meet Abdul and his family. Elaynna couldn't believe that her father had a good community network. All of his friends had moved down from Birmingham to Croydon. They all came in turns bringing lots of gifts and sweets. Some came to say their condolences for Yasmin's brother Wasim. An old wound had been brought to surface; Yasmin was reminded of the horror she went through when she had lost her brother to that horrible incident. Although she held up while she met all of Abdul's friends, that night she cried uncontrollably to Abdul.

Abdul was unable to comfort her, due to their living circumstances. When Elaynna and Qasim had fallen asleep he just held her hand and stroked her head to sleep. "You have changed Abdul, I don't know why but you have, I think that love that we had is dead now, our relationship is just physical now." Abdul knew what she was talking about but then brushed it off with an excuse that Yasmin couldn't think otherwise.

"You expect me to embrace you in front of our children? I have some shame Yasmin. Now the children are older we have to be careful, it can't be the same anymore. We can't live like newly wed forever."

Yasmin understood what he meant but then realized how he was quite loving and caring when he was in Pakistan, even when Elaynna and the boys were up to eight years old. He seemed to have changed after Qasim's birth.

"But when the children were of understanding age you were still quite loving and caring, things changed when Qasim was born, is there something that you aren't telling me." Abdul took a deep breath, trying really hard to not to let the word slip his lips, he tried closing the chapter once and for all.

"Yasmin the children are teenagers now, we are living in a friends house, there is no privacy and now life will get harder for us, I have to provide for the family so we can live a life of ease and buy our own house." Yasmin ignored him turning over to sleep. She continued to cry for the rest of the night, not because of the loss of her brother, but the loss of her husband's love.

Abdul found a job right away in a local factory that made their own vases. He had worked in a similar factory many years ago and still had the knowledge of how to weld the sand into beautiful vases; he even knew how to dye the colour of the fragile glass. He found another job in the evening working in a local grocery shop. He was happy to have found two jobs this meant he could easily save up the money to move into their own rented property. This also meant that Yasmin won't have a chance to complain about him not caring.

Being extremely busy with his two jobs, he found schools for his sons to enroll in. Elaynna was not bothered with until one day Mushtaq mentioned to Abdul that maybe Elaynna should go to school too. When they went to try to find her a space, she had missed her GCSEs, so the school suggested that she go straight to college to learn to read and write English. When Abdul went to enroll her in they said she would have to wait at least six months as that was when the new enrollment began. Until then Shabnam completely made use of Elaynna.

Poor Elaynna did everything, just like she had done at home. However this time it was worse. She wasn't allowed to go out. When Shabnam arrived from work she would sit and gossip with Yasmin, and then she would take Yasmin out ordering Elaynna to have dinner ready when they got back. This happened everyday, no body bothered to ask how Elaynna felt, did she want to go out to see the city? Having everything ready on the table, they took advantage of her innocence. The only fresh air she got was when she went out to put the washing on the line, or when she went to put the rubbish out. It had been almost six months since she had been in England, she hadn't seen one bit of it.

She was beginning to feel homesick and missing her grandmother and friends. At least she had someone to talk to there. Her grandmother could read her emotions in an instant and always knew how to make her feel better.

"Oh Dadi, I wish you was here." she cried to herself one day when no body was home. She learnt to be so orderly and efficient with the house work that Shabnam didn't lift a finger anymore. Although it was her house Elaynna was running it like a house keeper. HHH er mother was living the life of a queen; she would sit and watch TV all day not helping much with the house work.

Elaynna was treated like an overworked animal that was seen as a body with no feelings. Her father reassured her every evening that he will take her out soon, but he never got round to it working six days a week. On Sundays he would spend the whole day sleeping and catching up with his friends.

One day Elaynna asked if he had heard anything from their grandmother. Abdul informed her that soon they will be getting a telephone so she could talk to her.

"What is a telephone Abu ji?" asked Elaynna curiously. He smiled at her innocent question and pointed to the handset that lay in the corner of the room. She hadn't noticed that before, she thought it was another decorative piece. Abdul laughed at her and told her that it wasn't working before and now it had been fixed. He was waiting for a letter from his brother to tell him Aunty Imtiaz's home number so he could call her. It would be a bit costly but worth hearing his mother's voice, he added.

Elaynna totally forgot about going out and longed for the day for the letter to arrive. In a few weeks time the letter arrived with the telephone number at the bottom of it. Abdul called Elaynna one Sunday when her mother was out with Shabnam, her brothers had gone out to play football.

"Ammi! How are you!" he shouted down the phone, it wasn't a very clear line.

"I am fine my child how are you? Is everything ok? Where is my Elaynna? How is Yasmin and the boys, Beta I miss you all so much!" Jannat shouted back. Abdul's eyes filled with tears after hearing his mother's soothing voice after a long time.

"Yes Ammi all is well here! Everyone is praising Elaynna she is doing so well! She will be starting school soon!" he shouted once again.

"Here talk to her!" he handed the handset to Elaynna who started to cry as soon as she heard her grandmother's voice.

"Jee Dadi, yes everything is all well here! Everything is perfect! I miss you too Dadi!" both granddaughter and grandmother cried uncontrollably on the phone. Abdul put his hand on Elaynna's head telling her to calm down, he couldn't help crying also. All of a sudden the telephone disconnected, with a long tone on the other side.

"I had to use a card, it cost £5 for ten minutes, but it was worth it even though it wasn't a very clear line." He smiled assuring Elaynna. Feeling for his daughter he told her to get ready to take her out. Elaynna told him she had dinner to cook it wasn't ready yet.

"Don't worry about it; we will be back in time." She excitedly got ready and ran upstairs to get her cardigan even though it was summer.

It was early afternoon, the sun was out, it was a gorgeous day. Elaynna took deep breaths of air from her nostrils; the air went down her lungs feeling like a bird that had been let out of its cage.

"This way" pointed Abdul, and then he gave her a whole tour of Croydon. She was amazed to see all the clean shops and streets. He bought her an ice cream she ate it so quickly. They had a long chat and sat down on a bench when they got tired.

She felt wonderful bonding with her father for the first time. They didn't realize the time go by, the sunlight had confused them. She adored the beautiful curves of the city, the hustle and bustle made her feel excited. London is not so bad at all, thought Elaynna. What a clean country. When they turned back to go home, Abdul told her to not to worry, for soon she will be going to college to learn English and be able to make new friends.

When Abdul turned the key to enter the house, Elaynna felt something wrong in the air upon entering. Yasmin and Shabnam were back, they interrogated Elaynna where she had been and why wasn't the cooking done? What would they eat? Glaring at her, Elaynna felt guilty. She couldn't meet her mother's gaze; she apologized, when she went into the kitchen everything was done.

Her mother had done the cooking of the vegetable curry; the vegetables that she had chopped before she left. Deciding to quickly make the chapattis, while she was getting everything ready; Shabnam walked in with a frown on her face. Elaynna went to put the pan away; Shabnam grabbed Elaynna's hand and pushed it on the hot frying pan.

"Next time you leave the cooking like you did; the hot pan would be on your fair coloured face. How dare you leave everything after all that we have done for you." Shabnam hissed. Elaynna cried in pain. Suddenly Yasmin walked in, out of panic Shabnam held Elaynna's hand under the tap. Shabnam pretended that she didn't see Yasmin; changing her colours like a chameleon.

"Oh dear Elaynna you work so hard. Look what you have done, you have burnt your pretty little fingers, let them cool here under the tap." Yasmin noticing the incident, didn't bother to take a look; she walked out taking the dinner to the living room. She was still upset with Elaynna, because her husband had chosen to take her out rather than his own wife. With her he would make excuses that he was too tired and today all of a sudden he had time to take his daughter out leaving her to pick up the housework.

Shabnam smiled cunningly at Elaynna when the door closed itself behind Yasmin, "Now remember my warning, this time it was your fingers next time it will be your pretty face, oh and don't even bother trying to tell anyone about this, they obviously won't believe you." Shabnam shoved her hand back to her leaving the kitchen with a look of disgust.

Holding her hand in agony, Elaynna looked at her bright red fingers. They were badly burnt; the skin had blown up with air in it. She wiped her tears joining everyone in the living room.

"Are you ok beta? Shabnam told me you burnt your hand. How can you be so clumsy? you never burnt yourself in Pakistan especially when you used to make chapattis in the hot tandoor?" Abdul asked with his mouth full.

"I don't know where my mind was Abu ji I will be careful next time." Elaynna replied quietly. Her mother looked away eating in silence. Luckily it was her left hand that was burnt thought Elaynna, if she was seen eating with her left hand then she would have got in even more trouble.

That night Elaynna couldn't stop the tears that overflowed her eyes. Still shocked at the way she had been treated by Shabnam. I thought she was like my aunties in Pakistan. No body ever treated me like this before. Knowing that Shabnam was right that if she did tell on

Shabnam no one would believe her like when she told her mother about her teachers threatening her in school.

Rather than going to the school to investigate her mother made her stop going to school altogether, crushing her confidence further. It was her grandmother who believed her and showered her with the love and care that she needed, but now the way Shabnam had treated her, who is she to turn to now? This thought upset her even more.

CHAPTER 20

As weeks went by the days neared for her to start college. Shabnam tried really hard to stop her from going. She was worried on losing a free house maid. At first she tried to convince Abdul and Yasmin.

"Look I understand your concerns Shabnam but you also go out to work? I am sure there are men where you work? So why are you being so narrow minded for our daughter?" Shabnam knowing she had shot her own foot. Not interfering further she apologized and said she had had her best interests at heart since she was a young single girl. That last wording did make Yasmin nervous but she knew she couldn't argue against Abdul. Shabnam changed her plan to trying to scare Elaynna.

"Elaynna I know you are probably still upset with me." She said one day while Elaynna was hand washing the shirts in the bath tub.

"N . . . no w-w-what makes you say that?" she stuttered, still a little frightened of her.

"I know you are looking forward to start college. But it's a scary world out there Elaynna, they don't like us Pakistani people you know. You will probably be the only Pakistani girl there. They will laugh at your salwar kameez and make fun of you. Tell your dad you are happy to stay at home." Elaynna shuffled on the bucket turned upside down that she sat on. Her bottom was starting to feel sore from sitting there from scrubbing the darkened collars.

"I, I, I will try but I, I, I know he wont listen to me." She finally answered and then continued taking the stains out of the shirts with the hand held brush and washing up liquid, just the way Shabnam had showed her. Shabnam got really agitated with her answer that she slapped her head so hard that it hit the sink beside her. Confused and in the shock of the pain, Elaynna dropped the brush and shirt in the bathtub. When she caught sense of what had happened, Shabnam had gone. This time Elaynna decided that she would rather go to college even if she was made fun of, better than stay at home with all this donkey housework. The hope of freedom reduced the tears that fell into the bathtub.

Over the next few days Elaynna tried her best not to be alone with Shabnam, to avoid her she did extra work around the house. This seemed to pacify Shabnam to not to try bothering to keep her away from college. This made life a little easier for her, she didn't care about the housework, she was longing for fresh air and freedom again.

The morning arrived for her to start college. Her father took her once before to show her her classroom. She nervously got dressed that morning, a little worried what the college will be like. Even though when Kareem assured her that abusing students was against the law.

This made her wonder whether being abused was allowed full stop. Was it allowed for Shabnam to burn her hand or thrash her head and make her work like a maid? Obviously that was allowed because her own mother didn't seem to care, her own father called her clumsy when she was badly burnt. Her trail of thought disappeared when Rahim told her to hurry up to leave, whom was also joining the same college to do an engineering course. This gave her a little assurance that she wouldn't be traveling alone at least. As soon as they entered the college they went their separate ways, Rahim told her to meet him at the entrance at the end of the day. Her response was a nod as she nervously went to her class through the crowd.

Walking nervously with her head kept down, she realized Shabnam was wrong, nobody cared what she wore, and she wasn't the only Pakistani girl there. In her class there were several Pakistani women and some Indian boys who had come to learn English. There were also some Europeans in the class.

"Good morning class, and Welcome all to Croydon College." Not a single person replied; none of them knew a word of English. She handed them a piece of paper to write their names. Everyone managed to write their name apart from Elaynna. Elaynna didn't know how to read or write at all, that too especially in English.

The lady who sat next to her was an older Pakistani lady in her fifties. She understood what the teacher was saying translating to Elaynna. Elaynna appreciated the help but still couldn't do what the teacher had asked. "My name is Mariam," she whispered with a smile.

"This lady is very good; I failed last year that's why I have taken the course again." The teacher proceeded with the lesson.

214

"OK don't worry if you cannot write your name. We can start from the basics. Oh silly me my name is Mary Jane. You can call me Mary Jane no need to call me miss." Mary Jane was in her late forties with curly blonde hair. A very enthusiastic individual, who loved teaching, it was her passion.

Mary Jane began by writing out all the letters teaching them the phonics. Then one by one she went over to each table helping them spell out their names. Their homework for the day was to practice writing their names. There was a lunch break in between the lessons for an hour. Mariam introduced herself properly and showed Elaynna around the college. This was the first time in eight months that Elaynna felt she had found someone genuine and caring. Mariam's tenderness reminded her of her Grandmother. Being in a new country and with many new faces she didn't know whom she could trust.

That same evening when Elaynna returned home with Rahim. She saw her mother and Shabnam argue for the first time. They did not notice Elaynna saying hello to them, the dishes were left from the morning, for Elaynna didn't get a chance to do them because Rahim was rushing her. Yasmin sat on her bottom all day watching television. Rather than asking how her first day at college went, Yasmin shouted at Elaynna for keeping the dishes in the sink, she was expected to wake up early the following morning to do all the house chores before she went to college if she wanted to carry on her English classes.

Elaynna held tightly on to her exercise book and nodded in agreement. Quickly putting her books away in the store cupboard she began to make dinner. She wasn't sure whether she was dreaming or what ever happened in front of her was on purpose.

Whilst stirring the daal, she heard Shabnam and her mother laughing and joking in the living room while they watched the television. They had apologized to each other promising one another to not to tell their husbands.

That night after Elaynna tiredly put everything away she finally managed to do her homework in the kitchen at 11pm, yawning heavily while she tried to perfect her name. The first few lines were a bit messy and quite apart. Not giving up she spent all night trying to write her name just like Mary Jane had written on the top of her homework page close together neatly.

Her pencil withered as she spent another hour nearly perfecting her name as asked. "E-L-A-Y-N-N-A" she said to herself with a smile when could write her name without looking anymore. A tear fell from her eye onto the page of her name. For the first time in her life she was able to write her name all in one day of going to college. The emotions were a mixture of sadness and joy. The sadness overwhelmed her wishing her grandmother was here to see her doing all important work on a piece of paper, she would have been so proud that she had written her name, that too in English. The joy was that she had learnt to write her name in one day of schooling here. No matter how hard she had tried in Pakistan to learn, it just didn't work. She then packed her bag with her neat practiced work, ready to show Mary Jane and her new found friend Mariam. A spark of confidence arose in her for once in her sixteen years of life, wanting to show someone her written name but everyone had gone to bed.

The legs of the chair scraped on the tiled floor as she pushed her chair under the breakfast table heading to sleep. It wasn't an easy day ahead with housework before she left for college. Calculating on her fingers she would have to wake up at 6am to have everything ready so she could get to college on time.

Also hoping that she could show her father her new achievement the following morning, he would be so proud she thought. Finally retiring to bed she imagined herself being a doctor or a lawyer one day; maybe she will be the first to be a doctor in her family, how proud her grandmother would be. I can be anything now that I have decided to learn, she said to herself in the mirror whilst changing into her pyjamas.

The following morning Elaynna found it difficult to wake up, but she had to force herself out of bed when her mother screamed in her ear to get up and make breakfast. It was 6am; she quickly washed her face and headed towards the kitchen, serving breakfast to Mushtaq, her father and Shabnam. As they left for work, Elaynna started to prepare things for dinner, she half cooked the meal by having the spiced tomato puree ready and took the chicken out of the freezer. She kneaded the dough and left it aside to set. As asked she started to wash the dishes when Rahim and Kareem came into the kitchen demanding breakfast. They all had toast and tea with a bowl of porridge that Elaynna had prepared earlier. By that time it was 8.15am, Rahim told her to hurry and get ready or they will miss their morning bus.

Elaynna nodded and quickly did the dishes; she then took another glance at the kitchen when she finished wiping up the table and surface, making sure the stove was clean so Shabnam wouldn't have a fit when she got home.

Taking a deep breath she headed upstairs to get dressed. She had pressed the same outfit the night before. Knowing her mother would shout at her if she was to take out another.

"Elaynna! Come on we are running late!" Elaynna jumped when she heard Rahim shouting.

"I'm coming Rahim!" she shouted back. She quickly brushed her hair and did her plait while running down the stairs. Quickly wrapping her shawl around her head throwing it over her shoulder, "Bye Ammi!" they both shouted leaving the house. Yasmin got Qasim ready for school, when she got back she inspected the kitchen and made breakfast for herself.

An eyebrow rose when she saw how Elaynna had prepared dinner and kept the kitchen spotless. "I have trained her well. And Jannat said I was too harsh on her, look how she has organized everything just so she could go to college and learn. I have never seen such eagerness in Elaynna to learn, I am definitely doing the right thing." she said to herself.

On the bus ride, Elaynna couldn't stop yawning; her tiredness was brushed away with her excitement to show her teacher her homework. How she had mastered writing her name in just one day.

The bus was full of people going to work, school and college. Elaynna tried to observe them, the day before she was too shy to look around.

She observed the men in suits who had shiny gelled hair with a nice perfume; she hoped her husband would be like that one day, very handsome looking, well kept with a important looking job.

Some passengers were reading a book, while others had headphones on listening to music. Hoping one day she would be able to hold a book of importance and be able to read it with interest like the woman across her that was immersed in her book. The cover had a little boy on it holding a kite; she couldn't make out the writing, for it was too advanced for her to read yet.

The bus made a funny noise when they got off at their stop and walked to their college. They were a bit early; there wasn't much of a rush in the main hall. They departed their ways and headed off to their classrooms. Rahim's class was on the far side of the college. They never bumped into each other during the day. Elaynna smiled with her head up for the first time when she entered her classroom and saw Mariam, for some reason she felt a fondness with Mariam already. They exchanged greetings.

"You are looking very happy my child." Elaynna took out her exercise book.

"Look, I learnt to write my name in angrezi." Mariam stroked her head and gave her a thumbs up.

"Well done! Mary Jane will be ever so proud. Also you have written it so neatly." She then folded her book away realizing that she forgot to show her father that morning. But someone being happy at her progress meant a lot to her. Her eyes welled up a bit, Mariam looked into her eyes reading them instantly. She hadn't seen such a young girl with so much sadness hidden in her eyes. When this was the age of excitement and daydreaming.

"Thank you Aunty." Elaynna replied to her gesture. Before they could have any further conversation, Mary Jane entered the room welcoming everyone. Going around checking everyone's homework, she praised everyone for their efforts and told them that the homework would be getting harder soon; she loved a class that came back with complete homework.

At lunch time Elaynna looked around the canteen where everyone opened their packed lunches. She realized she had forgotten to bring her own lunch; her tummy was beginning to rumble when she saw everyone else dig into their food. She couldn't believe how silly she had been when she packed everyone's lunch the night before and totally forgot about herself.

She had been too eager to do her homework than to remember to prepare her lunch. Mariam sat across her and opened her lunch box. She had made egg sandwiches. Elaynna couldn't help but to gape at Mariam's food.

"Here, I made extra, I always end up making two big sandwiches. Please take one." Elaynna resisted at first, but the kind reassurance from Mariam made her to stop hesitating. She took one slowly, eating an egg mayonnaise sandwich for the first time. The taste seeming a bit unusual at first, but then she got used to the taste and devoured the whole sandwich. "What is it made of? I can taste the egg but what is the white stuff?" Mariam laughed at her innocence, "Its egg mayonnaise." Elaynna looked at her with query, she thought she knew all the kinds of English foods there was.

"Mayonaaz? Whats that?" Mariam laughed nearly spitting out her food correcting her pronunciation. "It's made out of the white egg and used as a flavored cream." Elaynna laughed with her. How silly could she be, she thought it was yoghurt but kept that thought to herself to keep her from embarrassment.

"Thank you Aunty for the lovely food, I am so silly I forgot to make my lunch last night I couldn't wait to get my first piece of homework perfect." Mariam smiled at her, and offered her half of her apple and got her a cup to share her tropical juice.

"Here take this." Elaynna felt comforted being saved by a meal when she thought she would have to starve until she got home, and wouldn't really have had time to eat she had to complete making dinner.

"Would you mind if I ask you something?" Mariam interrupted as they dug into their cut apple.

"Yes." Mariam paused for a second before asking her the question.

"I believe you are around 15-16 but why is there such sadness in your eyes?" Elaynna stopped chewing, she didn't realize that her sorrow was so apparent for anyone to read without her saying a word.

"Sadness? Oh you must mean tiredness. I slept quite late last night watching television." Mariam knew she was lying, but didn't intervene further.

"So how long have you been in the United Kingdom?" Elaynna told her almost a year repeating the question back to her.

"I have been here for nearly five years now. My son called me over here and made my stay indefinate, I asked him if it were alright for me to learn the language, I was getting rather bored at home. So here I am." Elaynna nodded listening with an interest.

The bell sounded off, indicating that the break was over. Elaynna helped her throw the rubbish away both hurrying to their class. They practiced their letter pronunciation their homework today was to practice the letter phonics; they will be learning how to read soon.

On her way home Elaynna couldn't help thinking how she noticed that Mariam wasn't really paying much attention to her lesson. Sitting there observing everyone and helped anyone when they got stuck by helping to translate. This made Elaynna wonder when she knew all the answers and was so good at translating then why was she having to repeat the class and how could she have failed when her English was very good.

Reaching near home she shrugged her shoulders to her thoughts, scraping her feet slowly towards home. Feeling rather tired from the long day she wasn't looking forward to the housework at all, her feet seemed to drag on the pavement feeling heavier in each footstep. In Pakistan when she used to come home from school her grandmother welcomed her lovingly offering her a snack and something cool to drink, she didn't need to do as much as she had to do here to obtain an education. It was the opposite here, she had to do everything even though her mother was home all day. Rahim knocked on the door,

Yasmin welcomed them in, Elaynna noticed that her mother had tidied up and vacuumed the place.

Phew, thought Elaynna, at least she didn't need to clean. Her mother was helping after all. Elaynna took her bag off and changed into her pyjamas, she didn't want her college clothes to smell like spices. She took out the chicken from the fridge and finished cooking dinner; while she cooked she hummed the pronunciation that Mary Jane taught them that day. For some reason her mother was in a happier mood.

"You look happy Ammi," she dared to say.

"Oh you will know why when your Abu comes." Confused at the answer, she continued cooking the rest of the meal. Shabnam had gone out, she didnt look as aggressive she had done the day before when she returned home. It was a Godsend for her to come home to a clean house with a cooked meal. That evening after dinner, after Elaynna had put all the dishes away making sure she made her lunch this time, she put in an extra piece of sandwich for Mariam and a Satsuma.

Elaynna showed her father how she had learned to write her name, who was sitting with Mushtaq and Shabnam while they were watching the news.

"Oh beta well done! I am so proud of you keep up the good work, I appreciate you trying." Elaynna felt a warm glow inside, she wanted to embrace her father, a hug was all she needed to replace the comfort she was missing.

Unfortunately ever since she had turned into a teenager her father had stopped giving her hugs, he still kissed her forehead though. "This means that we have double good news tonight." Everyone stopped in their tracks to pay attention. All of the boys stopped doing their homework while they lay on their fronts on the red carpet; they all turned to face Abdul longing to hear what he had to say.

"News? What news?" Mushtaq turned to Abdul. Yasmin smiled to herself, Shabnam thought Yasmin was expecting again.

"I had applied for a council property, now we have been given a three bedroom house with affordable rent. Alhamdulilah I feel so blessed! Mushtaq my brother you can have your house back, sorry for any problems caused or inconvenience." Mushtaq expressed his happiness to Abdul.

"I am so happy for you brother, but how dare you say sorry for any problems? You always paid your way around even though you were working so hard to save up to get your own space. Every time I rejected the rent money you forced it into my hands, Elaynna has taken such good care of the house and so has Yasmin. I am grateful for the time spent with you all. People can't usually live under the same roof." Shabnam wasn't really happy at all, she was losing a servant. She tried forcing a smile; Not wanting anyone to see her rage.

"I must say a lot of thanks to Shabnam for keeping up with us, especially how we used up your living room as a room, I am sure you want your privacy back." Yasmin privately winked Shabnam.

"No, no, you can stay for as long as you like, there is no problem." Shabnam finally spoke placing her tea cup on the table leaning forward.

"No Shabam you have done enough for us. How long will the four boys sleep in one room huddled together, they all need their space to study. We will always remember your lovely gesture for the time spent." She didn't want to make it obvious that she wanted Elaynna to stay to do the house work.

"So when are you planning to move, or when do you have to move?" Mushtaq queried.

"I shall get the keys for the house in a week, so if we count the days it is approximately 14 days exactly once we have cleaned and decorated a little. I have kept some money aside for furniture and decorating." Yasmin felt proud to hear that, my husband is so clever she thought.

"Yes one week should be enough to decorate, I will be happy to help, if you need anything." Abdul appreciating his friend's warm gesture placed a hand on his knee, "You have helped enough my friend. Thank you."

Shabnam followed Elaynna into the kitchen; having to release her rage somehow.

"I bet you must be happy that you are leaving; now I have to do everything alone again." Elaynna didn't respond she pretended she couldn't hear. An argument was the last thing she wanted.

"Well what have you got to say? The food you cook is rotton anyway, you won't do well in your nasty little college, now that you are showing off how quick you can be to achieve all the housework and get an education. No matter how hard you try you won't ever be able to learn a thing because you are so stupid!" she hissed in her ear. She pushed past her on purpose leaving her to feel so low in herself, like she was unable to learn.

This trampled on the little self esteem she had gained in the past few days. As much as she did not want to admit it, she knew she was quite slow to learn in Pakistan, everyone had said so. Elaynna thought she had left all that behind in Pakistan not expecting for it to come up to surface again.

She had buried those truths in Pakistan and came to England for a new beginning, how did Shabnam know that she had a learning difficulty? Maybe Ammi told her, she thought. She wanted to cry but for some reason a hidden happiness overtook Shabnam's curse.

They were finally leaving that horrible house and will be in their own home. A place that they will be able to call home, not feel like they were treading on egg shells all the time. Elaynna hugged herself with excitement trying to forget about Shabnams outburst.

CHAPTER 21

The following weeks were like hell for Elaynna. Shabnam made her work harder than before. Elaynna had to go to the new house every evening after dinner to help decorate as well as do Shabnam's housework. She was falling asleep in class and getting in trouble with Mary Jane for being behind on homework.

Mariam took Mary Jane aside telling her that she was having a few problems at home which will suffice soon. From then on Mary Jane was easier on her and said she could catch up when she was ready.

Within two weeks they were able to move in; Abdul had taken great care to buy everything to Yasmin's taste. This made Yasmin feel she was important again. While they waited for their cab, Yasmin thanked them again for their hospitality. Shabnam cried when they were leaving. She wasn't crying that she was going to miss them, she was crying because she would have to do everything herself again. They waved until their car was out of distance.

"Have you got everything ready?" Yasmin asked on the way.

"Yes, relax and have patience." Abdul answered annoyingly.

When they reached to their destination, the boys glared at the new three bed house. They jumped out of the cab upon arriving racing to the front of the house. Kareem beat him to it. Reaching inside they started exploring. Abdul had done a good job, it looked fresh and new. Yasmin was impressed with the furniture; there was a box room that Abdul had set up for Elaynna with a single bed and a wardrobe. He had set up a bedroom for the boys to share which had a bunk bed and a separate single bed for Kareem. Abdul went to buy groceries while everyone settled in their new home.

"The new house is your responsibility like you had at Shabnam's house, but I don't want you losing your sleep over it. Your eyes have become so dark, dinner will be your responsibility when you get back from college I will do the rest." Yasmin assured Elaynna, her mother expressed happiness after a long time.

That night they all slept like babies on the new beds. Yasmin was so excited that day, she especially got dressed up for Abdul, now that they had a room to them selves now. Abdul was also relieved to be alone with his wife again, no more whispering to each other or being careful of their words in case they were heard. Embracing each other until they fell asleep, they were out like a light; their bodies ached from sleeping on the floor.

Elaynna looked around her new square room, she had never slept alone before feeling a little frightened and excited at the same time. There was a wardrobe for her things and a small dressing table next to her single bed.

This was the first time she had her own space and a place to put her things. At first she thought she wouldn't be able to sleep, she fell into a deep sleep from the comfort of her new bed that embraced her tired body like a soft cushion. "Aaah" a sigh came out from her mouth when she drew the new quilt over her body.

That night Elaynna had a bad dream, she dreamt being accused for something, her mother dragged her out of college for it. When she woke up in the morning she didn't know what to make out of what the dream meant.

Elaynna thanked Allah it was the weekend. No college that morning, she could finally get some rest away from the witch she thought to herself. If only her grandmother was here she would have sorted Shabnam out in no time. All she wanted to do that day was sit and watch the new T.V. There weren't many channels but there were a few Indian and Urdu channels.

"Give me the remote and go make us our breakfast." Rahim grabbed the remote from her hands. "Hey!" Elaynna managed to say. She wouldn't dare argue with her brothers. He then switched it on to Tom and Jerry.

"Wait for Ammi and Abu to wake up then I will get breakfast ready." A few minutes later Yasmin walked down the stairs tying up her wet hair.

"Didn't Abu go to work today?" asked Kareem wondering why.

"No he is resting, let your father rest, it's the first night in many months that he is having a proper sleep. Elaynna what are you doing, get up and do the beds and make breakfast. I will start the tea and put the clothes out." She ordered heading off to the kitchen. Elaynna got up instantly, following orders without further ado.

Some Saturday this was she thought, she couldn't do what she wanted. Well at least they have their own home now, is all Elaynna could think of to reassure herself. Her father had woken up by the smell of the cooking. Elaynna joined her mother taking out the dough and started to make parathes. This was the first time her mother entered the kitchen in her presence, she would hardly cook a thing in Shabnam's house.

The boys all rushed to the kitchen when the smell reached their noses. They ate so quickly rushing back to the living room. Yasmin laughed at them nearly spitting out her food.

Yasmin and Elaynna ate in silence, when Elaynna had finished she quickly got up to do the dishes before she had to be reminded by her mother.

Elaynna joined her brothers; her body was aching from all of the work she had been doing in the past few weeks. Her bottom ached when she sat on the sofa giggling with her brothers while they watched the cartoon. Jerry had smacked Tom in the face with a frying pan. The pan reminded her of her time when Shabnam had burnt her fingers on purpose. A sigh escaped her mouth when she relaxed back in her chair. The horrific days replayed in her mind of the double act that Shabnam played with her. How someone could be so deceiving and never get caught, Elaynna wondered. "Elaynna, now you sit again? There is a lot to do; we have guests coming today and tomorrow to congratulate us on moving. Go and start cooking they will be here in a few hours. And go and shine the bathroom and toilet." Elaynna dragged her tired feet into the kitchen starting to prepare a feast.

The whole weekend consisted with guests coming and going. Her mother helped her until the guests came but then left Elaynna to do all the work alone from cooking to serving. While she was making tea she almost fell asleep, pouring it she almost burnt her hands, it just about missed her when she felt the spill on the kitchen surface. This routine carried on until Sunday night.

Elaynna went straight to bed that evening, television was out of the question it was too late, their father disapproved to let them watch television so late.

The following morning Elaynna headed for college, she was tired but that didn't bother her so much. She couldn't wait to tell Mariam her happy news. Doing housework in your home was a complete different feeling. Only her mother had a right over her to tell her off not that witch Shabnam. When she walked into her class Mariam looked at her in an odd way.

"Guess what Aunty, I have some great news." Mariam forced a smile, "Really? Please share, any good news will do . . ." Elaynna tried to observe what was different.

"We have finally moved into the new house now. I have my own bedroom and just a few hours on my bed you feel refreshed."

"Oh how nice." she responded looking away. Elaynna tried to figure out what was wrong with her; giving a hard look she noticed that she kept covering the other side of her face with her scarf. Before Elaynna could inquire any further Mary Jane walked in with her folder shouting good morning.

Mariam tried to avoid having conversation as much as possible. Being more concerned with keeping the right side of her face hidden. Elaynna couldn't focus on her lesson she was too worried about Mariam. Mariam was not her usual jolly self. They both yearned waiting for the lunch break. When the bell rang, Mariam scurried out of the classroom. Elaynna confused at her behavior rushed after her down the stairs.

"Aunty Mariam! Please wait!" Mariam stopped upon reaching the canteen; she found a corner and sat down when she would not be noticed. Elaynna followed sitting across her.

"Whats the matter, are you upset with me?" Mariam shook her head breaking into tears. Elaynna confused to what to do sat next to her placing an arm over her shoulder, just like her friends used to do when she used to be upset.

"Elaynna, I am depressed. My own son is against me. He uses me like a slave and believes what ever his stupid wife tells him. Last night he pushed it too far, while I was arguing with his wife he swore at me saying horrible things to me. When I tried to stand up for myself he slapped me so hard that I got a bruise on my cheek." Elaynna stunned to hear that, the Mariam she thought was a stable confident woman was just like herself, abused, neglected.

Elaynna wiped her tears for her; Mariam readjusted her scarf showing her the red mark on her face. Fortunately it wasn't a punch or it would have turned black and blue.

"My own son . . . Elaynna, I gave birth to him, he makes me do all the housework for his wife, and they make me babysit in the evenings so they can go out till early hours in the morning. I don't mind the house work, I like to keep busy, I also don't mind baby sitting for them, I love my grandchildren. But constantly being mentally abused that I am lazy and stupid from my daughter in law is not on. My son watches agreeing with her." Elaynna pitied her "I know how you feel . . ." Elaynna tried to reassure her, she knew exactly how Mariam was feeling. Completely torn and misplaced like you were born in the wrong family. Why did everyone take them for granted? Always finding fault rather than appreciating.

"Why didn't you mention anything before?" Elaynna soothed squeezing her shoulders, almost massaging them.

"I didn't want to be a burden, by now I was used to it. But last night was out of order; I can't believe he is my son." sobbing more onto Elaynna's shoulder.

"You think I come here for studying? This is my salvation where I can forget it all and have someone to talk to." Elaynna didn't ever say anything to Mariam about her own problems because she was used to keeping everything to herself, her grandmother had taught her to never let anyone know your business.

However her mother told her friends everything, she could hear all of their family business being discussed, when Abdul would arrive home the ladies would change the subject.

"My son brought me here because his wife could no longer do the house work and look after the children, day by day she made me work like a donkey and swears at me when I get things wrong." Elaynna unpacked both of their lunches. Elaynna then listened to her contently trying to give her hope that things would get better. Maybe if they studied they would get important jobs and make money of their own.

"Who will hire us with an English ESOL course?" Mariam laughed through her dinner. "Anyone, you never know." Mariam then plucked up the courage to ask Elaynna her story. At first she didn't know what to say, but now feeling a bond with Mariam, her wounds bursting to set themselves fee. Elaynna began her story from childhood to adolescence. Mariam remained shocked and amazed at her courage for her patience.

"So you can't read or write at all? But now you are doing so well. Keep it up. Remember being able to read and write solves ones many problems. Anything is possible then. You have your whole life ahead of you please don't be a typical housewife." Elaynna mumbled "Hmmm." Although she had been in her class for a couple of months she was quite behind compared to everyone else, it took her time to understand things. No matter how hard she tried, she found it hard to understand, because of this she lost interest in her studies again.

Mary Jane always excited her about learning when in class, she tried in anyway that she could.

Miss Shazia had made her detest the class room. All she did was use her as a slave beating her really badly when she didn't do her homework.

One day she remembered at the age of seven; she had come into school without remembering the homework set out the night before. They had to memorize a poem and write it neatly in their exercise books. Elaynna managed to copy the poem but she couldn't read it at all. Reading had always been extremely hard for her all she could do was make out were the letters that she had learned in the first year.

When asked to recite the poem in front of the whole class, not being able to memorize it, she stuttered in front of the whole class. The other girls laughed hysterically like she was a clown. Miss Shazia stormed towards pulling her hand out forcefully then began whacking it continuously with a whip until it had red bruised lines on it. When she went home crying that day telling her mother of the incident, her mother slapped her again scolding her it was her own fault for being lazy and not concentrating.

Having no one to turn to or anyone to understand her dilemma she began to hate her books she began to do what ever she could to avoid being brutally beaten from her teachers. To her fortune in England this was not allowed, the teachers here were so nice, eager to help you to learn. The first night she had learned to read and write her name, but now as the class was moving forward, Elaynna was having the same problem in catching up. No matter how hard she tried to concentrate, all she was good at was to copy the letters from the board; she managed to speak the language with Mariam's help. Mary Jane always knew how to get the students interested in the lesson, breaking down the lesson jumping up and down making it fun. But still Elaynna struggled.

Homework was always completed on Elaynna's end; Rahim would help her in the evenings, not by helping or explaining but by telling her answers to the questions and writing them out for her. Still she was learning bit by bit, she consoled herself.

"Who would think that we would have similar stories? So Shabnam is out of your life now? That's a good thing, but your mother is your mother, I'm sure she means well." Was all Mariam could say, she didn't want to make Elaynna feel worse. In all her life she hadn't heard of a mother bringing up her daughter in this way.

Daughters were usually close to their mothers and their mothers looked out for them even more than their sons because later in life daughters were known to be the real carers for their parents.

"Well there is this saying, that Sons will be sons until they get a wife but daughters will be daughters for the rest of their life . . . . I am living that . . ."

Elaynna thought it was a lovely poem,

"Wow what a lovely poem, it is true though . . ." Mariam couldn't help laughing at her gullible comment.

"It's not a poem silly, it's a saying." The bells suddenly went off, they then headed off to their class both feeling lighter than when they had come into college.

Both of them could not believe each others stories they couldn't stop thinking about them for the rest of the day.

Elaynna was brought up believing that children looked after and respected their mother more than anything in the world. She learned this from her father, who cared so much for his mother. The longer she thought about her parent's relationship Mariam's words echoed in her ear "Son is a son until he finds a wife, a daughter is a daughter for the rest of her life." No matter how close her father had been to his mother, he chose to live away from her and did whatever his wife told him.

He couldn't stick up for his children when he knew what was going on. Mariam pondered on Elaynna's story, her own mother locking her up in a room in such heat almost killing her? What had the world come to? Mariam started to miss her own daughter who was living abroad in Sweden; remembering how lovingly she had brought her up. They were inseparable until she got married. Mariam thought coming to London would help her with her loneliness; she did lose her loneliness but was turned into a slave. Having a similar story to Elaynna of only being allowed to go to college after the chores were done, in Mariam's case even when they were done she was picked on constantly.

They departed their ways after college and said their goodbyes for the day. After speaking their hearts out, college was beginning to become something that they both started to look forward to. It didn't matter anymore to Elaynna that she didn't understand her lessons anymore.

College became a place where she could let go and find the Elaynna that she wanted to feel and be. The Elaynna that was loved and cared for. Because of Mariam's support and shoulders to lean on, her mother's abuse had become easier to bear. They spent their lunch hour laughing at silly jokes sharing their lunch. Although there was a major age gap between them they understood each other very well, both had found a trusted friend.

Elaynna had never experienced such comfort apart from her grandmother. An academic year had almost passed, and Mary Jane was helping them to revise for their exams. Elaynna was struggling with her revision not knowing where to start. They had to take three different tests. One was for reading, one for writing and one for speaking.

The night before her exams Elaynna tried to revise confused for what she was preparing for. The speaking bit wasn't so bad; she could answer simple questions she knew she would do well in that bit. Mariam had rehearsed with her quite a few times. When she tried to read, all she could make out were the one to two letter words the rest were tricky.

In one year she had just about managed to learn the alphabet and write one sentence and that was "My name is Elaynna Aziz." That night she prayed so hard that she pass through the exams hoping to do her parents proud.

The morning arrived for the examinations, Mary Jane started with the reading and writing tests. Handing out a paper for their exam, they had to do a reading from the paper and answer the questions in writing. The test lasted for one hour.

It took Elaynna half an hour to read each letter on the paper not knowing what she was supposed to write on the separate sheet of paper. She just about managed to copy the date that was on the board writing her name at the top.

"OK class you have five minutes left to finish up your paper." Elaynna out of fear wrote down what she knew. 'My name is Elaynna Aziz.' She then folded her paper as soon as Mary Jane started to collect the papers.

"Go and have a break the speaking examination will begin in thirty minutes. See you in a bit." Mary Jane took the papers to the office leaving the class to carry on.

"Oh Aunty Mariam the exam was really difficult I hope I pass." Elaynna worried. Mariam agreed with her and told her the same assuring her to not to worry. Thirty minutes later Mary Jane returned to take the speaking tests. She called everyone one by one to the front in order of registration.

"OK so let's start with simple questions." Mary Jane asked them their name, age and where they lived. Elaynna did well in this test. Mary Jane gave her a clap at the end. This made Elaynna feel so happy for the rest of the day thinking she had passed her course. After all the examinations Mary Jane informed them that their results will be posted to their homes in august and if they passed they will move up to the second level, if not they can repeat the same class.

The last week before the summer holidays was the best week Elaynna ever had. Everyone was being so nice to one another and Elaynna had built some confidence, she was no longer so shy when talking to the boys in her class. They were no different to her brothers treating her with great respect.

They got to play lots of games and watch movies in class. English movies, so they could enjoy and pick up new words at the same time before the following year, the games they played were draughtboards, monopoly, including other fun board games.

On their last day Mary Jane told them each to bring a dish so they could have a leaving party together. Mariam bought rice; Elaynna brought chicken korma as suggested by Mary Jane. That last morning as Elaynna was cooking the korma, she felt her stomach churn like the way it did when she was leaving her grandmother, it worried her that this might be the last time she would ever see Mariam.

Who will listen to her problems? Or make her feel better the days she was sad. Mariam had similar thoughts when she reached college that day. The party was nice while it lasted Mary Jane showed them how to play musical chairs and pass the parcel. She went all out helping them to have lots of fun.

At the end of the day while they were getting ready to say their goodbyes, Elaynna couldn't help breaking into tears. The next six weeks were going to be difficult without having anyone to talk to. Mariam had tears in her eyes too when they embraced each other. "Don't worry Elaynna these six weeks will go by very quickly my child. We should see each other soon." Elaynna nodded wiping her tears with the back of her hand. Mariam took out a little gift, telling her she got her a little something in case she didn't get to return. This made Elaynna feel worse she hadn't thought to get her dear friend anything. "Please open it when you get home." they gave each other one last hug going their separate ways.

Elaynna opened her gift on the way home, she couldn't keep the promise of waiting until she got home. Unwrapping the gift she found a small trinket box made of silver steel. It looked like a mini treasure box with beautiful embroidery. As soon as she got home, she placed it on her wardrobe smiling every time she looked at it because it reminded her of Mariam.

CHAPTER 22

The holidays for Elaynna meant more house work, her mother made her do a spring clean and cook for the guests that kept coming and going. Her mother was expecting again. This meant Elaynna had to do everything, Yasmin was always ill, the pregnancy wasn't so easy like the first four. Yasmin was constantly vomiting, her hormones were playing havoc on her. All she wanted to do was to swear all day and nit pick at little things.

Once when Elaynna was dusting the television she threw her sandal on her back telling her she missed a spot. Elaynna couldn't remember her mother being so aggressive over little things when she was expecting with Qasim.

Elaynna prayed that she be blessed with a little sister. The age gap would be quite big but she didn't care, she longed for another girl in the house.

In the middle of august their test results came. Abdul opened the letters; first he opened Kareem's results, Rahim's and then Elayna's. He patted Kareem on the back when he opened his test result. Kareem had done extremely well in his exams especially in maths and science. He had passed all of his GCSE's; Rahim had also passed his engineering course. When Abdul opened Elaynna's letter, she had only passed the speaking test but failed the others. Abdul didn't say a word, looking up at his daughter. After a silence of five minutes he finally spoke.

"Whats the matter? I bet shes failed, shes always been so slow." Yasmin hissed. Abdul tried to save Elaynna's hide, he knew if Yasmin found out she would go crazy. "Well Elaynna you passed your speaking test . . . . but failed the others . . ."

Yasmin didn't take a minute to get up, immediately slapping Elaynna across the face.

"What is wrong with you?! You waste so much time not studying. Why do you think we brought you into the United Kingdom! We brought you here to study and learn and make something of yourself!" Yasmin screamed. Abdul felt helpless, he wasn't enjoying watching what was happening to his only daughter. He tried to calm Yasmin down nicely but it didn't work, until he had to shout at her for the first time.

"Yasmin will you shut up! It is not the end of the world. It says here she can repeat the class. The poor girl is slavering around all day how do you expect her to learn for Gods Sake?!" Yasmin gathered the moment to get to reality that Abdul was shouting at her. Pausing to think hard she answered him boldly.

"Well I learned how to read and write as well as look after my parent's home. If I could do it so should she, why does she have to get special treatment? You have spoiled her Abdul. That's why shes failed." Abdul held his rage; he didn't want to bring out all the poison that he had buried down in his chest for the past eight years. He knew exactly what his wife was like. If she was in the wrong she would never accept it. He thought she would have been smart enough to realize why he wasn't the same since Qasim was born. But today he had to let her know what he really thought of her.

"Children please leave the room. I need to talk to your mother." The four of them froze in their steps confused to what was happening.

"NOW!" he shouted at them. They all scurried out of the room as quick as their feet would take them.

"Sit down Yasmin!" Yasmin slightly frightened of her husband's behavior obeyed. "How dare you! Who the hell do you think you are?" Yasmin confused at his outburst didn't know what to answer back.

"What do you mean?" she protested.

"You know exactly what I mean." Yasmin tried to defend herself.

"I am doing whats best for our daughter." Abdul got up from his seat and shook his head. "So what I am doing for our daughter is wrong? I am spoiling her? In what way does she look spoiled to you? The poor girl works so hard and never sighs at the work that you throw in front of her. How do you expect her to learn? She scarcely has anytime for herself. As a mother, sorry, as a woman I thought you would understand her feelings. But no! All you care about is her working all day like a donkey." Yasmin looked down at her feet. "I know whats best for my daughter." She whispered.

"SHUT UP!" Abdul shouted at her. "Then you wonder why I am becoming distant from you. I am fed up of your nonsense." Yasmin stunned at his answer.

"Distant? So you lied the last time." Abdul nodded. "I know what you did to Elaynna, Ammi told me. Because of you she nearly died!" Yasmin froze shocked in her seat, her hands and feet felt numb with fear.

"Now whether you like it or not, Elaynna is going to college for another year, I want her to make something of herself. In Pakistan you didn't tell me why exactly you made her quit school. If Ammi or you had told me earlier that her teachers were abusing her rather than teaching her as well as making her do their housework, I would have gone down there to teach them a lesson or got them in trouble with the principle. But because of you she lost her right to education, and now when she has a chance here and is trying hard you are trying to ruin it again for her!" Yasmin didn't respond, she was beginning to hate Abdul for not siding with her, she still thought she was right and he was wrong, she was feeling incredibly guilty again for what she had done to Elaynna. Abdul had dug up an old conscience.

"But she failed Abdul can't you see she isn't up to all this studying. A woman's place is in the home. The more experienced she is in her housework and cooking she will fit in well with her in laws." Abdul gave her an angered look; he looked like his eyes would pop out of their sockets.

"She is going to keep going until she can read or write and you are not going to stop her. Why aren't you looking at the bright side she only failed the reading and writing test and passed the speaking? Doesn't that prove anything that our daughter is capable of something?" Yasmin was getting annoyed now and plucking up the courage to speak up to Abdul which she hadn't done before.

"Oh so you want to make her into a doctor or lawyer now? The freedom that you are planning to give her in this western country will ruin all of us. She will run away with some boy and leave us hanging in shame." Abdul walked off ignoring her now a final word.

"I trust my daughter, and I know whats best for her, it will be better for you to never to interfere in my decisions again."

Yasmin sat in her seat leaning back into her chair beginning to cry. Abdul had never spoken so crossly with her; he didn't understand what the western culture was like. She was just trying to protect her daughter from the western society. Beginning to wish she didn't give birth to a daughter, sons were better at least you did not have to worry about their welfare. Because of having a daughter she had now lost the love of her life, she thought.

The following morning Yasmin wasn't feeling too well, she stayed in bed all day. Mostly because she was still quite upset from the day before, Elaynna came to her aid giving her food in bed, constantly asking if she needed anything. Yasmin ate the food that Elaynna placed in front of her but did not utter a word of appreciation. Beginning to hate Elaynna for taking her respect away, no matter how hard Elaynna tried to speak to her she just looked the opposite way. She tried massaging her feet but Yasmin pulled away. Elaynna sad at her mother's disposition left her on her own, continuing with the house duties. She preferred her mother talking to her at least, even when she was constantly shouting at her or abusing her. This was the first time her mother was giving her silent treatment. Wondering maybe it was due to her failing she wished she had tried harder in her exams. Feeling responsible for the argument that her parents had had. Elaynna decided that her mother's silent treatment was justifiable; it wasn't easy bringing up four children, and being pregnant with the fifth.

A mother was the most important being on earth, she had to go through so much for her children, having to keep the child in her stomach for nine months and then go through such a hard labor to bring them in to the world. Thinking about this made her feel her mother had the right to be the way she wanted.

Her mother didn't talk to her for a whole week. Being normal with her sons, but silently out casting Elaynna. She didn't shout at her or pick at anything. Elaynna was beginning to feel hurt now, why was her mother treating her like an infidel. What had she done so wrong, when her mothers friends came for visits with their daughters, Yasmin spoke to Elaynna acting normal in front of them. However soon as they left she returned to avoiding her and not speaking a word to her.

One night Elaynna couldn't sleep, trying to think of ways to make her mother to speak with her again. She came to a decision that no matter what she will make her mother speak to her, no matter what her mother did in return, she will apologize and will keep apologizing until her mother accepted, even if she had to kiss her feet for it.

The following morning when her mother was in the kitchen preparing breakfast, Elaynna plucked up the courage to try to talk to her. Frightened as she was she didn't know how to start. It had been almost two weeks now without any dialogue. When she placed the saucepan on the stove, she tried to speak the words that she had been rehearsing in her mind the night before.

"Ammi, I am sorry to have hurt you, please talk to me again." Her voice croaked. Yasmin ignored her continuing to knead the dough.

"Ammi, please talk to me." Elaynna's voice now slightly raised and clear. Yasmin just slammed the kneaded dough bowl next to Elaynna and left the kitchen. Elaynna followed her into the living room after taking the saucepan off the stove. Yasmin sat on the sofa pretending to watch the television.

"Please Ammi, talk to me now, I will do anything for you to speak with me again. If you want me to pass this time I will make sure I do, no matter what." The ignoring continued further. A strength of persistence increased in Elaynna, she decided to go to her feet and touch them for forgiveness. Yasmin tried to move her leg; Elaynna hugged both of her legs and begged for forgiveness. "A aah!" shouted her mother in pain. Elaynna thought she was shouting out of annoyance, her tears deafened her senses,

"Please Ammi talk to me, I won't let go of your feet until you do . . ." another noise of pain came from Yasmin.

"A aah!!" Elaynna looked up and saw her mother clutching her stomach. She jumped to her feet asking her what was wrong.

"I'm in labor! I need the hospital now! Call your father!" Yasmin panted through the pain. Rahim and Kareem came running down the stairs after hearing their mothers cry for help.

"You look after Ammi; I will call an ambulance and Abu!" Rahim quickly called an ambulance which arrived within minutes. Elaynna quickly packed a bag of clothes for her mother and the babies' clothes. She had heard Mariam telling her something about being prepared when pregnant when you go into labor. Elaynna also packed some snacks for her mother; remembering she hadn't had any breakfast. Rahim sent Elaynna with Yasmin to the ambulance assuring her Abu would meet them there.

Upon reaching the hospital, the paramedics took Yasmin straight into the labor room, she was dilating quickly, Elaynna held her mother's hand the whole time, without realizing what was happening she was taken into the labor room with her mother. Within minutes Yasmin gave birth to a little girl. Elaynna could not stop crying tears of joy after viewing the most beautiful sight she had ever seen. The birth softened Yasmins heart a little; she was not happy, when she saw she had given birth to a girl. Another daughter to train like a soldier in this horrible world she thought, rather than being grateful for the birth of a healthy baby.

The midwife cleaned the tiny baby after weighing her and placed her in Yasmin's arms. The midwife told her the baby was seven and a half pounds. A perfect average weight, a tear fell out of Yasmin's eye when she looked at the baby. Another beautiful girl Allah had blessed her with, realizing she was being ungrateful before, made her emotional. Elaynna couldn't stop crying tears of joy, Allah had listened to her prayers, he had blessed her with a little sister.

Yasmin handed her over to Elaynna while the midwife and nurse cleaned her up. Elaynna looked at the new little member of the family.

"Aslaam Aleikum little sister" Elaynna whispered in her ear, kissing her cheek. The baby opened her eyes briefly staring at her. A skin tone of fair skin, and big oval eyes with a dimpled chin of features.

"Ain't she beautiful," the nurse said looking over Elaynna's shoulder. Without understanding what the nurse said, Elaynna nodded in agreement, she could tell from the nurse's expression that she had said something nice. The midwife took the baby from Elaynna's arms helping Yasmin to latch the baby onto her breast for her milk.

Breastfeeding being second nature to Yasmin, this was not a problem for her to perfect on the first try.

Elaynna offered her mother some of the snacks that she had packed. All Elaynna could find was malted biscuits and bread. Yasmin appreciated the gesture with surprised look, the gesture didn't surprise her, her responsibility and efficiency surprised her. There was a knock on the door, it was Abdul. Looking weary from his morning shift, he walked in like a proud father.

Elaynna was holding the baby again while her mother had something to eat. "Mashallah, What did Allah bless us with this time?" Yasmin still playing upset with Abdul. She didn't answer him. Elaynna walked over to her father to show him her little sister. By looking at the happiness on Elaynna's face Abdul could tell it was a girl. "Oh Elaynna, I should be congratulating you more than your mother. Allah answered your prayers, you always wanted a little sister and I told to to ask Allah in your prayers, and look mashallah you have what you wanted." He then gently took the baby from her arms to have a proper look.

"She is actually too beautiful to be your daughter Yasmin, she is definitely my daughter." Yasmin looked away with a frown; she tried to get up, giving up realizing she could barely move.

"Ammi, please rest I will look after the baby." Yasmin lay back to get some sleep. Abdul read the adhan in the babies ears, the beautiful words of Arabic soothed the baby to sleep. Lying her down in the cradle beside Yasmin, father and daughter tiptoed out of the room.

Abdul bought Elaynna some breakfast from the hospital café complimenting how much he was proud of her bravery for handling the situation so well. Elaynna blushed looking down stirring her tea.

"What shall we name your little sister then? Do you have any ideas?" he asked while sipping some coffee and taking a bite into his croissant. Elaynna shrugged her shoulders while she enjoyed her blueberry muffin.

"Hmmm, how about Sabah?" he asked thinking hard taking another sip. "Your sister was born in the morning, Sabah means morning dawn. I think it's nice, don't you?" Elaynna thought it made sense and it would be easy to pronounce she thought.

"Right, let me take you home, and we will bring something back for your mother. You will need to stay at home to look after your brothers."

A warm glow grew inside them on their way home. The boys were waiting to hear the happy news.

"Allah has blessed you with a little sister!" they all cheered with happiness congratulating each other. Now that they were all older having a little baby in the house would make their lives more exciting again.

"What have you named her?" Rahim wondered "Shazia?" he teased winking at Elaynna. This time Elaynna actually found what he said amusing. Abdul frowned at him,

"No, I have decided to name her Sabah." They all agreed it was a lovely name. "I will take you all to the hospital later to meet her, she looks like an angel mashallah, it reminds me of you Elaynna when you were born, you weren't that different apart from being half the size." Elaynna felt special when she heard that, smiling to herself she went into the kitchen to prepare lunch. Reaching there she looked at the horror the kitchen was in. Rahim walked in behind her proudly telling her how he made breakfast.

"So you made breakfast using the whole kitchen and so many dishes? Who is going to clean all this up?" she asked with a straight face trying hard not to laugh, but didn't when she realized she might hurt his feelings.

Rahim offered to help. She told him not to, it was bad enough that he fed everyone if their mother found out and saw the kitchen in the state it was she would go mental. Elaynna first scrubbed the kitchen spotless and then made lunch and soup for her mother.

Fortunately there was some chicken in the fridge. While she packed the goodies for her mother the thought of Sabah's face made her want to scream with glee. She couldn't remember being so happy, a little sister to be there for her and someone to talk to rather than being surrounded with boys all the time. A little sadness fell over her thoughts, if only her Dadi was there, the most important member of the family was missing.

"Elaynna, come quickly to the phone, I have called your Dadi!" shouted Abdul.

Elaynna ran as quick as her feet would take her to the phone.

"Aslaam aleikum Dadi, How are you?" hearing a sound of laughter on the other side of the phone. "Aslaam aleikum my sweetheart I am well, how are you?" Elaynna held the phone tightly, imagining she was holding her grandmother's hand. The clarity of the phone call was so clear; feeling her grandmother's presence right next to her.

"Dadi, I was just thinking about you and here we are talking to eachother! I am so happy today Dadi, Allah blessed me with a little sister." Jannat laughed with joy on the line, feeling happy to be blessed with another granddaughter.

"Yes. I know how badly you wanted a little sister, even when Qasim was born you hoped for a sister. But now Allah has heard your prayers, look after your mother and sister well now." Elaynna nodded on the other side, not realizing that she couldn't see her.

"Do you hear me beta?" Elaynna realizing her silliness replied yes.

"Ok Dadi, I will talk to you soon and we will try to send you pictures." She could see her father gesturing to return the phone back to him reminding her the cost of the call.

"Ok Ammi, take care of yourself. Did you get the money order ok? Ok sure . . . . speak soon." Abdul then hung up and asked Elaynna if the food was ready. Elaynna nodded and told everyone to come and eat while it was hot.

After lunch Abdul went to the hospital with the boys, he asked Elaynna if she wanted to come or stay to clean up. By looking at her hopeful face he laughed telling her to get ready.

"You will have to prepare the house before your mother comes home. You know what shes like if there's a single bit of mess." Elaynna nodded understandably buttoning her coat on.

On the way to the hospital Elaynna's attention was caught by a lady, who was holding a small baby. It was a little girl jumping up and down in her mothers lap, Elaynna looked at her admiringly, the baby caught Elaynna's glimpse and jumped up even more giggling. This touched Elaynna's heart, she wanted to go over to her and hold her. But she knew that the lady would find it offensive.

The bus stopped outside the hospital, they all got off jumping with joy. The four of them following behind Abdul, the boys impatiently jiggling while taking the lift to the maternity ward.

Yasmin was sitting up in her bed trying to eat the hospital food, too bland for her taste, but she knew she had to be careful in what she ate or the baby would feel the spices in her breast milk.

"Aslaam aleikum Ammi, how are you feeling? Wheres is our baby sister?" Qasim asked with a high pitched excited voice. Yasmin gave her boys a kiss on the forehead when they came forward to her, Elaynna expecting a kiss from her mother when she went close to hand her her soup, Yasmin ignored her, she dismissed the fact that she had kissed her sons but not her daughter.

Elaynna pretended she didnt feel a thing, but the pain felt like a sharp pin, she tried to ignore the pain while she unpacked her mother's food on the table in front of her, and then went to see Sabah in her glass cot where her brothers were already hovering over her like bees over honey.

"Hi Sabah . . . ." The boys said at once.

"Oh so you have decided on a name already then?" Yasmin asked with an tone of annoyance.

"You don't like it? We can change it." Abdul reassured her, "What does it mean?" Elaynna interrupted, asking if they could hold the baby. Yasmin nodded at her taking a sip from her soup breaking some bread to dip into it.

"It means morning dawn . . . I thought since she was born in the morning I thought that it was a suitable name." a sound of slurping came from Yasmin's mouth.

"Then lets keep that one." Abdul nodded and smiled at her, he then saw his four children each taking turns to hold Sabah. Elaynna showed them how to hold a baby carefully. They mimicked her like they never held a baby before.

"Stop it boys, shes just being careful, it's for your benefit." They stopped at once, asking for a turn. Elaynna would let them hold the baby each for a few minutes and then take her back. They tried to argue to hold her, but Elaynna was too overprotective of her. To stop the arguing Yasmin told them to put Sabah back or she will get in the habit of being picked up. Elaynna put her back obediently and sat down on the small sofa next to her brothers. A nurse walked in pleasantly greeting everyone.

"Right Mrs Aziz, you may be able to go home tomorrow. All is well with you, you are ready to go home and enjoy your new arrival." Abdul pleased to hear it, thanked the nurse for the support. The nurse took a quick look at the baby before leaving.

"What did she say?" asked Yasmin.

"She said you can go home tomorrow. Alhamdullilah everything is well." Yasmin was happy to hear it.

"Alright everyone lets get ready to go home. Your mother will be home tomorrow." Yasmin kissed the boys goodbye, apart from

Elaynna. Being ignored like the way she came in. Nobody noticed this apart from Elaynna. It felt like a pinch in the heart, her eyes burned with sadness walking out of the room saying goodbye. Nobody else noticed the difference in Yasmin's behavior. The excitement that Elaynna had come with, she left with a complete opposite emotion. Her mind raced back to the past, why had she not ever noticed her mother's difference in her caring nature. It then occurred to her the reason why she hadn't noticed it before. Her grandmother had filled that void for her, her grandmother would give her the physical and emotional love that she needed as a child. That her own mother hardly gave, all she gave her was abuse. Now her grandmother wasn't there with her anymore, she was beginning to realize what was missing in her mother's affection.

Surely a mother loved all of her children the same, then why the difference in the sons and daughters? Rahim, Kareem and Qasim were capable of their mother's physical love when they clearly did no housework then why was she not capable of her mother's love when she did everything under the sun to impress her? The mere thought of this occupied her mind the whole journey home. Why did her mother hate her so much? Maybe hate was too big a word to describe it, but surely there was no physical love there? Her thoughts had occupied her so much that she didn't realize when they reached home; she didn't even remember getting off the bus and entering the house.

Abdul asked Elaynna to get half of the house work done today so she could prepare properly for her mother's welcome the following day, he also told her to not to go overboard so she could get some rest too.

There was enough food for dinner; they didn't mind eating the same thing again. Elaynna's thoughts and the demands of the day had tired her out immensely. Even Rahim was being extremely nice to her, he was proud of her the way she handled taking their mother to the hospital being there for the birth. He told her to leave the dishes, he would sort it and join them for an Indian movie. Kareem frowned at this first but then joined in when Rahim loaded the video tape.

"I got this from my friend at college; he is so cool he has all the latest Indian films, and every Amitabh Bachan movie." They started watching the movie Sharabi, it was a story about a rich son whose father was so busy making money that he neglected him, and due to this the child became an alcoholic from a very young age. Watching this made Elaynna even more emotional, she felt her life was not different to the character in the movie; the only difference was he was rich and drunk.

Elaynna couldn't hold her tears at some of the scenes. Fortunately there was a happy ending, the father learned his lesson at the end after some tough trials, and the young boy found true love when he grew up. This helped Elaynna to have a restful sleep believing that there will always be light at the end of the tunnel.

CHAPTER 23

There wasn't any time to rest the following morning. Rahim pitied on her helping her with the cleaning, Elaynna managed to change and iron all of the bedsheets, made lunch and do all of the laundry. Kareem offered to do the dusting and cleaned the windows. Rahim vacuumed the whole house top to bottom; feeling impressed how well he could clean.

Elaynna decorated the Moses basket that her father bought that morning. She hoped to have a husband as caring as her father who was very considerate of little things for her mother. Well aware of their love for each other, feeling that her father loved her mother more than her mother loved him. The house was looking more than than new; they waited impatiently for their father to return. Elaynna had packed some wholewheat halwa that her grandmother used to make when Qasim was born. Liking the smell of it her brothers all ate some.

They heard a taxi arrive outside their door. All peering at the window they saw their father pay the taxi man and enter the house. Yasmin appreciated the lovely welcome ordering Elaynna to bring some water and inspecting the dust. While she sat down holding the baby, Rahim swooped in to hold her. Elaynna gave her the water asking how she was feeling,

"I am fine beta, the house is looking well." Elaynna embarrassed at the compliment asked if she wanted to eat, she had made her a special paste to eat with roti.

"No, no I am fine, I had the halwa you sent, I just want to go to my room to rest and get some sleep. Your father has bought some formula for the baby, since last night the baby wasn't getting satisfied with my milk, the nurses suggested I give her some formula on the side to keep her stable. Will you watch and feed her while I rest. I don't think I want to be breastfeeding her today." Elaynna pleased at the fact that her mother was communicating with her, and doubly pleased that she would be looking after her sister. "You can stop calling her the baby she has a name!" protested Abdul. Everyone laughed; he sent Yasmin to bed and showed Elaynna how to make the formula. She understood it in a jiffy and went to get the Moses basket from her mothers room. Yasmin was out like a light in her bed, so she tiptoed to get the Moses basket and closed the door behind her ever so quietly trying her best not to waken her with a single amount of noise. When she reached downstairs she noticed that Sabah was starting to cry, she first checked the nappy, it was dry, and then placed her baby finger to check if Sabah was hungry, Sabah sucked on to it quickly, this indicated to Elaynna that she was hungry.

Realizing this she paced her steps to the kitchen to prepare her milk. Jannat used to always do that with Qasim to check when he was hungry, and then push him in his mother's lap. Elaynna would find it amusing the way her grandmother would plonk Qasim onto her mother's lap for a feed. It reminded her of a bucket under a cow; the only difference was that you had to manually squeeze out the milk from a cow.

While the kettle was boiling Elaynna picked up her little sister rocking her in her arms, she calmed down in an instant. Elaynna then handed Sabah back to Rahim and went to the kitchen unwrapping the brand new bottle and sterilized nipple. Her father told her she only needed to feed her two ounces this meant two spoons measured on the scoop and two on the bottle. Once the formula was made she put it to her cheek to check the temperature. Being too hot; she placed the bottle in cold water for a bit and then carried the bottle into the living room. Abdul put the radiators on to keep the house warm for the little one.

When the milk was cool enough Elaynna began to feed Sabah who by now had fallen asleep due to the warmth of the house. Although she was asleep she took to the milk instantly drinking it within five minutes falling back asleep. Abdul told her that she would need to wind her on her shoulder. Upon placing Sabah on her shoulder, she did a burp instantly. Sabahs warm skin next to her cheek made Elaynna feel content inside. She wanted to hold on to this moment forever.

The warmth of love, tender love and care was in this little being that only came into the world a day ago. It didn't surprise Elaynna later that her mother wasn't showing any attention to Sabah, because she was a girl. "Don't worry we sisters are enough for each other." Elaynna whispered in Sabah's ear. Sabah had her cheek on the top side of Elaynna's shoulder. Her warm sweet milky breath swept up Elaynna's nose.

Elaynna gently placed a kiss on Sabah's nose, wrapping her back in her blanket, gently lying her down in the Moses basket. Abdul told her to take her upstairs to her mother, if she cried then to go to check on her. She obediently followed his instructions although she didn't want to take her upstairs, she wanted to have her close by.

Reaching her mother's room she could hear her mother's snoring, she sounded like a genie in a deep slumber.

Over the next few weeks before Elaynna had to go back to college, Elaynna fed, changed, bathed Sabah while her mother rested. Yasmin stopped breastfeeding altogether ever since she came back from the hospital, she didn't want to connect with Sabah. When the day arrived for Elaynna to return to college, Yasmin had to take over Sabah's care. Not once did she say to Elaynna that she did ever so well in taking care of such a small baby when she knew nothing about children herself, even if Elaynna was still a child herself, the burden of life just threw it self on her shoulders and she somehow managed to get through them.

The day that Elaynna had to return to college, the process was like a mother departing her own child. The separation anxiety was no different from a mother who had given birth to her own child and was returning to work forcefully because she had no other choice. That morning Elaynna prepared all the bottles that would be needed for Sabah for the day. All her mother had to do was to place the bottles in warm water and to feed them to her.

As Elaynna kissed Sabah goodbye, she reminded her mother what to do, for a second she felt they were in the wrong roles. Her mother should have been leaving and instructing Elaynna what to do.

Yasmin saw Elaynna's moist eyes when she departed Sabah. As much as Yasmin didn't want to admit to Elaynna how proud she was of her, deep down inside she was amazed at Elaynna's pressure resistance. No matter what she pushed on to her, Elaynna triumphs through, Yasmin thought to her self.

Yasmin was certain that Elaynna would do well with her in laws when she got married, but why couldn't she learn to read and write? Why was Abdul making that such an issue, he should just let her stay at home and do the housework and learn other new things. Yasmin remembered that her parents didn't let her go to school she still turned out alright with a good husband.

Elaynna left her home trying to not to let anyone see that she wanted to cry, when she sat on the bus her heart sank to the pit of her stomach, she buried her face into her hands, every time she closed her eyes she could see Sabah's face smiling and kicking her legs. The vision made her break into tears. She didn't care if she was in a public place, at least no one knew her. A lady sat next to her trying to offer her comfort by handing her a tissue. Forcing a smile back at her she accepted the tissue, each time she tried to stop her tears, her heart welled up more. Taking deep breaths didn't seem to heal the missing attachment. Elaynna cried all the way to her college, by then her head felt like it had been hit by a hammer, the crying physically drained her. Before she went to her lesson, she quickly splashed water on to her face in the toilets, checking her reflection in the mirror. The whites of her eyes had turned to a bloodshot red; she tried to splash them with cold water to bring the redness down. She didn't want to go into her class with bloodshot eyes and be asked numerous questions about what was wrong and be set off again.

All of a sudden the thought of Mariam came to her mind, hoping she would be in her class room; maybe she knew how to make her feel better.

The reminder of Mariam made her want to quicken her steps to her class. A last look in the mirror to check her eyes. She went closer to the mirror to check properly; her eyes were still bright red. I will just have to look down when I walk into my class, she thought. Walking into her class, she saw many new faces and a bigger class. She sat in the same spot she had usually sat in, in a way she was grateful for the new faces in her class, if there were her old class mates they would have come up to say hello and ask what was wrong.

Mariam came in five minutes later walking in with Mary Jane. Mariam looked at Elaynna giving her a big smile; Elaynna felt her presence, she looked up and returned her smile. Both were excited to talk to each other about their summer.

"Hi darling how are you!" Mariam came over quickly embracing her. They both squeezed each other so tightly, not wanting to let go. Mariam looked into Elaynna's eyes, a sense of worry crossed her mind,

"Whats wrong Elaynna? why are your eyes so red?" Elaynna took a deep breath holding back the fresh new tears that were about to overflow.

"Alright class, please settle down so we can begin!" Mary Jane interrupted when Elaynna was about to open her mouth. "I will tell you later in our lunch break." She managed to whisper.

The morning lesson was a struggle for both of them, impatient for their lunch break.

The bell sounded off; Mary Jane asked both of them to stay behind. While everyone left, Mary Jane went over to their table to talk to them. "I hope you can see that the rest of the class has moved up and only you two are left behind?" they both nodded at the same time. "Don't worry, I am not having a go at you two, I am just asking if there is any extra help you would like so you can move up this year? Especially you Mariam, you speak English so well, I don't understand how you failed last year and this year? Do you love me so much that you don't want to leave my class that you fail on purpose?" She winked at Mariam.

Mariam wanted to say yes, instead she laughed at her joke telling her she will try better this year, even though there was some truth in Mary Jane's words.

When they reached the canteen, Mariam held Elaynna's hand letting her pour her heart out to her. Mariam, moved by Elaynna's full on summer couldn't help welling up. When she finished telling Mariam everything, Mariam squeezed her hand and told her to be grateful that now she had a little sister to share the love she wanted to share with her mother. Elaynna nodded, finding comfort in Mariam's words. Reminding her that was the reason why she was so upset, from being away from her.

"Elaynna, stop being silly, now you will have something to look forward to everyday after college, Sabah will be waiting for you to come home. Being away a little will make your bond stronger, and I promise it will get easier to leave in the mornings." Elaynna wiped her tears, feeling lighter already.

Elaynna then let Mariam tell her of her summer. Mariam told her how she terribly missed Elaynna, being locked indoors for most of the summer. Her son and daughter in law made plans to go on holiday without the kids and left the children with her. That was the best week she had, she was free to do what she wanted and was able to take the children out to enjoy outings in the park, her son had left her some money to spend freely. However when her daughter in law returned the abuse continued, Mariam pulled up her sleeve to show her her arm of how she burned her arm while making rotis, her daughter in law walked by on purpose and pushed her onto the hot pan. Mariam said all her son could say was to be careful next time without looking at the extent of the burn.

"What wrong have we done to others Mariam that we are treated like this?" Elaynna asked looking down at her food, she had lost her appetite. All of a sudden she remembered something. "My grandmother taught me that when you are patient then Allah is always with you and he rewards you immensely later in life." Mariam appreciated the words of wisdom, telling her that her grandmother must be very wise.

It was true what Mariam said, Elaynna did have something to look forward to going home, feeling extremely excited to see her little sister. Elaynna had to come and go alone to college now her brother's timetable had changed. Elaynna bounced at the bus stop like she wanted to go for a wee.

"Come on bus, come on bus . . ." she kept saying under her breath. When the bus arrived she jumped on as quickly as she could, tapping her fingers on her books all the way home. To an onlooker it would look like she was tapping out of nervousness, but she was tapping to reach home as quick as time would take her.

When her stop came she jumped out running down the street. Her emotions changed as her steps took her quickly to her door. Out of breath she rang the doorbell Yasmin opened the door, quickly exchanging greetings. Elaynna ran past her looking for her little sister. Her eyes traced the living room, and then she realized she must be sleeping, it was time for her nap.

"Whats wrong? Are you ok?" Yasmin looked at her oddly, knowing really what she was looking for.

"Nothing, I was just looking for Sabah, is she ok?" Yasmin smiled reassuringly telling her she was asleep. "Was she ok? Did she miss me?" surprised at the words that came out of her mouth, she worried her mother would plonk her one. Yasmin actually found it quite amusing her inquiring like she had kept her in *her* stomach for nine months.

"Obviously shes OK. She was with her mother, and yes she did miss you." Those words made Elaynna feel a lot better, like a heavy burden had been taken out of her heart. The noise of Sabah's cry echoed down the stairs; the door bell had woken her.

Without a glance back to her mother, Elaynna ran up the stairs to check on her. Sabah seemed to have sensed Elaynna's presence in the room, smiling at her when she picked her up. Elaynna kissed her all over holding her in her arms tightly. Laying her back down for a nap, but now that Sabah had Elaynna she wouldn't settle back to sleep.

Instead Elaynna decided to let her play and checked her nappy. Yasmin walked in observing the bond of the two sisters.

There was definitely a difference in the way Sabah showed her preference to Elaynna compared to Yasmin. Yasmin ordered Elaynna to watch Sabah while she prepared dinner. Elaynna feeling grateful for this continued to play with her. Making funny faces at her, trying to make her laugh, she was only a month old, too young to giggle yet.

After dinner, Elaynna was told to tidy up and Yasmin took Sabah to bed with her. Now that she was back at college Yasmin told her she would do the night feeds. Elaynna insisted she didn't mind, any time with Sabah was priceless to her, be it day or night. Yasmin shook her head, "Your Abu would highly disapprove of it, and if you fail again he would say it's my fault. He already blames me that because of me you failed, I don't want to upset him further."

That was the first night Sabah slept in Yasmin's room, in the last three weeks, Elaynna would take Sabah into her room when she woke up once in the night. Having the Moses basket beside her bed made her feel more close to her. Elaynna tossed and turned that night she couldn't sleep. At two in the morning she heard Sabah cry for her feed. Yasmin tumbled out of bed, holding her screaming on her shoulder. Elaynna usually kept a thermos and a bottle for Sabah's feed for when she woke up in the night, when she woke up she would quickly place the made up bottle in hot water cuddling her, singing her lullabies while it warmed up to the right temperature. This would help her settle back to sleep within five minutes and no one heard her crying in the night.

But tonight her screams were being heard all over the house, waking everyone up. Yasmin waited for the water to warm up not knowing how to settle her back even after the feed.

"Elaynna! Elaynna! Please take her from me before I kill her!" shouted Yasmin from the kitchen. Elaynna ran out of her room without her slippers. The cold floor didn't bother her when she ran to the rescue of her sister. As soon as Sabah was in Elaynna's arms she calmed down instantly falling asleep within minutes. Yasmin shocked and confused at what she was seeing didn't know what to say.

"Ammi, if you are tired I can let her sleep in my room just in case she wakes up again so she doesn't disturb your sleep." Yasmin nodded rubbing her eyes going back to bed leaving the Moses basket outside her room.

The following morning, Abdul asked what happened the night before, Yasmin sarcastically told him that Sabah would not settle without Elaynna's magic touch. Abdul laughed and proudly said that his daughter had a magic touch in everything that she did. Yasmin upset at his comment spent the rest of the day shouting and abusing Elaynna, the same cycle of making her do everything began again in the house. This didn't bother Elaynna anymore, as soon as she saw Sabah's beautiful smile she forgot everything.

It amazed her that the little love and attention that she got from her little sister made her whole world a beautiful place to live in, it gave her the strength to do everything apart from doing her homework.

Mary Jane was getting impatient with Elaynan's lack of interest and incomplete homework, doing worse this year. Elaynna was always tired in class, but when she got home her energy seemed to come back in an instant.

By now Sabah was six months old and learning to eat. She no longer woke up in the night anymore this helped Elaynna to get a full night's sleep. Her father bought her a little cot that was now kept in Elaynna's room. There was barely enough room for it. He showed her how she could pull the sides down to make it easier to lift her up. For that Elaynna decided to keep one side down in the night so they could hug each other before falling asleep. In the morning Elaynna would lift the sides up before she left for college; she would take out the prepared meals to defrost for her mother to feed Sabah with.

Horror hit Elaynna one day when she came home from college. Yasmin was burning with fury holding a stick in her hand. Beside her were her brothers Rahim and Kareem, Elaynna looked at them questionably as well as worryingly, she was in trouble for something her senses picked up on the negativity, but she could not put her mind to what had she done? Yasmin stared at her like she was possessed with an evil spirit. Taking one step at a time, walking slowly into the living room, Elaynna tried to figure out what was wrong, the fear on her face grew for every step that she took.

Yasmin got up and grabbed her hand forcing her to sit down. "So why do you go to college? To talk to boys?" confused at the accusation, Elaynna looked to her brothers for help. Both looking down at their feet,

"I don't know what you mean?" Elaynna protested trying to free her hand. "Kareem told me everything, he saw you talking to an Afghani boy outside of your college. Tell me who the hell is he? What is your relation to him?" Elaynna trying to remember what was she was talking about, as soon as she remembered, before she could defend herself. Yasmin whacked her hand with the stick. Elaynna cried in pain, "He is just a new boy in the class!" she screamed in pain.

"Oh really so you have become friendly with him? That's why you so happily go to college, to show your beauty to Asian boys? I am so disappointed in you!" Elaynna tried to protect herself while she was constantly being hit with the stick, it was no use. To her dismay, Kareem had gone home to tell their mother, rather than to ask her who he was. Elaynna knew that even if she were innocent no body would believe her, they never did. It was a punishment for a crime that was an innocent talk for a minute. A new classmate was asking where their class was he had lost his way, he had also called her sister, did not even dare try to flirt with her.

Elaynna's tears and suffering meant nothing to her brothers; Kareem a brother whom she respected and trusted, how could he betray her in this way?

"You will no longer go to college! I am so disappointed in you! Let your father come so I can tell him what his precious little daughter is getting up to! And he blamed me for your failing, when you go there to talk to boys!" Yasmin drew saliva spitting on her face.

Every time Elaynna tried to speak, her mother slapped her mouth shut. The noise of the shouting and hitting made Sabah cry, the noise frightened her, seeing her big sister upset didn't help her either. "Take that little brat out of here Kareem!" Kareem picked up Sabah quickly rushing out.

With bruised hands Elaynna dragged her feet to her room, huddling her knees against her chest, Elaynna rocked herself back and forth crying uncontrollably. Her hands trembled with pain every time she tried to wipe her tears.

That night Elaynna wasn't offered any dinner, left alone in her room crying. The front door opened with Abdul entering the house carrying the shopping, he sensed something was wrong due to the atmosphere of the house.

"Whats wrong? Why does it seem like someone died in here?" trying to make everyone laugh. Yasmin told him what Kareem witnessed, Abdul quite furious for the fact that Kareem told their mother and not him first, he also asked what Elaynna's answer was. Everyone remained quiet realizing that Elaynna wasn't given the chance to speak.

"Go get your sister; I want to talk to her." Rahim went running upstairs; he knocked on the door, walking in without the permission to enter.

The room was dark with the curtains shut, Elaynna was huddled up in one corner of her room; only the noise of her sniffling could be heard. Rahim felt guilty he hadn't done anything to defend her, he didn't bother to ask her what had actually happened. He was quite confused at what Kareem had told their mother, he never saw Elaynna talk to anyone apart from her friend Mariam.

"Elaynna, Abu is here, he wants to see you." Elaynna got up without looking at him, she was fed up of life treating her this way. Abu is probably going to beat me as well, he won't be interested in the truth, no body is, she said to herself. Leaving her room in a no care attitude she slowly walked down the stairs to the living room. Elaynna stood in front of him like a criminal standing in front of the judge waiting to hear her further punishment for the interrogation had been done.

"What am I hearing Elaynna? How could you break my trust like this? Who is that boy?" Abdul asked her wearily, Elaynna without looking up answered in a low voice. "He is a new boy in my class, he was asking for the way to the classroom, he can't speak English and I was the only one he could communicate with in his broken Urdu. All I did was show him the way . . ." Abdul looked at Yasmin furiously after he saw the state of Elaynna's hands. "She is lying! Kareem said she was smiling whilst talking to him." Elaynna protested, "I was only being nice . . . He called me sister." Yasmin's rage grew again. "Oh so now you have answers eh? Abdul this is the reason why she is failing, she goes to college to impress boys!"

Abdul told Yasmin to stop talking. "Oh so now you are trying to make me keep quiet when I am speaking the truth? Truth hurts doesn't it Abdul? I don't care she will no longer go to college! If you don't listen to me I will no longer stay in this house!" Yasmin commanded without pausing.

Abdul tried to defend his daughter but it was no use. "What will she achieve staying at home?" he asked her trying to keep his voice down. "I don't care Abdul I cannot put my and your respect at the risk of her being seen with a boy. I can make her achieve a lot staying at home that is my problem not yours!" Abdul was getting annoyed with Yasmin's disrespect in front of the children. He felt helpless; he knew he could not argue further, there was no point.

From that night on Elaynna's education was put on hold once again. Elaynna wished she had at least one more to day to go to see Mariam for the last time.

A week later, Mary Jane called asking for Elaynna. Abdul was home that day, he informed her she will no longer be coming to college, Mary Jane said it would be nice if she could come just to collect her things. Abdul agreed promising to send her on the following Monday. When Abdul told Elaynna this, she was confused as to what things she had left at college when she used to bring her books home everyday.

When Monday arrived and Elaynna headed to college to get her things, Yasmin gave her an angry look when she got ready to leave for college. Elaynna ignored her quickening her steps to leave.

When she reached college she hurried into class, Mary Jane welcomed her telling her to sit down. Confused to what she was being told to do, she sat down next to Mariam while Mary Jane told the rest of the class to carry on copying the board. Mary Jane then asked Mariam to take Elaynna out in the hallway. They both walked out, Elaynna worrying what had happened.

"Why have you not been in college? Is everything ok? I asked Mary Jane to call your house and to get you here somehow so I could talk with you." Elaynna felt relieved at this, her wish had come true of being able to speak to Mariam for the last time.

"I got in trouble for a crime I didn't commit . . ." she started.

"Kareem saw me talking to the new Afghani boy in our class, you know Rasheed? All he did was ask me the way to the class a week ago, Kareem had come into college to fill in a form for his new course. He went home that day and told Ammi that I was talking to boys at college, so she said I wasn't allowed to got to college anymore." Elaynna finished looking down, wanting to cry again reliving the way she had been treated. Mariam's eyes saddened all of a sudden, her best friend would no longer be able to come to college anymore.

"Oh, I am ever so sorry to hear that . . ." Mariam started, trying to keep her tears in her eyes, not letting them to overflow. "I was hoping to come to see you for the last time, and you somehow arranged that, thank you so much." They both looked at each other in a worried way, Mariam finally plucked up the courage to speak again even though her chest was tightening with sadness. "All I want is for you to be happy." She then took out a paper to write her contact details. "This is my number and address, call me or come over when you can." Elaynna looked at her with trembling lips and started to cry. Mariam wiped her tears and held her close.

"I don't know what I will do without you . . . I will probably die with depression." Mariam rubbed her shoulder and said she wouldn't die of depression; she had Sabah, now at least she could be with Sabah twenty four hours a day.

This reassured Elaynna, that was how she had been coping. Then she wondered what she will tell her mother what she left at college, she didn't bring any of the college material with her. The same words came out of her mouth after thinking this.

"Not to worry, Mary Jane will give you some old books to take home." Elaynna felt relieved after hearing this. "I think I better make a move then, or I will get in more trouble if I take too long." Mariam nodded, and asked Elaynna to stay in the hall way while she got the old books from Mary Jane. Mary Jane came out with Mariam and gave Elaynna a big hug wishing her all the best. Mariam had told her she will be going to another college soon, she knew if she didn't say that, the college could further investigate and her parents will get in trouble.

CHAPTER 24

When Elaynna went home that afternoon, her mother made her wash all the windows of the house, she then made her cook dinner and clean out all of the cupboards. Sabah followed Elaynna around everywhere, seeing her little innocent face helped Elaynna carry on with her work without any complaints. When she retired to her bed that night, she lit a candle so she would not wake Sabah in the dark, she looked through her work, her hands fell on the first piece of homework she ever did.

Scanning it from top to bottom, her mind went back to that evening of how excited she was having the chance being able to learn again, the pressure of the household and no help from anyone made it difficult for her to learn. She sighed blowing her candle lying back to bed with moistened eyes.

Her eyes fell on Sabah's deep relaxation, she wished she was that little again so she could start her life all over again; the urge to trade places with her sister was strong. If she could start again she would concentrate in school and learn how to read and write and get an important job, something that her mother would highly approve of.

Then it occurred to her that no matter what she was to do to impress her mother, she hardly showed any appreciation.

Elaynna fell asleep watching her little sister slow rise and fall of her body in the dark. This soothed her to sleep, until she was awoken at 6am to do all the cleaning and to prepare breakfast. Her father looked at her worryingly, feeling helpless not being able to do anything for his beloved daughter.

One day one of Yasmin's friends Nilofar came for a visit. While Elaynna was washing the dishes in the kitchen, Sabah crawled in, the opening of the door helped Elaynna to hear of the conversation that was going on between the two women.

"You can't just let Elaynna sit at home after that incident. How will she learn about the world and learn how to deal with people." Elaynna picked up Sabah putting her ear close to the living room.

"I don't trust the men out there Nilofar, Elaynna already broke my trust, and then Abdul blamed me for her failing."

Nilofar mumbled, "If you won't let her educate herself she will stay a door mat and not learn anything new. Why don't you let her get a job?" Yasmin gave her an aggravated look.

"A job? Oh well done an even better place for her to disobey me." Nilofar put her hand on Yasmins thigh and whispered. "Look if you let her work, she will come home and hand her salary to you, she will earn money and you can spend it as you please." This made Yasmin to consider the deal opening up her cunning side.

"You can also start to put some of the money aside, so when she is of marriageable age you can use that to pay for her wedding jewelery, your life will be so much easier." Yasmin started to like the idea of Nilofar's suggestion.

"What about Abdul, how do I convince him?" Nilofar looked left and right to make sure no body was listening, although there was no body there, she put her voice even lower so that even the walls could not hear it. "Already Abdul is broad minded, he argued with you to let her go to college, when you suggest the idea of independence to him I am sure he won't say no. Also Abdul has lots of links; he can get her a job in a factory or something." Elaynna walked in purposely to check if there were any other dishes left, pretending she didn't hear anything. "Elaynna the pakoras that you made were great, thank you." Nilofar said kindly. "You are most welcome." Elaynna responded, taking the tea cups away into the kitchen, holding Sabah with the other arm.

Elaynna took Sabah upstairs to play with her, not wanting to eavesdrop anymore. Yasmin and Nilofar carried on their conversation. "That is a great idea Niloo, I hope it works." Niloafar smiled and whispered again, "of course it's a good idea, that is what one of my other friends does with her daughter."

That evening while retiring to bed Yasmin pulled out the subject of letting Elaynna to get a job. "I was thinking that we should maybe let her work . . ." Abdul looked at her curiously. "Let who work?" Yasmin realizing she started in a mid sentence. "Elaynna . . ." Abdul then changed his expression from a curious look to a surprised one. "Oh so you think she will be safe if she worked? You have been against her going to college and now you think it will be suitable for her to go out and work. You really are something sometimes." Abdul tried really hard not to get angry.

"Look, I feel bad as it is for spoiling her education, rather than letting her waste her time don't you think it will do her some good to earn some money for herself and her future? She will learn how to deal with people. What will she learn from staying at home?" Abdul thought that Yasmin was talking some sense for once.

"But where will she work? She has no experience." Yasmin pondered at that and then made the suggestion that she work in a women only environment.

"I am sure you have some links where she can work in a factory or something? A more ladies only place?" Abdul thought for a second and then realized that one of his friends worked in a sewing factory, which sewed curtains and bedsheets. That factory had mainly women working in the whole factory only some men who were supervisors and managers. His friend Shoaib was a manager there; he could try talking to him.

"I will speak to my friend Shoaib tomorrow. I am sure he can help." Yasmin excited that her husband was listening to her again; she slept peacefully after a long time imagining all the money that Elaynna would be bringing in so she could spend freely. Abdul had always questioned her before giving her any money; she hated having to explain what the money would be for and not being able to shop for other than necessities.

The following evening Abdul told Yasmin that he had somehow secured a job for Elaynna in the sewing factory, she would have to start in two weeks. Yasmin was surprised at the efficiency of her husband's contacts; it never seized to amaze her that whether they were in Pakistan or London Abdul had many good contacts who were willing to do anything for him. What was it that he had that everyone instantly loved about him? She wondered.

Now all she had to do was to convince Elaynna, which she knew wouldn't be a problem. It then occurred to her that she had to be nice in order to get her salary from her; a little sweetness would go a long way she thought. While Elaynna was finishing up the house work and putting Sabah to bed her mother came into her room uninvited. "Elaynna, beta . . ." Elaynna paused in her steps, hearing her mother call her so lovingly made her overwhelm, she hadn't been talking to her properly since the college incident. Elaynna got up instantly replying, "Ji Ammi ji . . . ." Yasmin pleased at her daughter's pleasant reply. "Well since you have proven to me that you were innocent in what happened at college, I have decided to let you go and get a job. I spoke to your father and he has arranged a job for you in a sewing factory, which will be starting in two weeks. Is that alright with you?"

Elaynna worried about what the work will be like, hadn't she had enough work to deal with already, "Well? Its up to you, it will give you a good chance to make some friends, and be independent, buying what you please . . ." friends, thought Elaynna, the only good friend she had, had been taken away from her, she was too frightened to get close to anyone again for the fear of losing them.

Her only friend right now was her little sister, who would listen and smile at her all day. "Whatever you want Ammi ji, I will do it." Elaynna accepted the proposal.

Over the next few weeks Yasmin would communicate with Elaynna more to gain her trust. Those two weeks of her age of seventeen were the most special to her, her mother was normal like other mother's were with their daughters. Her mother had stopped neglecting Sabah as well. She was now expressing more love to Elaynna and Sabah than to the boys. Elaynna even got compliments from her mother for the first time this made Elaynna yearn to be closer to her mother like she had been with her grandmother and Mariam.

Her brothers were too busy with studying and doing the newspaper rounds to notice. When Kareem heard that Elaynna was getting a job he tried everything in his power to stop it. Elaynna couldn't believe how much he had changed from being so understanding to being so narrow minded. Elaynna told him it was their mother's decision and to take it up with her. Although Rahim was quite supportive of her getting a job, he believed it will giver her more confidence and self esteem as an individual. When Kareem did take it up with their mother, Rahim and Elaynna were confused as to what she had said to him that he calmed down not bothering again.

The first day of the new job arrived, when she was leaving the house her mother gave her a kiss on the cheek and a hug. This brought tears to Elaynna's eyes, for this affection she was willing to do whatever it took.

The factory was local, it was a twenty minute walk there, her father showed her the way, and she was to go straight to reception. If she was ever lost she was to ask for Mr Shoaib, as much as she wanted her father to come with her she felt his work was more important than to be escorting her to work. Elaynna's legs trembled when she walked through to reception, there was a plump round English lady sitting at the admin, she had a suit which looked like it had raspberry jam on the breast of it.

"Hello Miss how may I help you?" she asked Elaynna in a friendly voice. "My name Elaynna, I come work, my first day." The lady looked at her up and down, with a smile she checked through some paperwork. "Oh Elaynna Aziz? Yes yes Mr Akhter told me about you. His office is on your first right. It will have his name on the front."

To Elaynna's delight she still remembered some English; she was able to communicate enough to ask for things and to introduce her self. She understood what the receptionist told her, she was to take a right turn to see Mr Shoaib.

Elaynna walked clutching her handbag tightly, and nervously knocked on the door that read

MR SHOAIB AKHTER. "Please come in," was the reply. A man clean shaved, wearing a suit sat at the table, he was in his fifties. Younger than her father, he had a wide broad face with dark brown eyes and black hair. The suit he wore had brackets on the side, his navy jacket hanging over his chair. "Aslaam Aleikum, you must be Elaynna, do come in." He spoke to her in Urdu.

Elaynna walked to the desk looking down. "Please don't be shy, please sit down. I know your father very well he is a great man. He was always there to help me, so I could not turn him down when he asked if there was a job available." Smiling at Elaynna waiting for a response, she continued to look down and nodding her head in agreement. He got up to show her the factory; she could smell a whiff of cologne when he walked past her. "Please let me show you the way. I have decided that your job will be to do the packaging, as you can't sew." Elaynna responded again with a nod.

He held the door open for her like a gentleman and took out a cigar from his pocket. Elaynna's jaw opened when she saw how big the factory was, it was never ending. There was so much more than just sewing. He introduced her to her co workers along the way, no surprise she was the youngest one there, there was also many Asian women working there. This helped Elaynna feel relieved that she wouldn't find it too hard to communicate and make new friends. They welcomed her warmly; her working partner was a lady in her thirties, an Indian lady who was a single mother. Her name was Poonam.

"Elaynna just get comfortable, Poonam will show you what to do." Elaynna was left again in a strange environment, but it was worth the love she would be getting from her mother later.

"Hi, my name is Poonam, you speak Hindi?" Elaynna smiled and nodded answering in Hindi. "Yes I can speak Hindi, its not much different to Urdu. My name is Elaynna." Poonam welcomed her and introduced herself. Elaynna felt sorry for her that she had to work so hard to provide for her children, her husband had died at such a young age, being left to look after her children by her self. Elaynna introduced herself and asked about the work place.

"Its not bad, we are a nice community here, a little bitching goes on but there will be that wherever there are will be lots of women right?" Poonam tried to make her laugh.

"I will look after you, don't worry, we have the most responsible job so we have to be careful how we pack or the reputation of the company gets a bad name." Elaynna nodded, pretending to understand. Poonam showed her the big steam iron that pressed all the sheets and curtains, then she showed her the card boards in which she was to wrap between them and then to pack them in plastic sheets, and adding the sticky company's label on. This wasn't so hard, thought Elaynna, looking fun and easy. Her first few hours went by quickly, Poonam was amazed at the pace that Elaynna worked.

They got through a lot in the first four hours of the day. It used to take more than a whole day to get that many done. Poonam tried to look for mistakes, but there were none to her amazement. "Wow! Elaynna I am so happy to have you in my team! At the rate that you are working you will get a months work done in a week!" Elaynna felt her cheeks burn with embarrassment.

"I have always been good at learning physical work; I am quite slow when it comes to reading or writing . . ." she mumbled just enough to be heard, without realizing it she had admitted her flaw. "Well at least you are good at something, I am good at nothing, it takes me ages to learn, what you did today, it took me a week to learn to do it properly. Let's go and have some lunch." She nudged her, on her way she showed her the lockers and the canteen. The canteen was full of women gossiping away, the aroma of different foods reached

Elaynna's nostrils, she could smell chicken, alu gobi, potatoes, cheese and onion, all sorts of smells.

Elaynna found a seat right at the end of the canteen, the women all looked up at her like she was famous, they were really bad at pretending to not to stare. Chatting away loudly, she could hear one woman complaining about her mother in law, another about her husband and a third talking about her weekend. The noise deafened her thoughts. Poonam sat across her, telling her to eat quickly they only had a thirty minute lunch break and a tea break mid afternoon.

Poonam's skin was slightly dark in colour compared to her own, she had medium lips and small oval eyes with a perfect nose. Her jawline was wide, she was rather attractive. Her skin looked really soft to look at, Elaynna wondered what it would feel like to touch. She quickly ate her lunch of the left over spinach curry sandwich that her mother prepared for her especially. She had placed some bits of cheese and cucumber in there. It's a pleasant taste, thought Elaynna. Food always tasted nicer when it was prepared by someone else.

The pips went for the lunch break to end; everyone scraped their chairs rushing to get back to work. "Elaynna there is the room to make tea in your tea break. Mr Akhter is so kind, he always has a nice selection of biscuits to have with our tea. I will show you later." Walking back to their packaging room, Elaynna looked at the time she couldn't believe it was 1pm already. Her day was flying by, on the way back she tripped over a bit of material falling onto a really fat lady, whom looking at you could not distinguish whether she was a male or a female.

"Hey watch where you are going you blind bat!" she spat pushing Elaynna to her feet. "I am so sorry, ever so sorry." Elaynna pleaded. The loud croak of her voice had frightened Elaynna, fortunately Poonam was with her. "Hey it was an accident, be nice! It's her first day; she is only a little girl." The woman gave her a pathetic look and ignored her.

"Please be careful when you walk through here, it can be very dangerous. You could have slipped on someone and got their hands sewn!" whispered Poonam to Elaynna. "Once there was an accident when the factory newly opened, someone like you accidentally fell on another woman while she was sewing and her hand got caught in the machine, her foot forcefully remained on the pedal riding over her hand like a saw . . . so please be careful . . ." Elaynna shocked hearing about the incident, asked what happened after that.

"Well an ambulance was called of course and she was taken into A and E, her hand was never the same again. It cost the company a great deal of insurance." Poonam finished the story when they reached back to their room.

Elaynna worked swiftly as she had done earlier in the morning. Mr Akhter came to check on her before tea time, really impressed with the neatness and swiftness of Elaynna's work on her first day. He examined each package; there was not one mistake, "Mashallah, Elaynna! You have done so well! I am so impressed with your work on your first day. How did you do this so well?" Elaynna fell silent not sure what to say, then uttered her first dialogue to Mr Akhter.

"It was all of Poonam's great support and well teaching." Poonam felt touched at her words, they had just met, and Elaynna was giving her credit rather than taking it all onto her self.

"Oh so you do talk? I thought you were mute!" Mr Akhter teased her. Elaynna went red in the face with embarrassment. Thankfully he left straight away after giving Poonam a thumbs up, she didn't want him to see her blushing.

"Come its time for our tea break, I think we can relax longer as we have done more than we needed to." Poonam then held her hand leading her to the tea room, she didn't want her to be having any accidents again, or it would be costly. Elaynna was grateful for Poonam's presence when they had to walk through the sewing room again.

The lady she had fallen on earlier gave her a dirty look growling at her like a hungry dog when they walked pass. Elaynna instantly looked away pretending she didn't notice.

When they reached the canteen, it was just the two of them. Their voices echoed walking through the empty space. "Come . . . come let me show you where we have our break." Poonam opened the door to the tea room; there was a small utility room. It had a kettle, a toaster and a microwave as well as a small fridge with a small sink.

Poonam poured some water from the tap into the kettle and put the kettle on. She showed her the tin of biscuits that had an assorted mixture. Elaynna was beginning to warm up to Poonam already, she was very caring towards her on her first day. Poonam placed the biscuit tin opened in front of her to pick out some biscuits. While Elaynna wondered which one to try "If you cant choose just bring the tin out we can have it opened in front of us while we sit."

Elaynna carried the tin out with her. Elaynna was feeling hungry again from the afternoon work; a cup of tea was just what she needed to brush the tiredness away. She picked out a bourbon biscuit and a custard cream dipping it into her tea.

A thought crossed her mind wanting to ask about the fat lady who was mean to her earlier, wondering if she would cause her any problem in the future.

"Poonam, that lady who was rude earlier; she won't cause any problem for me will she? Just that she looked at me in a scary way when we walked pass."

Poonam reassured her it was nothing to worry about. "She's just a bully, if she ever causes any problem just let me or Mr Akhter know; she envies anyone or everyone." Elaynna felt relieved that she had someone to look out for her. Another thought crossed her mind.

"How will I get paid? Does Mr Akhter pay us at the end of the day?" Poonam nearly spat her tea out laughing, noticing the innocence on Elaynna's face she stopped all of a sudden.

"Oh you are new to all this aren't you? Basically it will be paid into your bank account each month and we are given a pay slip that tells us how much we have earned that month." Elaynna knew nothing about what Poonam was telling her so she remained quiet pretending to understand. Thinking that her father had probably sorted it all out, he just hadn't told her yet.

As the bell went for the factory to close, Elaynna grabbed her possesions following the crowd to the exit. Walking out she heard a familiar croaky voice. "Oye! Clumsy girl! You better watch your back! You messed with the wrong person!" The fat lady walked off in the opposite direction sending chills down Elaynna's spine. Elaynna walked briskly home making sure that the fat lady did not see which way she went home.

CHAPTER 25

Elaynna reached home just after 5pm. Yasmin welcomed her with open arms and gave her a drink soon as she walked through the door. Sabah came crawling into her lap, Elaynna was so happy to see her she kissed her all over. Sabah giggled feeling ticklish from the kisses. Yasmin asked her how her first day of work was, Elaynna told her how well she had done that the manager was so proud of her.

Yasmin asked if she got paid. Elaynna told her what Poonam had told her, her co-worker. Yasmin nodded and said she will ask her father for the details. When Elaynna went to check the housework, surprisingly it was all done. Her mother told her to get some rest and then she can help prepare dinner later.

Elaynna skipped to her room with Sabah in her hand. They both played together while Elaynna changed and then they went downstairs to the living room to watch television until it was time to prepare dinner.

The following weeks went by ever so quickly whilst working at the new job. Elaynna worked really hard, her hard work paid off making her popular in the factory. Since she was able to quickly finish her work, the other co-workers would ask her for her help with their jobs. Due to Elaynna's efficiency and quick wit to learn the work the factory was benefiting so much that they were getting more orders than ever, work was always completed before their set targets.

Mr Akhter couldn't believe how much enthusiasm she had for her work. "She will go far one day; she has the abilities and matureness of a great leader." He told Poonam.

The day came for her first salary. Mr Akhter went around the building handing everyone their payslip. Elaynna opened it excitedly thinking she was to have cash in her envelope but all she saw was a payslip with her name and numbers on it. All she could read was her name and the amount she had been paid. Elaynna scratched her head, and realized she should ask her father, he always knew the answer to everything.

That evening when Abdul came home, Elaynna showed him her first payslip. He stroked her head saying how proud he was of her; Mr Akhter had told him what a great worker she was. Elaynna felt important for making her father proud of her, she asked what the payslip read. Abdul then went to the closet taking out her bank card and information. He explained to her what a bank was and gave her a card that she could use when she needed to take out money to buy something.

"You keep it Abu ji . . . What use is this to me." Abdul shook his head firmly, and told her he would rather die than to take his daughter's earnings. They were getting by well he was grateful for it. "It's your money you spend it as you please." Yasmin was waiting for him to say that so that Abdul would never interfere with the money that her daughter gave her.

The visions of how she would use the money crossed her mind. "I will show you at the weekend how to use the ATM to get the money out from the bank." Elaynna took her bank card trying to observe it.

"Keep up the hard work, you will go far." He told her folding his sleeves up to his elbows getting ready to wash to do his prayers.

Fortunately Elaynna was able to count and knew her maths up to a point being aware of the value of money. When she looked at her payslip she was amazed at the salary she had got for such an easy job. Even her mother was pleased that she got paid well for a first job, £750 after tax was not a bad income to them.

Elaynna didn't know what she should do with the money, looking at Sabah, she decided she will save her salary for her future and educate her well. The urge also rose into her heart to buy her some toys and new clothes.

After working out how the ATM worked, she asked her mother if they could go shopping. Ever since she came to the United Kingdom she didn't get the chance to explore any shops, she told her mother she wanted to buy Sabah some new clothes and toys. Yasmin agreed to take her at the weekend. Yasmin played the sympathy card. "You know your father doesn't ever give me any money, how am I supposed to go shopping. If I ever ask him he only gives me enough to buy what I say it is for."

Elaynna confirmed to her mother that her money belonged to her mother; she could have whatever she wanted from it.

"I would like you to give me £500 per month if that is ok Elaynna? It will help a lot with the things around the house and I can keep some aside for your marriage." Elaynna didn't question further agreeing to whatever her mother wanted from her.

The following weekend Yasmin took Elaynna to the local market. It was the biggest market that Elaynna had ever seen. She couldn't believe how colourful London was. In the two years she had come from Pakistan she had never experienced the shopping. Her mother told her that this was where she bought her groceries. There was a market stall for everything. Walking by each stall there was one more colourful than the previous one. Until they stumbled onto the children clothes stall, Elaynna saw a beautiful pink frock that she wanted to buy for Sabah as a gift. She asked for the price, "£10 madam, is it a special occasion?" Elaynna half understanding what the young slim man was asking. "Yes please one please." Was Elaynna's reply. "What size madam? How old is your little one?" Yasmin butted in and said they needed a size for a one year old. "Here you go madam have a lovely day." Walking on Yasmin bought a lot of things. She bought cardigans, make up and clothes for herself. Yasmin remembering the household decoration objects she had seen at Shabnam's house. A rug, frames with calligraphy, and some little household features were all bought.

By the time they got home they had lots of shopping bags, Elaynna also managed to buy a little toy doll for her baby sister. When they got home Rahim and Qasim were so excited to see the goods. They were surprised at the bags they saw, each hoping there was something in the bags for them. Yasmin took out the bag of fresh pastries.

Rahim and Qasim grabbed it like hungry cubs that were waiting for their lioness mother to return with a piece of meat. "I am sure I fed you before we left, why are you acting like hungry animals?" Kareem laughed at their behavior and being called hungry animals. "Oh shut up Kareem, you think you are so sensible all the time." Kareem walked off holding Sabah into the kitchen to get her a snack.

Yasmin carefully unpacked all of the interior items she bought to decorate the house with. Finding a place for each of them, the living room looked transformed with the rug and the mini features. "Aah, now my house looks inviting!" Elaynna agreeing that her mothers taste was elegant, the living room did feel warmer.

That evening when Abdul walked in, he thought he had walked in the wrong house. "Don't you like it?" asked Yasmin, when she saw his expression.

"Where did all this come from?" Abdul asked with a frown.

"Elaynna and I went shopping today. I had a little money saved up from what you had been giving me. I had been putting it together for some time." Elaynna stunned to hear her mother telling a bald face lie. She was tempted to but in but she knew that her mother would kill her. She didn't want to lose the new bond she had with her already.

"Hmm, I didn't know you were so good at saving." Abdul scratched his head looking impressed.

"I must say it does look a lot nicer in here now. Well done. Elaynna did you buy anything beta?" Elaynna still confused at her mothers lie didn't know what to say to her father. "Oh . . . I er . . . I just bought Sabah a dress and some toys." Abdul shook his head laughing. "Silly girl you should have bought yourself something too, first time you go out to the market and you buy nothing for yourself? You are a working girl now. You need to look after yourself. Maybe soon you will be promoted." Elaynna blushed at her father's compliments.

Later that evening it bugged her wondering why her mother had lied to her father. As much as she wanted to ask she couldn't bring herself to. Yasmin came into the kitchen while Elaynna was putting the dishes away about to leave for bed.

"Don't tell your father that you paid for the shopping today; you will understand what I mean when you get married yourself one day. No use telling these men everything." Yasmin whispered to her the way Nilofar was whispering to her six weeks ago. Elaynna nodded in fear, she could see her mother's eyes burning with threat looking deep into hers, even if there were no threatening words coming out of her mouth.

It pricked her heart to question her mother further, she felt like a stranger with changing personalities. Elaynna felt the urge to tell her that lying was a bad thing, Dadi always taught her to not to lie, it was a sin. But her mother was clearly getting away with it, and that too in front of the most spiritual person that Elaynna ever knew, Elaynna always thought that you could never get away with things in front of spiritual people. Whenever you spoke to them you had to be careful what you said, they could read into your soul. She thought her father had this sixth sense, clearly not.

Elaynna thought it was difficult to tell lies, but her mother was able to do this with no problem, her eyes didn't twitch once. At the age of seventeen she was struggling to learn the rights and wrong, she wished her grandmother was here. She always knew the answer to everything; she was wise having lived her life already.

That night Elaynna fell asleep crying again, she missed her grandmother so much that night. Who to follow and not to follow began to confuse Elaynna, nor could she read so she could gain knowledge from books. Her life was just work and work. That night she remembered her friend's, their words of warning that told her that she shouldn't be leaving school she will regret it one day. Today was her day of regret. Then she remembered how she had always been manipulated by her teachers, they would use her rather than to help teach her when she had difficulty understanding, they were all lies? The more she thought the more confused she became.

Months went by with Elaynna working and giving her mother her salary. From the money she had left, she would leave one hundred pounds to save for Sabah's future. The rest she started to use to cheer herself up with. From being taught to lie as the first lesson from her mother, Elaynna started to lie about being held back on work so she could go shopping and buy some new things for herself. A sense of style emerged within her, of wanting to look pretty.

She bought herself make-up and accessories. That feeling of independence made her so happy. The abuse from her mother died down for a few months when she gave her the regular payments each month. Elaynna felt relieved at this, if money was the answer for her to get peace and a closeness with her mother then she was prepared to do anything for that peace and quiet.

It was almost six months of her job when her mother told her off for spending her money so much on clothes and make up. "Who are you dressing up for? I thought there were no men in your factory? Who do you dress up for? You think I haven't noticed how you have started to wear make up every morning? I send you there for a lawful earning, not to flaunt yourself in front of everyone!" Elaynna ignored her feeling guilty when she didn't do anything wrong at all. How could she explain to her mother that she was growing up and was nearly eighteen? She had the right to do what she wanted. "Sorry Ammi." She would say to escape the further interrogation.

From that day on Elaynna started to apply make up when she got to work and rub it of on her way home. Yasmin lost her patience at times; she started to pressurize Elaynna when she got home to do all the housework, when she started the job in the beginning Yasmin wouldn't let her do a thing. Now that her mother had the money she needed to be more social. Yasmin started to socialize with her friends more by going to outings and meeting them at shopping centers.

When she was tired from all the shopping and eating all day she would shout at Elaynna to do the housework being tired from all the walking she had done.

Yasmin was careful to always return before Abdul got home, she knew he would disapprove of her going out so much. He didn't like many of her friends; he thought they were a bad influence on her. He knew this through various conversations from Yasmin like someone else was speaking through her; she was using words that were picked up from somewhere else. When he confronted her she shook her head and laughing it off saying he was being silly.

Elaynna was really starting to enjoy the company of her new friends at work. She developed a good social network, all of the women shouted Elaynna when she walked in, complimenting her sense of style spilling their gossip of the night before. Elaynna was still a bit of a door mat still doing what anyone asked her to; she didn't care if she was called that anymore either. When she helped other people it gave her a sense of meaning.

A year had almost passed and Mr Akhter increased her salary for all the hard work she put in. Elaynna kept this a secret from her mother, worrying that her mother would take more of her money. Mr Akhter wanted to promote her as a supervisor but because she was unable to read and write he had to withdraw his proposal.

"I am sorry Elaynna as much as I want you to be my supervisor, I can't offer it to you, and there is much paperwork to do and less physical work. I thought you could read and write that's why you were so good at everything. But never mind keep up the hard work. I will offer the post to Poonam, she has completed her GCSE's, like you said she trained you well." Those words pricked Elaynna's heart all day. Poonam is now going to be supervisor because she can read and write. She felt like kicking herself in the backside for not learning such a basic thing.

Everyone in the factory was literate, herself the only illiterate one. They had been wishing her well but the position had been given to someone else. Whenever the urge to learn arose inside her, something took that right away.

Elaynna remembered her taweez that night, which Jannat had given to her telling her what to do when she was in trouble. All she could ask was why was someone taking the reward for her hard work.

It hurt her that no matter where she tried to improve her life someone else always used her to their benefit and she was left behind as usual.

Suddenly she remembered her grandmother's words. That what Allah always does was for the best; she then realized that the promotion of supervisor for Poonam would help her greatly in bringing up her children. Realizing that Poonam's lifestyle was a lot harder than her own, she didn't have any children or bills to pay for. This thought made her feel instantly good in herself. Her loss was helping someone needy than herself. The more she thought about it the more she smiled to herself. God does work in mysterious ways. She thought.

The next day when Elaynna went into work, Poonam gave her a big hug of thank you, "This means so much to me Elaynna you can't imagine! Now I can give my children a better future by putting some money aside. Thank you so much Elaynna I wouldn't have done it without you!" Elaynna looked down fiddling with her scarf.

"Its OK, you deserve the supervisor role more than anyone else. Your children deserve more in life." Poonam then gave her another tight hug. Poonam's happiness warmed Elaynna's heart.

Slowly time flew by, Elaynna blossomed into a very beautiful woman. Mr Akhter couldn't help looking at her when she walked in to work every morning. Every colour would suit her skin. She looked after herself going shopping often. Her beauty was the one thing she prided in. It surprised her at how much compliments she received everyday when she wore something different.

"Your husband is going to be so lucky Elaynna! He will fall in love with you at first sight." They would tease her. She brushed off their teasing pretending she didn't want to get married.

But when she was alone she would imagine her ideal husband, she would marry a educated man with high values and religious qualities. Obviously he would have to be handsome to look nice next to her. On her 20th birthday she started to receive proposals from her father's close friends. Whenever she attended weddings or social gatherings with her mother she always got a proposal, Yasmin was surprised at the amount of proposals that were coming through.

Yasmin refused them, telling them that they were not looking for a son in law yet, she was still working and had many responsibilities. The thought of Elaynna leaving always made Yasmin worry that her money machine will end, and the freedom she was having now would also be taken away. Who will do the housework while she went out in the day to socialize with her new friends? Many thoughts like this worried Yasmin whenever she got a proposal.

"Why are you postponing her marriage? She is at the right age now. In Islam if you get a good proposal it's a bad omen to say no, because you are pushing away Allah's blessings, and then you don't end up with a good partner." Abdul questioned Yasmin one night.

"I am a mother, it's hard to let go of your eldest daughter. I am not ready yet." Abdul sympathized with her.

"Oh my darling, you know it is the way of life. It has to happen one day." Yasmin turned the light off without answering and went to sleep, refusing to discuss more, she knew she could do nothing about it.

A few weeks later Abdul told Yasmin he had found the perfect partner for their daughter.

"My childhood friend Rahman, you remember him? They live in Manchester; they have sent a proposal for Elaynna. I have asked them to bring their son so we can meet him properly. He said his son has his own business, he has a restaurant. Isn't that great? Where better to marry our daughter other than a family that we know so well!" Abdul exclaimed excitedly. Yasmin huffed pretending to be happy.

"So when are they coming?" she asked trying to act interested.

"In two weeks In shaa Allah. My friend Rahman is so organized he looked up in his diary and gave me the date for the weekend he is free. Otherwise he is busy for a good few months; he also has his own businesses to handle." Yasmin understood this was a good proposal, so she had to make another excuse in order to detour her marriage.

"Don't get too excited Abdul, you never know how people actually are until you live with them." Abdul nodded agreeing but then replied, "I lived with Rahman and have known him since we went to school together, we grew up together and I knew his family well, but I don't know why I just have a good feeling about this."

The following few weeks were like hell for Yasmin, dreading for the weekend for Rahman and his family to arrive. Yasmin took her emotions out on Elaynna; telling her she was lazy and useless. Elaynna confused at her mothers behavior tried to ignore her, she took Sabah to her bedroom to listen to her stories from school and let Sabah read to her, although she couldn't pick out the mistakes, but hearing her five year old sisters voice of being able to read always made Elaynna proud. Although she couldn't prevent her sister from her grammatical errors when reading, however she protected Sabah from their harsh mother, she didn't let her do anything other than to play and learn, she remembered how her mother used to always abuse her at the age of five. She remembered once when she was kneading the dough crouching on her knees, her grandmother was out, Elaynna remembered that she had kneaded the dough too thinly and made a mess on her clothes.

Yasmin pulled her away angrily slapping her hard across the face five times, telling her she was useless and to get out of her sight. That was the first time her mother lay a finger on her, getting worse each time she had made a mistake, to abstain from that Elaynna became obsessed to impress her mother. To this day she never understood why her mother was never happy, especially with her own flesh and blood.

Elaynna was informed about the proposal just a few days before, being reminded to look modest in front of them.

"Don't go wearing make up now, I don't want you looking desperate!" Yasmin hissed at Elaynna like it was her fault for being attractive.

The morning arrived when Rahman and his family were to come. Yasmin made Elaynna clean the house from top to bottom, also ordered to prepare lunch, they were coming all the way from Manchester so a feast was necessary.

Elaynna got more and more nervous as the hours on the clock changed, Elaynna totally exhausted by the time Rahman and his family arrived. Rahman came with his wife Balkees and their four children. The eldest was who Elaynna was to get married to, his name was Akram Ali. He came with two younger brothers Gulnawaz and Mukhtaar, and his youngest sister, Mahek. As soon as they entered they were welcomed nicely by her parents, Elaynna sneaked upstairs to change into the clothes she laid out for herself, her father had bought her a new dress just for the occasion. Something that her mother frowned upon, sneering at Abdul that he was wasting money for no reason.

Elaynna changed out of the curry smelling clothes feeling a new sense of energy when she put on the new shocking pink outfit. It had a beaded border with a matching dupatta, this was the first time she wore such a bright colour. She then combed her hair and put her hair in a puff with a French plait in a way that Poonam had taught her. After applying some moisturiser, she was urged to apply some make up. but after looking at her reflection she realized there was none necessary. The bright pink made her clear complexion glow. A knock on the door disturbed her thoughts, "Come in."

Her father walked in asking her to come to meet the family. "My, you look beautiful, come and meet your uncle Rahman, they are all dying to see you, they haven't seen you since you were five."

Elaynna put her dupatta on her head following behind after her father. Each step that she took following her father down the stairs, her nerves took over her. Stepping into the living room Rahman and his family all got up instantly to greet her. Elaynna kept her gaze down not meeting eye to eye with anyone; the heat of the room brought out a natural rose to her cheeks. Akram Ali couldn't take his eyes off her. He knew he wanted to confirm the proposal no matter what, he hadn't seen such a beautiful Pakistani girl. He thought to himself. Who was so elegant in her ways and shy in her presence, nowadays the girls were usually more robust and loud. From all the eligible girls he had seen, she was the first who was so shy. This was the quality he was looking for in a woman.

"So what do you do Elaynna beta?" asked Balkees, too shy to answer, her father answered for her saying that she had a good job in a local factory.

"Why? doesn't she speak?" Rahman joked poking Abdul on the arm.

"You know girls are shy, and my daughter is very shy. Elaynna beta go and get some drinks for the guests." Abdul ushered her out of the room. Elaynna returned with orange juice in enough glasses for everyone. As she walked around with the tray in her hand, she managed to get a glimpse of her future husband. He had black curly hair with dark eyes and a rough stubble beard. Elaynna found him very attractive; he came in a suit, looking very smart. Their gazes met when she handed him his drink, she looked away instantly not wanting to stare.

Later Elaynna laid out the lunch, Mahek and Sabah helped lay out the dishes for everyone.

"Elaynna has cooked everything, she is a fine cook." Said her mother, the first compliment in front of guests.

"Wow this pilaf is amazing Elaynna, you must give me the recipe." Balkees exclaimed after eating her first morsel. Everyone sat together to eat, the room was filled with the families.

Elaynna couldn't eat, she was too tired to eat from all the work she had done that day. The situation didn't help either. She just played around with her meal. Elaynna finally spoke when she asked Mahek to join her in her room to play. Mahek and Sabah followed obediently; Elaynna took the desert in later with the tea and then went to join the girls.

"Baji Elaynna you are the most beautiful girl I have ever seen. I wish I was as beautiful as you." Elaynna laughed at her compliment, "How old are you Mahek, tell me a bit about your family . . ." Mahek said she was eleven and that the whole family was a loving family, "My dad makes a special effort each weekend to be with us, he takes us bike riding, fishing and he also takes us to a lot of different places.

I hope you marry my brother." Elaynna laughed again at her blunt innocence.

She taught them a hand game they played in a circle. They laughed so hard until they were bursting for a wee. Abdul called Mahek to return to her father when they were leaving to go home.

"So . . . . Abdul tell me what your final answer? We love your daughter, but will your daughter like our son, more so do you like him?" Abdul smiled "Well I think I have no objection, as long as Elaynna says yes." Yasmin butted in, "We will decide an answer whether we want to say yes soon, all of sudden will be wrong." Rahman nodded saying he understood the dilemma.

Mahek came down telling her father she had had a great time. Adding if Elaynna could be her sister in law? They all laughed at her while leaving the house saying goodbye.

As they left Elaynna picked up the dishes, she overheard her parents talking in the living room. "Why did you tell them that Elaynna was illiterate?" asked Abdul sounding cross.

"They asked how much she was educated and I couldn't lie." Abdul shrugged in an annoying way. "Well at least Balkees is illiterate too, and she stood up for Elaynna when there was a bit of tense silence." Hearing her parents talk made Elaynna's old wounds come to surface again. Ever since she had started working, she had forgotten about her weakness. It saddened her to be reminded of it again. The little bout of confidence that had entered her today was drowned like an anchor thrown to the sea. Feeling she was a hard working donkey that knew nothing but work.

"Well Rahman said he will talk to his son and then they will decide if they will accept our daughter, he also wants us to think about it. I think I will say yes he is such a handsome boy with a good future laid in front of him." Yasmin mumbled under her breath wishing she could stop the alliance somehow.

"Well I think you are rushing into it. Let them get back to us first, we also need to talk to Elaynna if she is happy with the marriage or not." Abdul nodded in agreement. Elaynna felt happy to hear that her wishes would be granted, although it worried Elaynna what Akram Ali thought of her. It was down to him to decide if the marriage was to take place and then she would be asked if she was also happy to accept him. Deep down, Elaynna had fallen in love with him at first sight hoping he had felt the same, she did feel him look at her often and then to look away.

Abdul knocked on Elaynna's door as she was getting ready to sleep, without letting Elaynna to speak for permitting an entrance, Abdul entered her room.

"So beta what did you think of the boy? Do you like him?" Elaynna felt her cheeks burn up, she had never spoken to her father about such things.

"Abu ji why does it matter if I like him or not, I know that you will do the best for my future, so whatever you decide I am happy with." Abdul felt proud hearing this. "Actually it is very important that you like him, I liked your mother before we got married, and I fell madly in love with her as soon as I saw her. I know you are probably wondering why." Trying to laugh quietly so Yasmin won't hear him.

"But I haven't regretted my choice once, so if you like him you have to tell me now. You know why?" Elaynna confused at what her father meant, "Why?" Abdul smiled at her gazing deeply into her eyes.

"Because Rahman called me this evening to say they reached home safely, he said that Akram Ali has liked you and wants to marry you. So now I need to know now, what is your reply? Yes . . . or no?" Elaynna blushed even more, this time with happiness, "Come on I am waiting for your answer?" just then Yasmin walked in the door and stood in the doorway while Abdul asked her again.

"Whatever you want to do Abu ji, I will accept it, I have always trusted your decisions." Abdul smiled patting her head. "I will talk to Rahman tomorrow." Yasmin walked out with him knowing now that Abdul had got to Elaynna first there was no chance for her to stop the marriage.

That night Elaynna couldn't sleep with the joy of being accepted. She thought that Akram Ali would reject her because she was illiterate. He had seen beyond that and said yes to have her as his wife. This meant so much to her that it brought tears to her eyes. Finally she will be able to experience true love.

CHAPTER 26

The following morning felt so bright to Elaynna feeling excited about life. She couldn't help skipping when she was about to leave the house for work, she hadn't noticed her mother was watching. Yasmin pulled her on the arm forcefully when she opened the front door.

"No need to be so desperate, that's not how girls behave when their marriages are fixed. If you show that you are happy people will think you have no shame. I brought you up better than this!" she hissed.

Yasmin didn't realize how hard she was squeezing her arm until Elaynna howled in pain that she let go walking off in the opposite direction. Elaynna was brought to tears upon leaving the house, the tears streamed down her eyes like the River Thames while she walked down the street to work. Why was it so hard to be happy? Why did her own mother keep doing this to her? The moment she had little joy her mother would take it away like she was undeserving of it.

By the time she reached to work she quickly wiped her tears and walked in to her department, her friends were confused when she ignored them.

"Looks like she's had another fight at home." Poonam said to one of her friends. "Let me go talk to her." Poonam joined her in the room where they had first met. Poonam kindly bought her a cup of tea and a croissant; aware that Elaynna mostly left the house without breakfast.

"Whats the matter my darling? Did your mother say something to hurt you?" Elaynna ignored her trying to hide her sorrow. "If you won't tell me how can I make you feel better?" Elaynna wanted to scream and shout the pain she was feeling, but it was useless, she knew nothing good would come of it. She tried to bury all the hurt down in her chest.

"Elaynna what is the matter, come on, wont you tell me? I thought we were close?" Elaynna started to sulk in her hands, the pain had come to surface again, the pain in her arm reminded her more of the hell she had experienced in her life.

"Why does everyone hate me? What wrong have I done to this world to be treated this way?!" She screamed, Poonam had seen Elaynna upset before but never this upset. "Why whats happened?" Elaynna wanted to pour her heart out to someone before it would burst. But she had been holding on to this ever since she could remember. She had been taking all the abuse from her own like she was adopted.

"There was a proposal for me this weekend, and now the wedding is fixed." Poonam smiled thinking that Elaynna was upset because she didn't want to leave her family. However she was proved wrong.

"So you are upset that you will have to leave your family?" Elaynna shook her head asking her to shut the door. Poonam worryingly shut the door, and sat in front of her. Elaynna didn't know how the words came out of her mouth but they did. They came out in the order of

Qasim's birth to Akram Ali's proposal, her mother's continuous taunts, it hurt her when she saw her mother's friend's daughters treated completely differently compared to her self. Elaynna told her about the college, how she had lost her first good friend who was also abused by her family. And now when her life was stable again from giving her mother the requested amount each month, nothing changed.

Poonam gave Elaynna a big hug and wiped her tears, she held her close against her chest. The warmth of her chest soothed her torn heart. "Shhhh . . . ." Were the soothing words that came out of Poonam's mouth. "Its OK, its all OK . . . . nobody hates you." Poonam let Elaynna hold her and cry until she needed to. Five minutes later, Elaynna let go and wiped her tears feeling a whole lot better.

"Let me go get you some hot fresh tea, I will be back." Poonam being the supervisor was an advantage to Elaynna. It had been nearly two hours in telling Poonam her story. Poonam came back in with some fresh hot tea and Elaynna's favorite biscuits. "Now eat something and let me talk." Elaynna blew her nose and took a sip of her tea. The taste of the hot tea made her shiver, her whole body had gone cold from crying. She felt drained but lighter at the same time. "Elaynna I know you are a lovely person, but if you keep dwelling on the past you will never be able to move on. Now is your chance to make your life the way you want it to be. Akram Ali chose you because you are special. Let your mother be as she is, she must have some personal issues that she is taking out on you. But never mind, you have to be stronger, and focus on your wedding, and be happy for it."

Elaynna felt Poonam's words made sense. "Like you said you are close with your father and he has always been there for you, use him as your weapon. I am sure you mother will not be able to do anything to ruin your wedding. You just have to be the sensible one." Elaynna took in the wise words that Poonam tried to teach her.

"And look we all love you here at the factory .... why? Because you are a lovely person and very special to us! Because of you this factory has found its proper legs. So be proud of yourself. Also when you get married I want you to go and get yourself an education. Because education is one key that opens many doors of wisdom." Elaynna nodded saying. "Thank you."

As the weeks went by there were many visits from Rahman and his family, sometimes Abdul and Yasmin and Sabah went to Manchester, the families got to know each other more. Yasmin's jaws opened when she saw Rahman's house. He had built his own house designing it himself, it had many rooms and a swimming pool. Rahman never boasted about his wealth, he always said he was content.

His son had his own apartment where they will live when he got married, after a few months of staying with them of course.

Yasmin was impressed when she heard this; she couldn't believe her daughter's fortune starting to be happy for her.

A date was set for their wedding; they were to be married within six months. In the month of June, the month of perfect weather. When her father told her this she couldn't believe the wedding would take place so quickly.

"You will have to hand in your notice at your workplace Akram Ali doesn't want you to work. So now we have six months to prepare your wedding. We must call your grandmother to join us." After hearing the mention of her grandmother Elaynna wanted to jump leaps and bounds, she missed her so much.

A few weeks later Abdul said he had sorted out Jannats visa and she will be there the following week. Yasmin aghast as she was upon hearing her mother in law would be arriving soon, she had to fake her excitement, under all costs she could not let Abdul see her disapproval.

Elaynna kept her eyes on the door while she busied herself with her housework. Sabah even helped when Elaynna told her to not to. It suddenly occurred to her that what would happen to Sabah when she went to live in Manchester? Ammi will eat her alive like she made me do everything from that age, she worried. The distraction of her grandmother arriving made her snap out of her fears.

"Dadi!" she screamed running down the stairs to embrace her. They embraced each other so tightly, letting go until it cooled their hearts. Both overwhelmed in their reunion.

"Oh my . . . Elaynna you are a woman now! You have blossomed in to a beautiful woman, you were always beautiful but now I say you are stunning, God save you from the evil eye." Jannat then looked around looking for her second granddaughter. "Wheres Sabah?" Sabah sneaked out from behind her mother, coyly stepping forward. Jannat held her face and kissed each cheek, Jannat then stuck her tongue out at Sabah making her laugh. The night involved with lots of catching up and Jannats approval of the marriage. Elaynna watched her grandmother lovingly, trying to observe her, how her grandmother had aged, not because of old age itself, but because of their separation. She had stopped dyeing her hair, she had let it stay white, her bones sticking out showed her lack of appetite.

That night Elaynna slept on the floor of her room letting her grandmother sleep on her bed. Poonam's words came to her while she lay staring at the ceiling, good things were happening to her already, the maternal love of her life had returned, now everything was possible. Her mother wouldn't abuse her now that she had the protection of her grandmother. The sound of her grandmothers snoring helped to sleep peacefully for the first time in five years. Elaynna turned on her back looking up at her grandmother's face that glowed in the dark with the street lights shining into her room.

"I love you Dadi," she whispered under her breath dozing off to a deep sleep.

That night she had a dream that she was getting married to Akaram Ali, she wore a green dress and was having henna applied to her hands with all of her friends surrounding her. Lots of people arriving with many gifts, each one would come up to her to tell her she was the most beautiful bride that they had seen.

Her dream was disturbed when she had to wake up to the sun shining in to her room, ushering her to wake up. When she looked up at the bed, her Dadi was no longer there. Elaynna rubbed her eyes trying to rub the sleep out of them, she stumbled out of her room, the smell of parathas awoke her senses. Rushing to the bathroom, she quickly washed her face, eagerly running downstairs.

"Come beta come eat, look at you, you look like a stick! Working in a factory and then coming home to do the chores. I know what your mum is like." She had so badly missed her grandmother's parathas, she went over to her grandmother hugging her tightly from behind placing a kiss her on the cheek. "I missed you so much Dadi." Jannat tapped her cheek with watery eyes, "Now come on go and eat." slowly everyone woke up following Elaynna, they all joined in to eat.

"Wow Ammi your parathas are the best. Haye I missed them so much!" Abdul exclaimed. Jannat told him to stop buttering her she needed the butter for the parathas. Everyone loved the irony in their grandmother's joke.

Rahims tea nearly came out of his nose laughing.

"Go on Dadi, let me take over you eat, shall I make your favorite omlette?" Jannat winked and nodded as she sat down at the breakfast table. "I want some too!" Qasim shouted.

The next few months flew by with the preparation of the wedding, Jannat helped with most of the things. Yasmin told Abdul that she had put some money away for the last few years from Elaynna's salary that they could use to buy the jewelery for Elaynna's wedding. Abdul refused the money furious at her for taking it from her.

"I was only saving it," Yasmin pleaded.

"You know what children are like, they don't know where to spend their money and end up wasting it." Abdul was so angry he wanted to hit her, but he held onto his anger.

"I also have been putting money aside for her wedding. If the money becomes less then we will buy less. But I refuse to use her money. I tell you this you return it to her and she can have it as spending money and use it for something useful." Yasmin was annoyed at herself for telling him, now that money was to go back, if she hadn't told him she could have used it for herself or the other children.

Yasmin had saved approximately £5,000 to use for her wedding. What will Elaynna do with £5,000? Yasmin thought that she could have bought herself some new jewelery with that money, but now if she did use it Abdul would know.

One night while Elaynna was alone in her room, Yasmin went to her to tell her about the money planning to keep it somehow with Elaynna's permission.

"Beta you know the money you have been giving me the last few years, I used to keep some aside to use for your wedding but your father refuses to use it. He told me to give it to you." Elaynna surprised at her mother wasn't sure what to say,

"How much is it?" Yasmin took a deep breath and told her, "£5,000" Elaynna shocked in her mothers reply.

"Well do you want it? What will you do with it?" Elaynna thought for a moment, "You keep it then." Yasmin gave her a pathetic look.

"What will I tell your father then when he asks me? He said to give it to you." Elaynna thought again. "Then just keep it until I need it. I will tell him I gave it to you to look after." Yasmin wanted something more.

"How about we buy some of your jewelery with it and I can buy something too." Elaynna nodded trying to do whatever made her mother happy.

Yasmin walked out feeling like she had accomplished something great. Now she was going to get some new golden jewelery with this money and then put the rest away for when she needed it. If Abdul asked she had Elaynna to cover for her and proof to show it went to good use.

The following few months went by even more quickly, as the wedding approached nearer and nearer the pressure increased more and more. Yasmin was more aggressive than ever, she made Elaynna prepare everything herself from the decorations to the gifts for the guests. Elaynna handed her notice in at work. She was to work until a month left for her wedding. Mr Akhter was upset to let her go, but he knew she had no choice. Elaynna invited everyone at the wedding, including Mr Akhter. When she gave the numbers to her father for the wedding, he was shocked to see that there were more than thirty friends of hers of who were attending the wedding, but he just smiled and said it wasn't a problem.

"You know more people than me." He teased her. The month before the wedding were both sad and happy moments for Elaynna, her friends came to see her every evening and did lots of singing and teasing.

No body could miss out that there wasn't a wedding happening there. Yasmin would force a smile whenever they arrived, she hated their laughing and giggling every night. One night she told Elaynna to tell her friends to not to come anymore they were not invited. Jannat heard her; Yasmin had mistakenly left the door open.

"I was quiet because I had come into your home, now that my granddaughter is getting married, the poor thing is still doing everything to please you and yet you have no sympathy for her happiness? Can't you see how her face glows when her friends come over and sing her wedding songs? It is a happy occasion Yasmin, and I will not let you ruin it for her or anyone!"

Yasmin turned red with embarrassment; she couldn't look back up at her. Without answering she went to bed early. This made Elaynna want to cry, she thought she was the cause of her family's distress. When ever there was a matter which involved her, she had made her family fight with one another. She felt it was probably the best thing for everyone that she was leaving. No longer will anyone fight because of her, she felt she was a big shame to her family. Another night went by with silent tears, this time the snores of her grandmother didn't soothe her.

Only a few weeks were left to the wedding, the house was always full of people, some coming to congratulate some giving their gifts in advance for the bride and groom. Many family friends who gave valuable gifts of gold.

One day Elaynna's boss and staff came to give their gifts. They presented her with household gifts. Mr Akhter and the whole factory teamed up with a decent amount of gift money, they were quite generous with their choice of gifts. She was presented with a small award ceremony, an idea Poonam came up with to prove to Elaynna's mother the importance of her daughter in the outer world. She was presented with the best employee ever award. Especially made, her name was printed on it. Although she could not read it, she was translated the meaning. It touched her heart to hear what it was for; Jannat smiled proudly giving Yasmin a look of disgust for always putting her daughter down. Then one by one all of the staff gave her a gift, a toaster, a kettle, dinner plates, cutlery, saucepans, hotpots and much more.

The whole living room was filled with gifts just from Mr Akhter and the factory. Yasmin got fed up serving them tea and snacks, she was eager for them to leave so she could have her living room back. Elaynna sat in awe by their lovely gesture being unable to get up from where she sat to say goodbye at the door, two weeks were left for the wedding she was strictly house bound.

She didn't mind so much since she had done all the shopping needed with her grandmother. Time crept to the last week of the wedding, Rahman and his family came to stay with mutual family friends so they could do all of the rituals together, taking turns to attend each of their childrens wedding rituals.

Constant singing began in each household. Elaynna was meant to do nothing but enjoy the rituals, her mother as usual not sympathizing with the situation made her do all of the housework. Every morning she made breakfast for everyone and any guests that stayed over. Jannat was extremely saddened when she saw how much her daughter in law had changed. She was unable to say anything as there was always some family friends staying over. It wasn't the habit of Jannat to make a scene in front of others. Watching her granddaughter's behavior brought tears to her eyes, why was her own mother so unjust to her daughter? Elaynna could see her grandmother's sad eyes, she would go over cheering her up that she didn't mind doing everything it helped her to keep her mind off of things.

While Elaynna worked in the day doing the housework, she had to attend the evening rituals with a fake smile, the rituals were making her more depressed, what was the need, she wondered, a simple Nikkah would have been appropriate. Every evening when women gathered to sing and play the drum, Elaynna was expected to dress up and sit in a corner without looking up or being able to join in, otherwise she would have been accused of having so shame.

She would have rather sat in her room and looked out of the window, at least she would have been able to move and act freely.

The last few days made Elaynna and Sabah grow closer, when Sabah learned that her sister was moving away, she would not stop following her sister around. She even followed her to the bathroom.

"Although I am going, I will always be here when you need me. We can talk on the phone everyday." Sabah twirled her hair feeling uneasy about the change.

"What if Akram Bhai doesn't let you call me?" Elaynna stroked her hair embracing her tightly. "If he doesn't let me call you I will take

you with me and we can tackle him together! We can beat him up!"
Sabah giggled holding her tummy.

"Baji you are so funny, I hope he is good as the prince charming that
I read to you from Cinderella." Elaynna started to cry, but didn't let
Sabah see the tears run from her eyes, "Yes I am sure he is the Prince
from Cinderella."

The last night before the wedding was near, Elaynna's friends fussed
over her while they got her ready for the henna night, they had kindly
decorated the whole house in flowers, the smell was enchanting.
Elaynna's grandmother had bought her her henna suit from Pakistan;
it was a parrot green with silver embroidery, just like the one she had
dreamed about. The salwar was baggier than usual, and the kameez
came to her knees, her hair was up with white fragranced flowers
bordering around the plait. The scarf was huge and heavy with a
silver beaded border. Her friends adorned her hands with flowered
bracelets. When she looked at herself in the mirror she could not
recognize herself, Sabah said she looked like a princess. Elaynna
placed her hand on her cheek smiling weakly.

Her friends brought her down while the elders sang henna related
songs. The sound of the drum made each heartbeat of Elaynna's race
faster and faster, her plain fair cheeks turned pink with embarrassment
when her friends held her bridal scarf above her head while she
walked down into the living room.

Soon as she entered the aunties changed their songs to praise of beauty.
As she sat down, everyone swarmed to her one by one wanting to
kiss and compliment her. Each one of the guests put a small amount

of henna on her palm and applied some oil to her hair. Sabah sat by her feet holding the tray of the henna and oil for the guests. Yasmin looked at her from a distance and prayed deep down in her heart that her husband and in laws treat her well.

Elaynna was then sat again in a corner while henna designs were planted on her hands and feet. Elaynna felt excited for once in her life, she was leaving behind a house of hatred and starting a whole new life with a man who accepted her regardless of her illiteracy. He was a man she wanted to serve for the rest of her life and try to forget the past, and be able live a life of dignity.

THE END

ACKNOWLEDGMENTS

I would like to thank each and everyone who have helped me to complete this novel. As much as I remembered about my culture I tried to base around it in this novel. I would personally like to thank my parents for their moral support, especially my father for believing in my abilities. I would like to thank all those that knew about this novel and their ongoing support. My husband Naseer Uddin, who helped me with some of the names of the characters, he played the most role in helping me complete this novel. He let me stay up at night to complete it. He did not once complain when I would drop everything to write, and edit this book. He took over the care of our daughter and the cooking so I could build my dream. Thank you, Naseer. My friend Saiqa Aziz who always believed in me, pushing me to complete fulfill my dream. Many thanks to you. I would also like to thank my friend Uzma Anwar who proof read it for me telling me she enjoyed it through and through, also playing a part in some of the editing process. I would like to thank William Blake for his help in designing the cover, capturing the cover exactly as I wanted it to be. A big thank you to everyone that knew about this book taking form, and believing in my imagination. May Allah bless you all. I would like to give my most thanks to the readers who will read this book and help in raising a contribution to the Malala Fund, helping to provide an education for the needy. God Bless You!